Taboo 2: Locked In

Taboo 2: Locked In

Yoshe

www.urbanbooks.net

Urban Books, LLC
78 East Industry Court
Deer Park, NY 11729

ISBN 13: 978-1-60162-430-7
ISBN 10: 1-60162-430-1

First Printing January 2011
Printed in the United States of America

10 9 8 7 6 5 4 3 2 1

Distributed by Kensington Publishing Corp.
Submit Wholesale Orders to:
Kensington Publishing Corp.
C/O Penguin Group (USA) Inc.
Attention: Order Processing
405 Murray Hill Parkway
East Rutherford, NJ 07073-2316
Phone: 1-800-526-0275
Fax: 1-800-227-9604

Prologue

"Good morning, staff," the warden said, greeting the morning roll call filled with correction officers.

Some officers said good morning as well, and some saluted him.

"I decided to take the time out to talk to you about a serious problem. I've been getting a lot of phone calls from the inspector general's office with allegations of corruption that may be going on in this particular facility. This is unacceptable. These inmates are not your friends."

The warden continued. "You are not to go beyond the scope of your duties as a New York City correction officer to provide these detainees with anything but what is required within the minimum standards. I'm pretty sure that you know what your job consists of, and you realize that you are here to uphold correction law and adhere to the rules and regulations of the department. If I find out that someone is breaking these rules, I will make sure that you will be removed from this command. Now, keeping your job is your job, and I hope that I won't have to make that decision for you."

The warden gave the roll call captain a nod, signaling for him to proceed. The captain began briefing the roll call and then called out names for post assignments. After everyone received their posts, roll call dispersed. A small group of female officers immediately began whispering among each other.

"You know who's one of the people that the warden was talkin' about, right?" said CO Watkins. She was the facility gossip queen who made it her business to know what was going on at work.

"No, who?" asked CO Porter, a heavyset female with a pretty face.

"He's talkin' about Howell. You know Howell. The one who has Five North steady?" asked Watkins.

CO Harris interjected, "Oh, yeah, that's Deputy Dog's fiancée."

CO Butner laughed. "Now why are you callin' Deputy Simmons 'Deputy Dog'?" The other officers snickered along with her.

"Because he's a dog. Can't you look at the man and tell that he's a dog?" Harris asked. "He was messin' with Howell first, had a baby on her with some officer from C-95, then him and Howell got back together and God knows who else he's doin' right now. Damn shame that he—," Harris began.

Watkins cut her off. "Girl, please! That's old news! I'm just talkin' about Howell. Now she has a child of her own. Only the father of that baby isn't Deputy Dog."

Porter opened her eyes real wide. She was the new jack of the small clique, having only been on the job two years. "So who is her baby daddy then?" she asked.

"An inmate," said Harris. Porter and Butner looked at each other in amazement.

"Are you serious?" asked Butner. "How do y'all know this?"

"We just know. That's been the rumor around here for the past two years. Her son has her last name and everything. If that was Deputy Dog's baby, then why doesn't he have his father's last name, right?" asked Watkins. All the ladies nodded their heads in agreement. "Not to mention, Howell rolls with Captain

Phillips, another ho who's been known to mess around with inmates."

Porter shook her head. "Those hoes are so scandalous! Why would someone risk their job like that? I couldn't do it. I need my job."

Harris gave Butner a pound. "I second you on that. Howell must have some real self-esteem issues. I mean, she's a pretty girl; why she would want to deal with an inmate is beyond me. Isn't she and Deputy Dog supposed to be gettin' married?"

"I heard that, too," said Watkins. "But I also heard that the inmate she supposedly had the baby by, last name is Gordon. He used to be housed in Five North a few years ago."

"Girl, I know who you're talkin' about!" said Harris excitedly. Porter and Butner looked on. "I remember that inmate. His name is Rasheed Gordon. He was a tall guy with locks in his hair. Nice-lookin' guy, too. Yes, he was."

Butner and Porter laughed at Harris. Watkins didn't. "Please, girl. Gordon, or whatever his name was, was an inmate. I don't look at inmates in a sexual manner. I am not physically attracted to them at all! I just don't like them and I dare one of these nasty-ass crooks to try to holler at me!"

Harris rolled her eyes at Watkins. "C'mon, Watkins. You are goin' really hard right now. If a man is nice lookin', he's nice lookin'. Bein' an inmate has nothin' to do with it. A man is still a man."

Watkins turned her nose up. She was adamant about her opinion. "Well, I wouldn't mess around with an inmate, I don't care how fine he is, and I damn sure don't want to be around any officer who fucks with one. If I even see an officer gettin' too familiar with an inmate, I'm reportin' them to the inspector general's office." Watkins looked down the corridor. Sierra

Howell was walking toward them. "Oh, wow, speakin' of the devil. Here goes the little fraternizer right now," she whispered.

When Howell arrived in front of the four female officers, she said hello to all of them with a smile on her face.

"Hey, girl!" greeted Watkins, putting on a fake smile. Harris, Butner, and Porter just waved.

"Good mornin', ladies," said Sierra. "How's everybody doin'?"

"We're fine, Howell," replied Harris. "So how's Five North treatin' you?"

Sierra shrugged. "Eh, it's okay. I've been there for a while now so I'm used to it."

"You have a son, right?" asked Watkins.

"Yeah, I do. He's two years old now," replied Sierra.

"That's sweet. How is he?" Harris asked.

"Oh, he's doin' good, girl. Gettin' big and gettin' into everything," Sierra said with a laugh. "You know the terrible twos." She paused for a second. "Well, let me go to this search. I'll talk to y'all later. Have a safe tour, everybody."

They all waved at Howell and watched her walk off. "That's a damn shame," said Harris.

"Inmate-lovin' heifer," said Watkins, shaking her head. "So disgustin'."

Chapter 1

Rasheed

It was 8:32 in the morning in Atlanta, Georgia and Rasheed Gordon couldn't sleep. He turned over and stared at the caramel-skinned beauty lying next to him. The woman was snoring, exhausted from the good loving that he had just given her for the last two hours. Rasheed put the sheet over her curvy frame and sighed as he sat on the edge of his bed, trying to figure out why he still felt unfulfilled.

When he thought about it, he really didn't have anything to complain about at this point in his life. What man wouldn't want what he had? Rasheed only had access to a different woman every night, money in his bank account, and a nice roof over his head. What could be missing from his life? For one thing, he had a beautiful baby boy, that lived in Brooklyn.

After pondering the thought for a few moments, Rasheed finally came to the conclusion that he didn't want to live in Atlanta anymore. After living there with his older brother, Karim, for almost two years, it was time to go back home. The bottom line was that Southern living wasn't for Rasheed Gordon, a native New Yorker. He thought that Atlanta was a great city, and looked even better on the videos that flashed across his television. The novelty of living in a new city had worn off.

Karim Gordon had made a substantial amount of

money in real estate and promoting in the city of Atlanta, but Rasheed knew that it was no place for a man like him. Down there, he was an unknown, merely a shadowy figure that lurked behind his big brother. He yearned to be back in the five boroughs, in his Bedford-Stuyvesant neighborhood, where he was a shining star and loved by many.

At the beckoning of Karim, Rasheed thought that his life would be much better in Atlanta than it was in Brooklyn. And it was. It was just too slow for him. Rasheed found himself missing the fast-paced action of New York City and the eclectic mix of people who lived there.

The Gordons were a well-known family in their Bedford-Stuyvesant neighborhood. Miss Carrie, the matriarch of the clan, raised all seven of her children along with Karim and Rasheed right on Halsey Street. They were close knit, and even through tough times, death, or incarceration, they were supportive of each other.

Karim and Rasheed came to live with Miss Carrie when they were only seven and five years old, respectively. Their mother, Lavon, was murdered by their abusive father, Jihad, who eventually killed himself too. It was an adjustment for the brothers, who had lived the early years of their lives under the strict rules of their Muslim father.

For Karim, the living arrangement worked out fine, but Rasheed proved to be the hardheaded child. The shock of losing his parents to such tragedy obviously had a long-term effect on him. He chose to follow in the footsteps of his much older uncles and become one with the streets, as if he had something to prove. Unfortunately, it took him numerous scrapes with the law and brushes with death to see that the streets didn't have love for anyone.

After his oldest uncle, Peppy, was killed by Dominican drug dealers, the surviving Gordon brothers—Nayshawn, Shaka, and Kemper—did a 360-degree turnaround. They took their hustling proceeds and obtained all sorts of businesses: a tire and autobody shop, a construction company, and younger sister Carrie opened a beauty parlor.

Ironically, Miss Carrie was a registered nurse for many years and was more than happy that her unruly children had finally come to their senses. Even though his uncles got their lives on track, Rasheed still chose to sell drugs and live a reckless lifestyle when he had access to jobs and money. He had to admit that the jail bids that he had done were because of some bad choices he'd made in the past. But it was the streets that he craved that caused him to have no regard for the law.

Rasheed walked over to the huge stand-up mirror that was tucked in the corner of his oversized bedroom. He looked in the mirror, wrapped his long locks in a ponytail, and flexed his prominent biceps, posing from every angle. Rasheed smiled and patted his chest.

A nigga looks pretty damn good to be thirty-three years old, Rasheed thought.

Looking at his reflection also made him think about his mother, Lavon. She was a gorgeous woman, with long, wavy hair, and her skin was the color of bronze, inherited from her own mother, Miss Carrie Gordon. Even though Rasheed had heard it numerous times, it wasn't until adulthood that he realized that he actually was a male replica of his mother. He moved closer to the mirror to inspect himself. Rasheed shook his head in amazement.

"Damn, I do look like Mommy," he said to himself. "God bless her soul."

Rasheed looked around the room and sighed. He

had recently expressed to Karim how he felt about moving back home. Rasheed knew that any mention of him wanting to leave Atlanta would not sit right with his serious-minded brother. Preparing himself for an argument, Rasheed felt his heart beating rapidly through his chest as he called out to Karim from his bedroom.

"Yo, Karim!" Rasheed shouted. "Can you make my plane reservations for me?" Realizing that he was kind of loud, he turned around to look at the sleeping female in his bed. She didn't flinch. Rasheed shook his head.

This broad looks real comfortable in my bed and I can't even sleep right now, Rasheed thought. Rasheed shook his head. He was going to be kicking her out real soon.

A laugh could be heard coming from the kitchen. "Hell no! You're a grown man with your own money. You can make your own reservations. That's the problem now. You're always waitin' for somebody to do somethin' for you."

Rasheed walked out of his bedroom. He slowly walked down the stairs that led to the kitchen area.

"C'mon, Karim. Are you serious? Can you make that call for me? You know that I'm not good with things like that and the money isn't an issue. It's just that I was all set to go to New York this week!" Rasheed said with a sour look on his face. He was also anticipating being home in time for the second birthday of his son, Messiah. It looked like that wasn't going to happen.

Karim stood in the kitchen wearing a Ralph Lauren robe and slippers while fixing his breakfast. He was just as handsome as Rasheed, just shorter and stockier like their deceased father, Jihad. Although they were brothers, their differences were obvious. Karim was the calmer of the two, and while he didn't take mess from anyone, he was the logical thinker. Rasheed was the brother who was quick to fight or pick up a weapon to settle his disagreements with violence.

Karim believed that he had too much invested and had worked too hard to throw away his life for that kind of temperament. This was one of the reasons why he wanted Rasheed by his side. His brother was the wild child of the Gordon family and Karim thought that moving Rasheed to Atlanta was a good idea, especially after he was shot in New York almost three years ago.

Annoyed with the constant talk of Brooklyn and Rasheed's refusal to conform to their laid-back lifestyle, Karim was secretly glad to see him go at that point.

After pouring some egg whites into a frying pan, Karim turned the fire down to medium and looked at his younger brother.

"I done already told your stubborn ass—if you wanna go back to Brooklyn, then that's on you," he replied. "That means make your own plane reservations for your trip. I don't want no part of it."

Rasheed rubbed his hands through his neat locks. "Sounds like you have an attitude because I wanna move back to New York." He looked around the spacious four-bedroom house that Karim called home. "Don't get me wrong, this is a nice layout, but I gotta get outta here, man. Ain't nothin' down here for me," Rasheed exclaimed.

Karim turned his eggs over and checked on his turkey bacon that was frying in another pan. He poured some Tropicana orange juice in a glass and sipped it. After a few seconds passed, Karim looked at Rasheed.

"So what am I supposed to do about that? You've been livin' down here for the last two years and some change, and even made a good name for yourself here in Atlanta. You had the opportunity to reinvent yourself, to become a better man and make an honest livin'. Now you wanna throw all this shit away to move back to Brooklyn? You're crazy!"

Karim placed the glass of orange juice on the granite countertop and waved his hand at Rasheed.

"All I can say is that if you move back to New York and you get into some more shit, don't call me!" Karim added, taking a bite of some toast.

Rasheed smirked. "So it's like that? Don't call you, huh?"

Karim turned his back to Rasheed and continued to prepare his breakfast. "You know, Rah, you was never a nigga who listened to any reason. You always had to be the one to do the exact opposite of what anyone told you to do. But you'd think that after all you went through in New York, you would wanna stay here in Atlanta."

Getting even more aggravated with Rasheed's request, Karim turned around with the cooking spatula in his hand.

"Now, I'm not Nana, I'm not Nayshawn or Shaka and I damn sure ain't Kemp, who cosigns a lot of your bullshit. The first time I suggested that you move to Atlanta, you wanted to bring your thievin' girlfriend, Tamir, down here with you. I said no to that. Then you dumped her for Sierra Howell, the correction officer you met when you were locked up on Rikers for your last parole violation. Now when you're released from jail, you have nothin' but drama with Tamir and Sierra goin' at each other's throats.

"So I give you another invitation to come down here, to put all of that drama behind you when Tyke, Sierra's ex-man, comes home from jail. This opens another can of worms because you and Tyke never got along with each other growin' up. You and Tyke started beefin' over Sierra and he ends up killin' Tamir to get back at you! Then to keep him from killin' you and Sierra, you put a hit out on him!"

Karim continued as Rasheed just stood there, with a

bored look on his face as he listened to his own drama. "So after all that, you end up gettin' shot by some homo-thug dude named Scooter who you were locked up with on Rikers. By this time, you had no other choice but to move down here.

"Last but not least, you moved to Atlanta and you discovered that you and Sierra might have a child together. It's just too much. Can't say that I really blame Sierra for not wantin' to be with you, Rah," he added.

Karim went back to preparing his breakfast.

Rasheed began to pace back and forth. "I see how you feel about me, 'Rim. All of these years I'm thinkin' that you got my back, and now you're actin' like I'm a fuckup."

Karim made his plate and placed it on the island. He pulled up the leather stool and sat down to enjoy his meal. Before answering his brother, he blessed his food and stuffed some egg whites into his mouth. Rasheed stared at Karim in amazement.

"Are you just gonna ignore me now?" Rasheed asked with a pleading look in his eyes.

"Yep. I'm ignorin' you. Do what you wanna do. You wanna go back to Brooklyn? Go outside and push that fuckin' Range Rover that I copped for you up 95 North. I'm done with this conversation."

Rasheed held his hands up in the air. "You're sayin' that I have to drive up to New York now? I wanted to be in New York in time for Messiah's birthday! This is my chance to make it right with Sierra and if I don't get there in time—," Rasheed protested.

Karim cut him off with a chuckle. He shook his head and picked his plate up from the counter. He walked toward his bedroom.

"C'mon, man! Now you wanna see Messiah and make things right with Sierra all of a sudden? Who do you think you're foolin'?"

With that, Karim walked in his bedroom and slammed the door in Rasheed's face.

Rasheed stood in front of the closed bedroom door. He couldn't believe that Karim had dismissed him like that. They were like Frick and Frack since he moved to Atlanta and Karim made it his business to involve Rasheed in most of his dealings. But Rasheed was tired of doing what Karim wanted him to do. It was as if he didn't have a mind of his own.

Rasheed trekked back upstairs to his bedroom and stood in the doorway. From there, he looked at all his bags. For a brief second, he realized that he would be going back to a place where he had left heartache and misery behind. That wasn't the problem. Rasheed just had a nagging desire to go back and finish what he'd started.

There were so many mistakes that he made then and the new man in him wanted to rectify them. One of those unfortunate decisions was denying himself the pleasures of watching his son grow up. Regrettably, Rasheed did not have a civil relationship with his son's mother, and he wanted to change that.

The last time that he was in New York was exactly a year and a half ago when Messiah was only six months old. Rasheed had made it his business to contact Sierra to let her know that he was going to be in town for a few weeks, and that he wanted to spend time with his son. She seemed doubtful about seeing Rasheed and equally hesitant about allowing him to see Messiah. After some convincing, they eventually met at a neutral location, at the suggestion of Sierra.

Rasheed remembered that day like it had just happened. He pulled up in his truck and Sierra pulled up in a brand new BMW X5. She had told Rasheed to meet her by the Jefferson High School football field in East New York and she would bring the baby there.

Even though it seemed a little inconvenient for the both of them, Rasheed was happy that he would finally be able to lay his eyes on his baby boy once again.

When Sierra got out of her truck, Rasheed felt his heart flutter. Sierra looked beautiful in her sheared mink jacket and tight-fitting jeans. Her long hair was stuffed into a cashmere beret and her lips glistened in the winter sunlight.

"Hello, Mr. Gordon," she said, approaching him with a bored look on her face. "You're lookin' good."

"What's up, Sierra?" Rasheed replied with an attitude. He could have kicked himself for being nasty with her, but the sight of her always seemed to make him angry. "Why do you have me meetin' you on this side of town? I'm not good enough for you to drop my son off at the house?" he asked, irritated.

Sierra sighed. "Why do we always have to go through this crap, Rasheed? You know that I'm still employed with the Department of Correction and I don't want to go anywhere near Halsey Street. You never know who may see us together."

Rasheed threw his hands in the air. "You know what? I don't have time for this. Just let me see Messiah. I'm not even goin' through this shit with you again. I keep tellin' you that I don't give a fuck about you being a CO, all right? If I cared, I would have been on the phone with the inspector general's office gettin' your ass into major fuckin' trouble. It's not like I don't have the evidence to do it."

Sierra bit her bottom lip. Rasheed knew that when she did that, she was pissed off. A smile of satisfaction came over his face. He had hit her where it hurt. He had won that round.

"You know, Rasheed, I'm really tryin' to make this thing we have . . ." Sierra said, trying to hold back tears, pointing back and forth between the both of them. "I'm really tryin' to make it work for the sake of Messiah. I just don't understand why you are so angry with me. Is it because I moved on?"

Rasheed walked to Sierra's truck, not trying to acknowledge anything that she was talking about. He didn't feel like conversing with Sierra about their relationship. It was Messiah's time now and every moment that was spent with him was precious.

Sierra lagged closely behind and climbed into the driver's seat of her truck. Rasheed opened the back door and slid into the backseat, next to Messiah's car seat. When he closed the door, he immediately removed the baby from the seat. Messiah was half asleep and sucking on a pacifier. His body jerked when his father pulled him out of the seat. Rasheed inspected Messiah carefully, with love in his eyes.

Rasheed looked at Sierra while holding his son in his arms. He softened up a bit. "I'm gonna answer your questions once and for all, okay? Just let me get some time in with my baby boy."

Sierra rolled her eyes up in her head. "Yeah, okay," she sarcastically replied.

Rasheed looked at Sierra, and, for a split second, he thought about choking the hell out of her. But while holding the baby in his arms, nothing else mattered at that moment.

With Messiah dozing in and out of sleep, Rasheed sighed. His paternal instincts kicked in and he yearned to experience more of those special moments with Messiah. This meant that he would have to clear the air with Sierra so that they wouldn't have any more misunderstandings.

"I'm gonna say this and I'm not gonna repeat myself. You know the reason I have an attitude is because, yes, I feel that you should be with me. We went through a lot to be with each other, and at the end of the day all

I can say is, what was it all for? So the only way that you gonna get any type of reprieve from me is if we be together and make this right. We have a child and I just want me, you, and Messiah to be a family, Si. Is there somethin' wrong with that?" Rasheed paused. "So don't come at me with the 'am I mad because you moved on' shit! No, I'm mad because I can't move on! Now does that answer your questions?"

Sierra didn't respond. Instead, she sighed loudly and turned around in the driver's seat. She pulled out her cell phone and began talking to one of her girlfriends. Rasheed stared at her for a few moments, and then looked down at his beautiful baby boy.

The smell of Baby Magic made Rasheed forget that he was upset with Sierra. Messiah had opened his eyes and stared at his father. Rasheed made a funny face and the baby began to giggle, spitting the pacifier out of his mouth. Messiah looked a lot like his mother, inheriting her dimples and slanted eyes. But everything else was him all the way, from the pointy nose to the lips and reddish-brown complexion. Messiah was a sight to behold. Rasheed knew at that moment that even at six months his son was going to definitely break some hearts.

As Sierra yapped on the phone about nothing special, Rasheed sat in the backseat of her truck, growing angrier by the second.

"Yo!" he shouted out. Sierra took the phone away from her ear and gave Rasheed the look of death. "Can I just have a peaceful moment with my son without hearin' all that chitchat?"

"Who are you talkin' to?" she asked Rasheed. Sierra went back to her phone call. "Girl, look, I'm bein' rudely interrupted. I will talk to you later," she explained to the person on the phone. Sierra hung up the phone and put it in her bag. She then turned around to the backseat to face him.

"What the hell is your problem, Rasheed? I would think that you would be happy that you're holdin' your son in your arms. But you over here all up in my business and actin' like you want my undivided attention!"

Rasheed kissed Messiah, carefully placing him back in the car seat. He then put the pacifier in the baby's mouth, watching as Messiah happily kicked his thick legs. Suddenly, Rasheed reached over the front seat and grabbed Sierra by the neck. As she struggled to breathe, she attempted to remove his strong grasp, but to no avail.

"Get the fuck off me!" Sierra uttered. He began to shake Sierra so hard while choking her that he didn't realize that he was banging her head against the car window.

"Who do you think you are?" Rasheed calmly stated. He pulled Sierra's face close to his. "I'm tired of you disrespectin' me, Correction Officer Howell. I'm tired of you actin' like I had no part in makin' Messiah, and I'm tired of you talkin' down to me!"

"Get off," she whispered. Sierra's face was turning red and Rasheed finally loosened his grip. He had blacked out. She instantly began coughing and rubbing her neck. Tears ran down her dimpled cheeks. "You fuckin' bastard," she muttered.

While his parents were struggling with each other, Messiah was crying hysterically. As he attempted to calm the baby down, Rasheed instantly regretted putting his hands on Sierra. Being from the streets, he didn't know any other way to settle his disputes.

Messiah quieted down when Rasheed put a bottle in his mouth. "I think it's time for me to get out of here," Rasheed exclaimed, opening the back car door to get out of Sierra's truck.

The winter cold hit him in the face like a brick. He

kissed his crying son, whose bottle fell out of his mouth, on the cheek. He felt like crying himself. Rasheed already knew that when he put his hands on Sierra, Messiah was going to be nothing but an afterthought in his confused mind.

At this point, Sierra was hysterical. "I hate you, Rasheed Gordon! I regret the day I ever laid eyes on your ass!"

"Is that right?" Rasheed chirped with a smug look on his face. "Well, I'll never regret fuckin' with you!"

Suddenly, Sierra flew across the front seat and tried to punch Rasheed in the face. He would have thought that after getting choked she would have calmed down. But she didn't. He was convinced that Sierra loved that type of drama.

As she attempted to hit him again, he grabbed her small fists and pulled her to him. At that moment, Rasheed began kissing her. Straight out of a scene from the movies, Sierra allowed herself to succumb to passion, and reciprocated. Messiah instantly stopped crying and began smiling, as if he felt the love radiating from his parents.

Rasheed got out of the truck and got into the passenger seat next to Sierra, where they continued their kiss. They were all over each other, massaging each other's body parts. The interlude was so hot that the windows of Sierra's X5 began to steam up. After a few moments, Sierra finally pulled away from Rasheed.

"I can't do this, Rah," Sierra said, wiping the saliva from her lips.

Rasheed put his hand in Sierra's crotch area. He could almost feel the heat coming through her tight-fitting Citizens of Humanity jeans. He turned her face to his and began kissing her again.

"Si, I apologize for puttin' my hands on you. But I'm not gonna lie, I still love you. It's killin' me knowin' that you and Lamont are happy, that you two are raisin' my boy together and I can't have that with you. I really want us to be with each other."

Sierra sighed. The tears began to flow again. "But, Rasheed, you know that I can't be with you anymore. Our lives are goin' in two different directions."

"But you want to be with me, don't you?" Sierra looked away and wouldn't answer him. He knew what that meant.

Opening the door, Rasheed got out of the truck and stood there staring at Sierra for a few seconds before he spoke.

"I love you and Messiah, but I can't stand by and watch Lamont take my family away from me. So I'm gonna step back and just leave y'all alone for good."

"What are you talkin' about, Rasheed? Don't you wanna see Messiah anymore?"

"I love my little man, but if me and you can't be together, there's no need for me to come around. I can't continue to meet all these different places just so I can see my son. It doesn't make any sense. This shit hurts too much."

Sierra started the engine. Rasheed could tell that she was irritated. He didn't care about her feelings; he was just being honest with himself. What was wrong with him wanting to have a relationship with the mother of his child?

"Close the door and lose my fuckin' number!" Sierra yelled at him. "I can't go through this shit with you anymore! Good-bye, Rasheed. Have a safe trip back to Atlanta!"

Rasheed closed the door and Sierra pulled off. It seemed as if everyone he loved left him. As he watched her truck disappear in the distance, he walked back to his own vehicle and cried like a baby.

Not wanting to get all teary eyed thinking about

that day, Rasheed knelt down on the carpeted floor and rounded up all the things that he would need for his move. As he looked around at the many bags he packed, he was beginning to think that driving to New York wasn't such a bad idea after all.

Rasheed got up and walked to the side of the bed that the woman was lying on. He shook her softly and she awakened almost immediately, dazed from sleep.

"Hey, sweetheart," he said with a smile on his face. The woman smiled back and reached for him. Suddenly, Rasheed turned serious. "Get up, put your clothes on, and get the hell out."

Chapter 2

Sierra

As the gates in the corridor of the Rikers Island correctional facility opened and slammed closed, they were a constant reminder to the inmates that their freedom was no more until the judge banged his gavel. Riker's Island was known for housing some of the most violent criminals in the city, and at any given time, any one of the many facilities could be in an uproar. To the naked eye, the hallways of the facilities looked impeccable. Unfortunately, underneath the numerous paint jobs and heavy wax buildup on the floors, there had been much bloodshed.

In the past, this ill-fated situation had occurred due to inattentiveness of staff. Most of the correction officers had become complacent and insensitive to the needs of the convicts during their time in jail. They made the job more about themselves, coming to work to socialize and fraternize with their fellow coworkers, as opposed to policing the jails. Female officers pursued the males in hopes of gaining a husband. If all else failed, they opted to become pregnant in order to obtain 17 percent of the male officer's paycheck.

For the some male COs, their goal was to have sex with as many women as they could. Obviously unaccustomed to the attention that they received from the women employed with DOC, they became caught up in getting themselves trapped with someone else's leftovers. It was as if they compared themselves to a celebrity of Denzel Washington's caliber. When these types of personalities meshed, it was never a happy medium. It was more like a soap opera inside of the department, as people gossiped about each other, committed adultery, and stabbed each other in the back for positions and sex partners. All of this caused nothing but strife in an already highly stressed work environment. On the outside looking in, it was completely different world; for the officers that worked there, it was their normalcy.

The corridor was empty as Correction Officer Sierra Howell took the long walk to her post. The heavy Folgers keys dangled from her waist as her childbearing hips swayed from side to side, and a walkie-talkie protruded from the back pocket of her uniform pants.

For some reason, she was feeling a little anxious but couldn't figure out what her problem was. Although she was blessed to have a great family, a good man, and a career, Sierra had been feeling that there was some trouble looming in the distance. It was as if someone or something was going to try to throw a monkey wrench in her life. Sierra hoped that she was only being paranoid.

Sierra grew up in a Brownsville housing project as the only daughter of Marjorie and Steven Howell. When she was nine years old, her father was killed in a car accident. Even with her father's untimely death, she was still a model child growing up: very respectful, obedient, and not giving her mother one problem. But as Sierra came into her adolescent years, she began yearning for a father/protector figure.

So at fifteen years old, Sierra began gravitating toward the "bad boys." To her, they represented masculinity in the highest form. They were the alpha male to Sierra, ready and willing to go to war for the ones they loved. It comforted her to know that her man was there to make her feel safe and protect her from harm. Unfortunately, she continued to have those same beliefs when she became an adult.

Sierra watched as the inmates filed in and out of the cell to retrieve their breakfast trays. She yawned as the monotony began to get to her. She looked at her watch and saw that it was 6:15 a.m. The inmates would eat their breakfast, watch some television, and lock in the cells in the next forty-five minutes. The time couldn't go fast enough.

It was almost 7:00 a.m. when the feeding was completed. Sierra instructed the inmates that it was time to lock in their cells. After closing the last cell, Sierra sat at the desk and proceeded to make her logbook entries. As she was doing this, she thought about Rasheed. Five North was the very place that their relationship had begun.

Sierra first laid eyes on Inmate Rasheed Gordon in Five North. He was carrying on a conversation with the other inmates and looking like he did not belong there. His looks were what initially caught her attention, and she was immediately physically attracted to the fine specimen of a man. Of course, at that time, Sierra thought that he was just another pretty thug; the Department of Correction had plenty of handsome men being detained in their jails. But after watching him for some time, she noticed that there was a redeeming quality about Rasheed that she just could not place her finger on.

Rasheed was so laid-back and charismatic, it seemed as if he was used to getting what he wanted whenever he wanted it. Most of the inmates gravitated toward him as if he was the most important person in the world, and Sierra couldn't figure out why.

The curious side of her wanted to know what made him tick, only that was impossible when she knew that she had taken an oath as an officer. Fraternizing with the likes of Rasheed Gordon, or anyone with a book and case number, was off limits.

After a few months of Rasheed being housed in Five North, the sexual tension between them became too much to bear. Sierra held her composure as the charming prisoner persisted. It became increasingly hard for her to resist him. When it was time for his release, Sierra couldn't resist the urge to feel his lips on hers. She gave him a passionate kiss right inside of his cell before he was released to go home. Rasheed was taken aback by the gesture, but little did she know she had opened Pandora's Box. She had given him all rights to pursue her aggressively. Through a mutual friend, they linked up when he came home, and the rest was history.

Sierra never thought that she would put her profession on the line for love. She didn't think that she could possibly be "desperate" enough to deal with a former inmate. Not only did she have a rendezvous with Rasheed, but she had a baby with him as well, something that she hadn't planned. Did she regret having her baby? No, she did not. But Sierra knew that it was no excuse for her unprofessional behavior. Never in a million years would she suggest that a correction officer, a man or a woman, have an affair with someone who was in DOC custody.

At one time, Sierra wanted to believe that Rasheed was the best man for her. He was fiercely protective and that was something that she loved about him. She had tried to convince herself that everyone made mistakes, and even a thug like Rasheed could change with a good woman by his side. She was wrong.

Rasheed painted a blissful picture of perfection and

she believed in him. She believed all of it. Actually, he turned out to be a manipulative control freak when it came to her and stopped at nothing to get what he wanted. When things didn't go his way, that temperamental, controlling Rasheed always managed to resurface. This was when Sierra noticed the disturbing similarities to the men she had to babysit every day. Rasheed would probably never be able to understand that the decision Sierra made to end their relationship was not about her; it was about Messiah.

Messiah deserved to have a decent male role model in his life, and Lamont Simmons was that and more. He was an assistant deputy warden, had worked for the Department of Correction for almost twenty years and, of course, was a great provider for their family. Part of that equation was Trey, Lamont's only son. Sierra smiled thinking about how much she loved her family, and she wasn't going to allow anyone or anything to ruin it. Not even Rasheed.

Later that day, during her meal break, Sierra decided to visit her fiancé in his office. Lamont was the tour commander for the facility, and the captains of the jail would report to him first whenever he was on duty. He would then give a report to the deputy warden and warden on what was going in the facility. Sierra was proud of Lamont's accomplishments, considering he had come a long way from being the neurotic jerk he used to be as a captain.

Lamont's office was located inside of the control room, much to Sierra's dismay. Every time she went to see him, Sierra got the nasty looks of disapproval from the control room staff, but she didn't care. A lot of correction officers, especially the women, talked about Sierra behind her back, giving her a full visual of how bland their lives probably were if they had to focus on her. They had their noses in the air, some of them forgetting that before they were hired by the Department of Correction, they were once welfare recipients or flipping burgers at McDonald's.

One of the things that gave her great satisfaction was that she had carte blanche to one of the most attractive men in the facility. It was all the ammunition Sierra needed to keep female officers hating on her.

When Sierra arrived at the control room, she knocked on the window and watched as an officer with an attitude reluctantly let her inside. Sierra looked the woman up and down with a smirk on her face, and walked straight to Lamont's office. Out of respect for his privacy, she did their secret knock, and he told her to come right in. Sierra walked in and locked the office door behind her.

"Hey, beautiful," Lamont said, looking shockingly handsome in his white shirt and top-model smile. She walked over and gave him a kiss on the lips. Sierra was about to pull away when Lamont pulled her back, this time putting his tongue down her throat. Sierra gladly reciprocated. After a few moments, they finally came up for air.

Sierra wiped the lip gloss off Lamont's mouth. "Damn. What was that for?" she asked.

Lamont smiled. "I don't know. I feel extra horny today. Can I have you?"

Sierra chuckled. "You want me right here? Right now?"

"Yeah, why not? Is there a problem with that?"

"I guess not. It's not like you're not accustomed to havin' sex on the job."

"Please don't start that shit, Sierra. Why do you always throw that in my face? That was like forever ago."

"It wasn't forever ago and it was with your half sister," Sierra replied, rolling her eyes.

"Okay, so Monique is my half sister. I didn't find out that she was my half sister until after we had sex! You know this already!"

"What a way to meet!" Sierra sighed.

Lamont shook his head. "As I said, it was my half sister, who I'd never met or ever discussed until after we had relations with each other. That was a chance meeting." Lamont sucked his teeth. "Can I get some lovin' or what, Si? You're blowin' my high right now with all this 'I had sex with my sister' talk!"

Sierra smiled seductively while Lamont watched her drop her uniform pants to the floor. Sierra stood there in her panties and licked her lips as she watched his erection protrude through his pants.

"Ready for me, baby?" he asked with a smirk.

Sierra gave Lamont the "come hither" look. She turned around with her behind facing him, and pulled off her lacy underwear. As she bent over, she put her right leg on the desk. Lamont was able to see her ass cheeks spread, exposing her fat pussy lips from the back. He was immediately turned on. He pulled his rod out of his pants and began rubbing himself.

"Wow, now you know that gets my dick so hard, Si."

Sierra turned her head around with her ass still spread wide open. She held one cheek open, this time exposing the pinkness of her sugar walls.

"So what are you waitin' for, baby? Come and get this."

Lamont looked at the door nervously. "Did you lock the door?" he asked.

"Of course I did, Lamont! Come on and get some of this good-good so that I can go to my post, baby! Hurry up before an alarm goes off!" Sierra ordered with an anxious look on her face.

Hopefully, an alarm in the jail wouldn't go off. This would only mean that there was an inmate disturbance somewhere in the facility or officer needed assistance. As an assistant deputy warden, Lamont would have to respond to the response area to make sure everything went smoothly. This meant that Lamont and Sierra would have to make it quick. This would only make their interlude even more exciting.

Lamont walked over to Sierra and kneeled down on the floor. He submerged his face into her sweet-smelling pussy and began sucking on it from the back. Sierra kept her mouth closed in an attempt to keep from screaming with pleasure, as Lamont's expert tongue lapped up her juices. He tickled her clitoris and licked her asshole with his tongue, while Sierra wriggled in delight. He grabbed her ass cheeks and opened them wide enough so that he could get to every nook and cranny of her vagina and the crack of her ass.

"You taste so good, baby," Lamont whispered, breathless from the adrenaline flowing through his chiseled body. He then stood up and dropped his pants to the floor. Grabbing Sierra by her long hair and slightly pulling her head back, he inserted his oversized penis inside of her. Lamont moaned and began stroking it real slow while he massaged her clit. Their bodies moved simultaneously, with Sierra tightening up her vaginal muscles around his thick rod. Lamont grabbed her small waist and shoved himself deeper inside of her. They both were in ecstasy, totally oblivious to their surroundings.

"Ooh, fuck me harder, baby," Sierra moaned softly. "I love this dick, you know that?"

"I know, baby, I know," Lamont replied. "And my pussy isn't going' nowhere!"

Lamont ground Sierra's pussy and she threw it back with a vengeance. The only thing that could be heard in the office was the ornery voices on the walkie-talkie and Sierra's wet pussy making gushy noises. Lamont began to get more excited and Sierra felt as if she was about to explode. He watched as his rod went in and out of Sierra's hot box. It was glistening from her juices. They managed to continue with their sexual interlude for at least fifteen minutes. They both felt the pleasure mounting.

"Baby, cum in me, please," she whispered. Lamont leaned over and began kissing the back of her neck. He knew that it was Sierra's hot spot. "Oh, oh, Lamont, I'm cummin', oh, I'm cummin'," Sierra whispered.

Lamont covered Sierra's mouth as he pushed deeper. Suddenly, Lamont's body began to jerk as he ejaculated inside of her. Sierra fell against the desk, with Lamont resting his body weight on her, spent from the quickie. After a few seconds of trying to catch their breath, they finally gathered up enough strength to clean themselves up. Lamont handed Sierra some baby wipes he kept stored in his desk drawer. After they were fully dressed, he collapsed into the recliner chair and Sierra sat on his lap. She kissed him on the forehead.

"I love you, you know that?" she said, gazing into his eyes.

He smiled, displaying his pearly whites. "I know you do, baby girl. I love you, too."

Sierra sighed and stood up. She wrapped her tousled hair into a ponytail. "I have to go to my post now smellin' like hot sex on a platter. They need to have a shower in this office." Lamont agreed. "Look, I'm cookin' tonight. What did you want to eat for dinner?"

Lamont shrugged. "Cook whatever you want, baby. I got to stay here tonight for the three-to-eleven shift. I won't be home until later on tonight."

Sierra sulked. "I don't like this new position, Lamont. You've been doin' too much overtime lately."

"Well, when I got promoted, you knew this is what this position entailed. It was no secret."

"Yeah, okay, I just hope that . . . Forget it," Sierra began with a sad look on her face.

"Hope what?"

"I just hope that you're really doin' the overtime."

Lamont stood up with his six-foot-plus frame towering over Sierra. She was only five feet two in height.

"Now why would you think that I'm lyin' about overtime, Sierra? You don't trust me now?"

Sierra shrugged, and sucked her teeth. "I do, but—" Sierra replied.

Lamont cut her off. "That's real fucked up, Sierra! After all we've been through, you have the nerve to ask me am I really doin' overtime? What about all the times that you snuck Messiah to see his father?"

"Now where the hell is that comin' from?"

"It's comin' from your insecurities, that's where!"

"My insecurities? I don't have any insecurities!"

"Yes, you do! First of all, you're always throwin' Monique in my face when I already told you that after I found out that she was my half sister, I was disgusted with myself for havin' sex with her. After all that you come in here talkin' that mess about how I fucked her in the control room! I let it go, so why can't you?"

"I'm not gonna argue with you, Lamont. Just be where the hell you say you're gonna be and we won't have a problem. It isn't like we never had a problem with you lyin' to me before!"

"There you go again!" Lamont walked to the door. "Just go to your post, Si, because this is not the time or place to be arguin', okay? I'll see you when I get home."

"It's not the time or place to argue but it's the time and place to fuck me, huh?"

Sierra folded her arm across her breasts and pouted. She didn't want to leave the office on bad terms with her sweetheart.

"I'm sorry, Lamont," she said, and tried to hug him. Lamont's body stiffened up.

"Yeah, all right. Just go back to your post, Sierra. I'll talk to you later."

Lamont opened the door for her and she walked out. Sierra turned around to say something else, but he closed the door in her face.

Chapter 3

India

Fraternal twins India and Asia Charles were gorgeous women, to say the least, and their names fit their facial features to a tee. India was an olive-complexioned beauty with long, dark hair and high cheekbones. Her prominent features also included her straight nose and prominent jawbone, bearing a strong resemblance to a black Pocahontas. Her twin, Asia, was the color of French vanilla ice cream, with a pie-shaped face and slanted eyes. With her jet-black hair and pink, pouty lips, she looked like an Asian princess.

Born and bred in Bedford-Stuyvesant, they were raised in poverty by a single mother. They could recall standing in long cheese lines with their mother, Khadijah, and playing with their bald Barbie dolls on the dirty floors of many welfare centers. On the other hand, Khadijah was always a hustler. She begged, borrowed, and stole from wherever and whoever to make sure that her daughters was taken care of. She also taught them never to trust men and to use them, if necessary. She taught them to use what they had to get what they wanted.

"Twins, y'all know that the game don't change for no one," Khadijah would say to her eleven-year-old girls while sitting at the kitchen table of their sparsely furnished Section Eight apartment on Jefferson Street. She would have a glass of Remy Martin in one hand and a Newport cigarette in the other.

"Y'all see your mama? I make sure that y'all have food on this table, clothes on your back, and a roof over your head. You wanna know how I do that?" Khadijah asked, taking a puff of the Newport and a sip of her drink. "I take, shake, and bake, if I have to."

India, who was the spitting image of her mother and the more inquisitive twin, had a confused look on her face. "What is take, shake, and bake, Mommy?"

"I will take whatever I have to, I will shake my ass if I have to, and I will bake me a crack pie and sell it just to feed me and my babies if I have to. I don't give a fuck about what I have to do to make sure that me and my babies are good, and you girls shouldn't either. As for these triflin' ass men out here? They ain't good for nothin' but some sex and some dollars. Love don't live here anymore, babies," Khadijah said, blowing smoke through her pointy nose.

India and Asia giggled. They loved when their mother talked like that. Not only did it make them knowledgeable before their time, but they incorporated their mother's attitude through their adolescence and adulthood as well.

When they became teenagers, it was nothing for the twins to be in the streets as late as they wanted to be. Khadijah was their best friend, never giving them any boundaries. She treated her daughters as if they were her equal. The twins had no regards or respect for anyone else but their mother. They became superficial and materialistic, not knowing how to be anything else. Khadijah had raised them to be this way.

Although the Charles twins were two physically beautiful girls, they had character flaws. Their ghetto mentality and their incessant need for drama stunted their growth and maturity. They turned into refined thieves at fifteen, and then at eighteen, they began living it up by stealing the identities of innocent, hard-working people. They used this hustle to their advantage by hitting up department stores all over the East Coast and ruining the lives and credit of others.

During this time, they bypassed urban labels like Rocawear and Baby Phat, and opted for high-end designers, such as Marc Jacobs and Azzedine Alaïa. Asia and India committed these crimes with no thought of how it affected people, as long as they kept themselves decked out in the hottest couture items and kept their pockets lined with cash.

It was only after their best friend, Tamir, was murdered that they both decided that it was time for them to finally get their acts together or become a statistic. Tamir was found dead in Nassau County, Long Island, off Exit 18 on the Southern State Parkway. She had died at the hands of Tyquan Williams, a resident thug, who eventually met his own demise a month or two after Tamir's death.

Surprisingly, the twins' mother was equally spooked by Tamir's murder, and finally came to her senses. She decided that she didn't want to lose her daughters to the streets. After this scare, and at the beckoning of Khadijah, the twins made the decision to turn their lives around. India and Asia decided to take a few civil service tests for city jobs.

The first one to call them was the New York City Department of Correction, and they happily accepted the positions of correction officers. Even the Charles twins had to laugh at the irony of the career path that they chose. The only question was did they really change for the better? Only time would tell.

India sat in the spacious living room of the two-bedroom apartment she shared with Asia. While she sat on the couch, painting her toenails, Asia stepped out of the shower with only a towel wrapped around her curvaceous body.

"I was thinkin' that we should have been had a job like this, girl," India said. "We're makin' good money and still got bitches hatin' on our swag."

"I know, right?" replied Asia while applying lotion to her body. "That's because we be comin' to work every day lookin' fly as shit. What I can't understand is how these broads are makin' all that money and still be lookin' half-assed! Those uniforms are an upgrade for them!"

India had other things on her mind. She wasn't worried about any female officer except for one, and that was Sierra Howell.

"Speakin' of half-assed broads, I'm really ready to get at that chick, Sierra," India said, blowing on the candy apple red nail polish on her toes. "I don't like that bitch."

Asia laughed while she stood in the doorway of the bathroom, lotioning her nude body. "Don't you see her at work every day?"

"No, I don't see her every day. If only she knew that I was Tamir's friend, she would probably have a fit."

Asia waved her sister off. "Well, she doesn't know that we're Tamir's friends, India. She doesn't even know that we exist."

India fell back on the couch in her living room. "You're right, but it's about to be on. I can't believe that I ended up in the same facility with the bitch." India looked over her painted toes. "I just miss Tamir so much. I can't believe that she's been dead for almost three years now."

Asia walked toward her bedroom. "I miss her too. She was our buddy." They both paused. "I wonder what's up with Rasheed?" Asia sighed. "Tamir was my homegirl but that didn't stop me from wantin' to give her man some pussy back then. Shoot, I still want to give him some."

"You're a whore, Asia!" India yelled out from the living room.

Asia laughed. "Call me what you wanna call me. But he wasn't tryin' to mess with me. He was all into Tamir. If he would have been with the program, man, I think Tamir would have had some problems!" She looked up in the air, like she was talking to her deceased friend in heaven. "Sorry, Tamir, girl!" Both of them laughed.

Asia continued as she walked into her bedroom, "But, oh, well. Since I can't have Rasheed, I just settled for a few correction officers, who just happen to be payin' like they weigh. Let them other females give up the puss for free. I'm not doin' it," she said with an attitude.

"Is that what you're doin', you little trollop? You're sellin' coochie to those clowns? They are so corny and I can't stand any of them. I don't even want their money. They can keep it. Those guys on the job act like they're so special. You would think that they're some A-list celebrities or somethin'. I guess they feel like that because they are layin' up with a couple of them desperate correction hoes. I just don't have time for any of their shit," India replied.

Asia laughed. "Well, you can go ahead and keep comin' home with that probationary new jack paycheck of yours. I think I done made top pay just from fuckin' with a few of them CO niggas. I can keep my own paycheck right in my checking account!"

India looked at her sister and smiled. "Do your thing, sweet pea. You know what Mama always said: 'Men ain't good for nothin' but fuckin' and that money.' It sounds like you got a good hustle goin' on."

"I do," Asia agreed. "So what's up with this Sierra chick? You gonna get at her or what?"

"Hell, yeah!" India replied. "Sierra is the reason that Tamir is dead now. If she wouldn't have started messin' with Rasheed, Tamir probably would have still been alive today. Who knows? Tamir and Rasheed probably would have even gotten back together. Sierra's ass is gonna get her payback but I'm gonna do it the smart way. There don't have to be no fightin' involved—no violence. I might just even befriend the stinkin' bitch."

Asia came out of the bedroom with giant rollers in her hair. "Why don't you just fuck with her man? Give her a taste of her own medicine so she can see how it feels. Didn't you say that her man is an assistant deputy warden in your jail?" she asked.

"Yes, he is, and I like that idea," India responded. She pulled her long hair up and pinned it on top of her head. "I have to meet him first and gain his trust. I don't know how I'm goin' to do that though." India looked at her twin suspiciously. "So while I'm tryin' to get up with Sierra's man, what are you goin' to be doin', Miss Hot Pants?"

"I'm gonna be workin' on Rasheed," Asia announced. "If Rasheed ever comes back to Brooklyn, I'm all over that."

India playfully rolled her eyes. "Now how are you goin' to do that when Rasheed is in Atlanta? He is not thinkin' about you."

Asia shook her head. "Whatever, heifer. Personally, I don't see Rasheed stayin' in Atlanta for too long. He'll be back because that nigga is a Brooklyn dude at heart. And when he comes back, I will be right here with open arms—and legs, too!" India couldn't contain her laughter.

The next day, after roll call, India watched closely as Sierra walked through the crowd of officers. She had been watching Sierra for some time now and saw that the woman didn't really socialize with her coworkers. She stayed to herself most of the time.

Once roll call was dismissed, everyone dispersed to go to their posts. India trailed closely behind Sierra, happy that they were headed in the same direction. This would give her the opportunity to finally meet the woman she despised so much.

Sierra walked into a waiting elevator and India walked briskly to catch it before the doors closed.

"Hold the elevator!" India yelled. Sierra held the elevator and peeped out the door. "Whew! Thank you," India said as tried to catch her breath. She looked at the stoic Sierra and spoke first. "Hello."

Sierra smiled. "Hello. Are you goin' to the fifth floor?" she asked, pressing the fifth floor button.

India smiled back. "Yeah, I have Five West today. What post do you have?"

"I have Five North. That's my steady housin' area," Sierra replied.

"Okay. That's cool."

The door opened on the fifth floor and they both stepped out. They waited for the officers to open another gate that led them to their respective housing areas. Before Sierra walked to the North side, India held her hand out and introduced herself.

"By the way, I'm India Charles, and you are?" India looked at the name tag on Sierra's uniform. "Howell?"

"Pretty name, India. My first name is Sierra."

"Thank you. So is yours."

"Are you a new officer? I don't think that I have ever seen you before."

I was in the control room yesterday when your man kicked you out of his office, bitch, India thought. She put on a phony smile. "I've been here about a year and a half. I'm still on probation, though. I hope I make it off."

Sierra shook her head. "You'll pass your probation. Don't worry."

India looked at the sleeve of Sierra's long-sleeved shirt. On one sleeve, she had two hash marks, each representing five years. This meant that Sierra had ten years or more on the job.

"I see that you're not a new jack. You've been there and done that, huh?"

Sierra sighed. "Yeah, I guess I've seen it all over the years."

You haven't seen anything yet, homegirl, India thought.

Sierra knocked on the window of the control room. The officer opened both gates on the North and West sides to let them into the housing areas.

"Take care, Howell. Maybe we'll get a chance to talk again real soon."

Sierra waved back and smiled. "Yeah, Charles, that would be nice. I'll talk to you later. Have a good day."

Once India walked onto her post, her smile instantly disappeared. Doing Sierra Howell dirty was going to be easier than she thought it would be.

Chapter 4

Lamont

It was the day after the argument between him and Sierra. Lamont was sitting in his office, pondering the future of their relationship. Lamont had noticed changes in Sierra since he had been promoted to assistant deputy warden, and he couldn't help but wonder what was going on with her. She was starting to become more suspicious and subliminally accuse him of cheating on her. It almost felt as if they were going backward in their relationship.

He had no idea why Sierra couldn't see that he was a changed man. Ever since they made their commitment to each other once again, Lamont had made it his business to reconstruct his negative traits. He loved that he finally had a stable home environment, something that he'd yearned for since his mother left him and his father. Lamont was six years old at the time.

From that day he promised himself that if he ever was fortunate enough to settle down with a good woman, he was going to do the right thing by her. Sierra was that person, and he made sure that he did whatever he needed to do to make her feel secure. But how many more snide remarks about his previous infidelities could he take?

Lamont leaned back in the chair, rubbing his chin. He couldn't understand women and their thought processes. Here he was, a good provider, good father, and a good man, and Sierra seemed like she was waiting for their union to fail. In the past, Lamont had cheated on her and Sierra moved on. He promised Sierra when they decided to get back with each other that the second time around was going to be much better. At least he thought it was.

Before they got back together, Sierra was involved with Rasheed Gordon, a former inmate from Five North. Lamont was surprised at her. He would have never thought that Sierra Howell, a self-proclaimed perfectionist, would have ever compromised her career for anyone, especially a crook.

After that, Lamont could not stand by and listen to other officers drag Sierra's name through the mud. Some even resorted to making up falsehoods without having any burden of proof. Lamont found himself defending her honor a few times, almost coming to blows with one of his good friends a few years ago.

"Yo, L, I've been hearin' some things about your girl, man," said Kaseem Brown one day while they were both in the captains' locker room getting dressed to go home. Kaseem and Lamont were good friends ever since coming to the correction department seventeen years before. They were even promoted to captain at the same time.

Lamont frowned at Kaseem. "What have you been hearin'?" he inquired.

Kaseem closed his locker and sat on the bench. "I know you heard the rumors. Tell me that you heard the rumors."

Lamont had heard the rumors, but that's all they were to him—rumors. He didn't want to entertain the Department of Correction gossip mill, especially when it came to his people.

"Nah," Lamont lied with a straight face. "I haven't heard anything. Why?"

Kaseem shook his head. "Dude, people around here are talkin' about Howell. I heard that she supposedly had a relationship with an inmate! Isn't she pregnant?"

Lamont stopped getting dressed. "C'mon, Kas. Don't you see that big-ass stomach of hers when you come over to the house? Yeah, she's pregnant, man!"

Lamont's heart fluttered because no one knew that the baby wasn't his, except him, Sierra, and his half sister, Monique Phillips, and she wasn't telling a soul.

Kaseem sighed. "Damn, L. I know that you can't be that stupid. I think Howell is playin' you, homie!"

Lamont frowned and stood up. "What the fuck do you mean, she's playin' me? How do you figure this?"

Kaseem sensed the hostility in Lamont's voice and body language, but that didn't stop him from running his mouth.

"I keep hearin' that she was involved with this one inmate. The guy's name was, um, what is this crook's name? Anyway, I do know that he was in Five North at one time." Kaseem tapped his feet on the floor and looked up in the air like he was desperately trying to remember the name of the inmate. "Damn! I can't remember the crook's name, but isn't Five North her steady housing area?"

A smile came over Lamont's face. "Yeah, it is. So what the hell is really good, Kas? What are you tryin' to tell me, man?"

Kaseem stood up. "I'm sayin' that you may need to get a DNA test when that baby is born. You never know, but Howell just might be pregnant by some crook and not you, man! Heard that she was havin' sex with that dude in his cell and everything. Listen, if that is a crook's baby and you stay with this chick, you are goin' to be raisin' his bastard child. Truthfully speakin', you don't need to be associated with her!"

Lamont's body tensed up. He looked at Kaseem, and,

from the expression on his so-called friend's face, he
saw that he was dead serious.

"You gotta be kiddin' me, right, Kas? You seriously
believe that my woman is pregnant by some inmate?"
Lamont asked, leaning his head to one side.

Kaseem nodded his head and puffed his chest out
a little. "Yes, I am serious! You're my boy and I can't
stand by and watch you get played like that. You know
how some of these broads are, L. We done laid up with a
few of them and you know firsthand that they're easy as
shit! To be honest, they're not above lettin' one of these
grimy-ass crooks get some of the skins, too. I just can't
knowingly fuck behind one of them motherfuckers!"

Suddenly, Lamont pushed Kaseem against the lockers.
Kaseem had a shocked look on his face and pushed
Lamont back. Before they could actually fight, two
other captains walked into the locker room just in time
and rushed to break it up.

"You disrespectful piece of shit! You're gonna actually
sit in my face and talk about my girl like that?"

Kaseem straightened out his wrinkled uniform shirt.
"Fuck you and your bitch, L! You always been a fuckin'
sucker for a ho! All you're doin right now is tryin' to
turn a ho into a housewife!" Kaseem yelled out.

The two friends tried to rush each other again, and
the other two captains stepped in to try to get them
to reason with each other. After a few moments, their
colleagues managed to calm them down. They were
still angry at each other, of course, but their close bond
was broken. It wasn't until after Messiah was a year old
that Kaseem came to Lamont and apologized for his
hurtful comments. Lamont accepted his apology and
they managed to repair their friendship.

Although his delivery was sort of harsh, Lamont
knew that Kaseem was only looking out for his best
interest. Lamont appreciated the gesture, but when

it came to Sierra, the love of his life, he always got defensive. Not to mention, it wasn't easy accepting that she had actually had a child for Rasheed and not him.

Lamont realized that Sierra bearing a son for Rasheed was only karma for his actions in the past. During their previous relationship, Lamont had an affair with Deja Sutton. Deja ended up pregnant with Lamont's first child. Sierra was devastated by this. Lamont felt the same way when he found out that she was pregnant by Rasheed.

After having a baby with a woman he had cheated on Sierra with, was he really at liberty to say anything about how Messiah was conceived? If it was a problem, Lamont only had one choice, and that was to let Sierra be. But it was obvious that he could not do that because she had a hold on him.

However, after he and Kaseem had that altercation, Lamont knew that he was a different man. Hearing how his buddy felt about Sierra and women in general, Lamont was disgusted. At one time, Lamont would have entertained Kaseem's views about women.

The old Lamont was a player extraordinaire, and breaking women's hearts was a game to him. It gave his ego a boost to see a woman break down over him, because he was an insecure, narcissistic jackass. Lamont was doing to women what his mother had done to him, and that was rip his heart to pieces when she left him and his father. It was his revenge on womankind, but how could he tell anyone this? Lamont portrayed the image of a ladies' man knowing that he was really the one who was afraid of being hurt.

So even though Sierra's prior relationship with Rasheed was forbidden to many, Lamont learned to not care about what was being said about them. Sierra was a good woman, and, most importantly, his woman, inmate's baby mama and all.

***

Sitting in his small office, Lamont smiled. He didn't want to fight with Sierra over petty bullshit, so he called her post.

"Howell. Five North," Sierra said, picking up the phone on the first ring.

"Hey, baby, how are you?" Lamont asked.

"Fine. You?" she replied in a curt tone.

Lamont chuckled. "Okay, okay, I'm sorry about yesterday. You didn't even wanna give me none last night and you know I can't have that. I need my stuff anytime I want it!"

Sierra chuckled too. "You can only get this when I want you to have it."

"I hear that!" Lamont replied. "Anyway, what are you doin'?"

Sierra sighed. "Nothin'. I'm doin' that same thing I do every day and that's babysit these grown-ass men." She paused. "Oh, yeah, some new jack introduced herself to me today. Her name is India Charles."

Lamont frowned. "Don't know her. There are so many new officers in here after that class came out of the academy last year. They salute me so much; I don't even stop to look at nametags anymore."

"She looks real familiar, though. I just can't place the face."

"Well, maybe she looks familiar because you may have seen her around the jail, you never can say."

"Yeah, you're right." Sierra paused and changed the subject. "Lamont, I'm so sorry about yesterday. You shouldn't have to apologize to me. It's just that I really love you and I don't want to be hurt again. I have a habit of gettin' with someone and the person turns out to be a different person. I'm older now and I can't afford to do that anymore. You say you love me and I believe you. I just don't wanna find out years later that you never loved me at all. I would be so crushed."

"I know, baby, I know. I'm not here to hurt you, okay? And let's not forget that you're a heartbreaker too."

Sierra laughed. "I thought I was that chick, shoot, you couldn't tell me nothin'! But I shut that down a long time ago. I've been through too much over the past few years."

"The both of us."

Sierra heard a loud buzz in the background and she jumped up to see the red lights in the corridors spinning. That meant that it was an alarm. Lamont had to go.

"Baby, I'll speak to you later," said Lamont.

"Go ahead, I hear the alarm. Be careful."

Lamont hung up the phone with a smile on his face. He snatched his walkie-talkie and ran out of the control room to the response area.

Chapter 5

Anwar

Anwar Jones arrived on Riker's Island from the Brooklyn courts. He walked into the facility intake area with a serious attitude and a frown on his face. He looked around at all the inmates who were being temporarily held in the large cell areas, waiting to be housed. He felt out of place from the rest of the scruffy-looking men who eyeballed him.

Anwar was decked out from head to toe in casual high-end clothes, from the Moncler spring jacket to his True Religion jeans, down to the brown Louis Vuitton sneakers on his feet. The David Yurman dog tag that he wore around his neck glistened in the dimly lit area, and his Mont Blanc spectacles gave him the look of a scholar. Anwar's caramel-colored skin looked freshly scrubbed in comparison to the graying skin of some of his future cellmates, and most of them were younger than he was.

As he walked past the officers that worked the area, his Dolce & Gabbana cologne lingered in their nostrils.

"Yo!" Anwar called out to one of the officers standing nearby. "What pen you wanted me to go in again?" he asked.

The officer looked up. "That pen over there," he said, pointing to an empty pen in the corner.

Anwar looked at the officer up and down. "Yo, ain't that the 'Why Me?' pen? Why are y'all puttin' me in a cell all by myself?" he asked, referring to the pen that officers used to isolate disruptive inmates.

The officer laughed and used his pen to point at Anwar's attire. "Man, look at all that designer stuff you have on. I don't want to put you in the pen with everybody else and somebody try to take them expensive sneakers off your feet and the shirt off your back! Fuck around, they might even go for the pants, too!"

Anwar smirked. "C'mon, homie, do I look like I'm pussy to you? Just put me in the pen with the regular niggas! I'm a G! They know better than to fuck with me!"

The officer looked at Anwar and hesitated for a moment. He didn't want to be responsible for anything jumping off in one of the pens because someone tried to get the well-dressed man for his things.

After a few seconds, the CO walked toward the Brooklyn pen and opened it. Anwar walked in and sat on the bench by himself. The CO shrugged and went back to his paperwork. Anwar looked around at the other new admissions and smirked to himself. He was thirty-five years old, and most of the inmates in there looked like little Similac babies to him.

Anwar was a professional convict, just like more than half of the inmates being held at Riker's Island. He hailed from Bedford-Stuyvesant, starting out as a young knucklehead roaming the streets. He caused havoc for no apparent reason at all and grew to become an adult with no regard for human beings. He portrayed himself as an honorable man to those he claimed to care for. Unfortunately, during this bid, Anwar would find out that he had love for no one, and eventually would realize that he had no loyalty to anyone, not even to himself.

He remembered being on the Island, back in the

day, when he and his crew used to get it on with the Puerto Ricans. It was nothing but alarms and waves of response teams coming to the housing areas on Rikers back in the early '90s. There were riots and slashings, all kinds of incidents happening in the jails, and Anwar was a part of that history. Anwar was a different type of dude; a regular guy he wasn't. Unfortunately, the Department of Correction was going to find that out.

Anwar sat on the hard bench, leaned his head back against the brick wall in the pen, and closed his eyes. When he did this, Anwar felt someone sitting down next to him. He immediately opened his eyes.

"What's good, my nigga?" the man greeted him. Anwar checked the guy out to see if he met the necessary requirements to be in his presence.

"Who are you? Do I know you?" Anwar asked while admiring the expensive Michele timepiece the guy was wearing on his wrist.

"Damn, B, you don't know who I am? It's me, Scooter!"

Shamel "Scooter" Abrams was a street hustler/ stick-up kid from Harlem. He was a direct descendant of Senegalese parents, who had done everything but disown him due to his trifling ways. Influenced by negative people, he chose to follow an untraditional lifestyle instead of the customary West African traditions that his parents had instilled in him. Scooter had been in and out of jail since the age of fifteen, and he continued his jail stints into his adulthood. The streets and jail were all he knew.

Anwar tilted his head back. He remembered the face. "Oh, shit, what's good, homie?" They gave each other a pound with a hug. "Yo, you all right, son? What you doin' in here?"

"Yeah, yeah, I'm straight. They just got me in here on some bullshit assault charge. I've been home for a minute and now this." Scooter checked out Anwar's expensive clothing and was impressed. "I see that you still be chillin'."

Anwar smiled. "What you mean? I stay fly all day, every day. If you know me, then you know that."

Scooter laughed. "Yeah, you right. What you doin' in here, B?" he asked.

Anwar sighed. "Man, these bird-ass cops was supposedly doin' a routine traffic stop when they pulled me over. They was talkin' about how my registration was fucked up on my G35 convertible. Okay, cool. I'll take that, but you ain't gonna pull me over, tell me to get out my shit, try to frisk me, and then wanna search my fuckin' vehicle. I went in on them dudes and they arrested me for obstruction and resistin' arrest. So now I'm in the bookings, right, waitin' for my case to be called. A nigga thinks he's goin' home, right, but when I went to court, I got remanded into custody. Now I'm here on this rock, man. I'm tight because I'm supposed to be done with this shit."

Scooter rubbed his bald head. "Me neither, B." He looked around and leaned over to Anwar. "You know I used to fuck with this CO broad in here, right?" Scooter said, totally off the subject.

Anwar yawned. "Oh, yeah?" He couldn't care less about Scooter's sexual exploits. He just wanted to go home.

"Yeah, man. I smashed that pussy in my cell and everything."

Anwar put his hand under his chin. "Word? What's the broad's name?"

"Miss Phillips. Monique Phillips. That was my bitch."

Anwar shook his head. He wasn't feeling the way Scooter was running his mouth, which was a no-no in jail and on the streets. With Scooter mentioning the female officer's name, Anwar took this gesture personally, because he was presently seeing a correction officer named Deja Sutton.

"Word? So that was your chick or your turn?"

Scooter smiled. "Nah, that was my chick. That woman was in love with me."

When Scooter turned his head briefly, Anwar noticed the long slice on the side of his face.

"Yo, what happened to your face, man? Who cut you like that?"

Scooter's hand went for the keloid scar on his face. "Yo, this dude snuck me when I was upstate," Scooter lied. "In the Green," he added, referring to the Greenhaven Correctional Facility.

Anwar shook his head and inspected the scar. "Damn! Somebody got your ass real good, too."

As Scooter continued to run his mouth, Anwar tuned him out and watched his surroundings. He saw a few females walking in and out of the receiving room, which was where inmates were held, but one in particular caught his eye. She came in there to drop off a worker to the intake officers who were working with the new admissions. Anwar watched as she sashayed across the intake in her fitted uniform pants.

Scooter fell back against the wall as if he had seen a ghost. "Did that bitch walk out yet?"

"What bitch? And why are you actin' all paranoid and shit?"

"I'm talkin' about the female officer who just walked in here and dropped an inmate off."

Anwar looked around. He didn't see her anymore so he figured she had walked out already. The pen that they were sitting in was toward the back, and she would not have been able to see them unless she walked over there.

"She's gone. You had a problem with her, son?" Anwar asked.

"I ain't really had no problem with the bitch. That chick is one of Phillips's homegirls. I don't need them

broads to know that I'm in here again if I can help it. I
hope they don't put me in Five North!"

Anwar shrugged. "Who gives a fuck about where you
go, son? This is jail. Plus, it's no way that you can hide
from two broads that work here."

Scooter wiped the sweat from his bald head with the
back of his hand, while Anwar gave him a strange look.

"Why was you avoidin' that chick anyway?" Anwar
asked.

Scooter sighed and leaned his head against the wall.
He closed his eyes.

"Her name is Miss Howell," Scooter said. "Don't you
remember her? She works in Five North."

"Miss Howell? That's who that was?" Anwar asked,
looking towards the door.

"Why? Do you know her?" Scooter asked.

Anwar folded his arms. "Yeah, yeah, I remember that
broad from Five North," Anwar lied. He knew of her,
all right. He had just never seen her in person. "She's
cool, I guess," he said. "I don't really know that much
about her."

Scooter smirked. "Yeah, that's the bitch that was
fuckin' with that dude, Rah. You know, Rasheed?
Rasheed with the locks in his hair? He's from the Stuy?"

"Nah, I can't say that I know that cat," Anwar replied,
telling another lie.

*Of course I know Rasheed. That's my brother from
another mother,* he thought. Curious to know what
Scooter had to say about Rasheed, Anwar played along
with the man. "I probably know him by face, though.
Why? What happened?" he asked.

Scooter leaned in closer to Anwar. He wanted to
make sure that no one heard what he had to say.

"Well, that CO bitch, Miss Howell, is Rasheed's
baby's mother!"

"Is that right?" Anwar replied, although he knew that
already.

"That's right! He was fuckin' with Miss Howell around the same time I was dealin' with my broad, Miss Phillips. He was in love with that chick, too."

"I could see that happenin'. She seems like she's an official chick."

Scooter sucked his teeth. "Please! Nobody can't tell Miss Howell that she ain't the flyest shit poppin'! Bum-ass bitch! These broads ain't shit, B! That's why I treat 'em the way I do!"

Anwar didn't know that the man before him was living a "downlow" homosexual lifestyle. Scooter had sex with women sometimes, but he actually preferred men.

Anwar looked around at the officers at the desk. After being subjected to Scooter and his excessive talking, being alone in that "Why Me?" pen wasn't such a bad idea after all.

"Well, I'm the one shot that bitch-ass nigga!" Scooter blurted out of nowhere.

After he said that, Anwar officially marked him as a clown. One of the things that a person shouldn't do while he's in jail is snitch on anyone, especially himself. Anwar thought that Scooter might have known better, but it was obvious that he didn't.

"What bitch-ass nigga? Who are you talkin' about?" Anwar asked with an annoyed look on his face. He just wanted Scooter to keep quiet at this point.

"I'm talkin' about Rasheed. When I was locked with him, like, three years ago, he got me set up. Just before he was about to go home, he got these two Blood dudes, Pretty and Valentine, to try to cut me. I don't know why, because me and Rah ain't never had no problem with each other; at least, I thought we didn't. So one day, I'm in my hood, mindin' my business, and who do I see? I see Rasheed! I went and pulled a gun out of my stash and capped one in his ass!"

Anwar realized that Scooter probably had gotten that cut when he was on Riker's Island after all. He could see Rasheed being responsible for that.

"So, is that the reason you're in here now? Because you shot bitch-ass Rasheed?"

"Nah, this is for some other shit," Scooter replied.

Anwar shook his head and smirked. He then got up and walked toward the front of the pen. An intake officer walked by. Anwar gestured for him to walk toward where he was standing.

"When y'all told me that I had to go in that pen by myself earlier, I didn't want to. But look, man, this motherfucker behind me hasn't stopped talkin' since he got in here. Personally, I don't want no dealings with that dude. Could you just put me in that pen over there, my man? Please. Damn!"

The officer glanced at Scooter, who was running his mouth with someone else in the pen.

"Wow!" exclaimed the officer. "That's that snitch, Abrams. I don't blame you, man. Nobody wants to deal with that dude anyway."

The CO looked at an empty pen and took that assortment of keys off his belt. He opened the gate for Anwar to walk out.

"Yo, B!" Scooter called out. "Yo, where you goin'?"

Anwar sighed loudly. "See what I mean, man?" The CO who took him out of the pen laughed.

After a few hours passed, Anwar lay down on the hard bench in the pen. He blocked the loud walkie-talkies and the other noises that were associated with jail. Scooter had him stressed out. What was only supposed to be a routine traffic stop had turned into an arrest, then turned into him being sentenced to ninety days on Rikers. Now that Scooter had decided to confide in him about the shooting of Rasheed, Anwar had no other choice but to finish him off. After what Rasheed had done for him back in the day, he owed his friend that much.

Chapter 6

Rasheed

Two days later, in Bedford-Stuyvesant, Rasheed parked his black Range Rover on Halsey Street. He sighed as he thought about the good memories that were near and dear to him. Feeling a little nostalgic, Rasheed gathered up enough strength to walk to the back of his truck and remove his luggage. Listening to the rustling of the tree leaves, he took in the spring air while listening to sounds of the city. The city was so different from the south, and he knew that, after this time, he wasn't going to trade it for anything. With the exception of his brother, Karim, who he loved more than life itself, his family was in Brooklyn, and this was where he was going to stay.

As he was putting his suitcases on the sidewalk, the door to the house opened. It was his uncle, Kemper Gordon, the youngest son of his grandmother. Rasheed and Kemp were so close in age that they had been raised like brothers. Rasheed always acknowledged the fact that Kemp was his uncle, though, out of respect and admiration for him.

"Yo, what's good, nephew?" Kemp greeted him with a huge smile on his face. He gave Rasheed a tight bear hug.

Rasheed laughed. He hadn't seen Kemp in about a year. The last time they saw each other was when Kemp visited Atlanta.

"What's poppin', Unc? How you, man?" asked Rasheed.

"I'm good. Can't you see that?"

Rasheed checked out the expensive pair of Gucci loafers on Kemp's feet. He nodded while checking Kemp out from head to toe. "I can see that you've been doin' your numbers."

Kemp helped Rasheed with his bags. "Yeah, a little, but, Rah, listen to me. I got something important to tell you before you go in the house."

Rasheed stopped in his tracks. "What's up? Is everything okay?"

"Ma didn't want me to tell you and Karim because she didn't want y'all to worry, but she's dyin', son. She has aggressive ovarian cancer and it spread. She's not goin' to make it. We were goin' to put her in hospice, but . . ." As Kemp continued to talk, but Rasheed didn't hear anything else Kemp said as he walked in the door and stood in the foyer.

He didn't know whether to be upset at Kemp and his family for not saying anything to him about his Nana, or to be angry at Karim for wanting to keep him in Atlanta. He figured that being angry with anyone was pointless, especially at a time like this.

Rasheed tried to catch his breath. He felt as if he was about to hyperventilate. Kemp followed him inside and went to hug him. Rasheed softly nudged him away.

"Where's Nana, Kemp?" Rasheed asked with tears in his eyes.

"Rah, look—," Kemp began.

Rasheed cut him off. "Fuck all of that! Where is my Nana?"

"We just brought her home from the hospital. She's in her bedroom. Karim will be here in a few days, too. I just called him today to tell him the news. That was when he told me that you were drivin' up."

"So why didn't anyone call me while I was on the road?"

Kemp shook his head. "That isn't any news to hear while you're on the road, man. We just wanted you to get here safely."

Rasheed walked down the long hallway. On the walls, he observed the pictures of their large family. There were pictures of him and Karim in elementary school, old school pictures of his aunts and uncles, including two ten-by-thirteen pictures of his deceased mother, Lavon, and his uncle, Peppy. Rasheed felt his throat tighten up as he thought about Nana, the one woman he loved more than any other woman in the world. She was the woman he loved just as much as he'd loved Lavon Gordon.

He opened the double doors to his Nana's master bedroom. When their home was being remodeled, the Gordon sons made sure that their mother had upscale sleeping quarters. She had a king-sized, four-poster oak bed, which was sitting on top of a carpeted platform inside of her bedroom. Nana also had a nook area, where there was a small love seat and a thirty-two-inch television mounted on the wall. A beautiful chaise longue was in front of the huge window, and Nana was sitting in it, with a chenille throw wrapped around her frail body. She was still a very lovely woman, even with her bald head and sickly appearance.

Miss Carrie looked up and saw Rasheed standing over her. He kneeled down on the floor beside her. He could tell that she was weak and that any day she was going to take her last breath. She kissed Rasheed's forehead and he put his arm around her skeletal frame. He instantly began crying.

"Don't cry, baby," Miss Carrie whispered. "I lived a good life and y'all have many memories of me. I don't want you to fret or fuss over me, okay?"

How am I gonna live without you, Nana? Mommy is gone and now you're dyin' on me . . . What am I gonna do? Rasheed thought.

Rasheed wiped his eyes, but he couldn't stop the tears from flowing. "But, Nana, you are the only mother I had for the last twenty-eight years! I don't know no other mother but you! Mommy died and, and . . ." Rasheed drifted off.

"Rah Rah, don't do that!" she scolded. "I can't help what's happenin' to me, it's God's will. It's my time, baby. I know that you don't want me to leave this earth, but, baby, I'm sufferin', I'm in pain, and the fight is over."

"Nana, please! You have to fight it."

"Now, Rasheed, I've been takin' care of you children all my life and I'm sixty-eight years old! Now it's time for me to be taken care of and God is goin' to do just that. The only thing that I ask of you is to let me see my great-grandbaby before I leave this earth."

Rasheed sighed. He didn't know how he was going to accomplish that last request because he and Sierra did not see eye to eye. His grandmother was not aware that he hadn't spoken to Sierra in months, and he didn't have the nerve to call her now just so his Nana could see Messiah on her deathbed. Rasheed didn't know what he was more afraid of: Sierra's response to his request, or his reaction if she said no.

"Okay, Nana, I'll work on that."

"Please, baby. That's all I ask of you," she said while rubbing his face.

Rasheed sat next to his grandmother and watched her until she dozed off. He put the throw across her shoulders and walked toward her bedroom door, looking back at her one more time. His body began to shudder with sadness, and he finally got the strength to turn the doorknob. As he walked down the hallway,

Kemp was in the family room, shooting pool. Rasheed collapsed in Kemp's arms and they both began bawling.

Later that evening, after putting away his things, Rasheed decided to hit the streets. The night was still young and the weather was exceptionally nice. He needed to clear his head.

Rasheed looked at his phone dozens of times, debating whether he should call Sierra. He knew that she had a new life. Any dealings with him would only be a distraction for her, but this was a life or death situation. His grandmother was dying and she had made a request. Now it was his obligation to fulfill it.

Needing a moment to regroup, Rasheed decided to take a ride around the neighborhood that he cherished so much. Rasheed turned down Lewis Avenue and headed toward Hart Street. He was going to ride around to see if he saw any of his old cronies, just to see if anyone wanted to get a drink or two with him.

Rasheed thought about Anwar Jones, who was one of his closest friends. He hadn't seen his ace, Anwar, since he moved to Atlanta, and he needed to see him now. Maybe seeing an old friend could help lighten the stressful load that he was carrying.

When Rasheed turned the corner on Hart Street, he parked near Roosevelt projects, which was to his left. No one was outside, which was highly unusual. He looked at the time, and it was only 7:00 in the evening. There, he finally found the courage to pick up his cell phone to call Sierra. He silently prayed that the conversation would be smooth sailing. He didn't need any more stress.

As Keyshia Cole's "You Complete Me" caller tune played, Rasheed leaned his seat back and waited for Sierra to pick up. He had changed his cell number, so he figured that the number was unfamiliar to her.

"Hello?" answered Sierra. "Hello, who is this?"

"What's up, Si," replied Rasheed. "It's me, Rasheed."

There was silence on the other end. "Rasheed Gordon?" she said sarcastically with a slight chuckle.

He sighed. It looked like he was going to have to kiss a little ass. Anything for his Nana.

"Yes. It's Rasheed Hakim Gordon. How are you?"

"I'm fine."

"How's Messiah?"

"He's excellent. Oh, yeah, by the way, he's two years old now. His birthday was yesterday. Remember?"

"Yes, I remember. I wanted to make it here in time but I thought I was goin' to fly up. I took the drive up instead. Look, I'm not callin' you to cause any drama, and I really don't want to bother you, bein' that you moved on and all, but I'm gonna be in New York for good and I was wonderin' if—"

Sierra cut him off. "Wonderin' what, Rasheed? Wonderin' if you can see Messiah?"

"Yes, that, too, but seriously, Sierra, my Nana is dyin'. She was diagnosed with ovarian cancer. It's in its last stages and she only has a few weeks to live. Her last request to me was to see Messiah. I mean, this would mean everything to me and her."

"I don't know. Let me think about this, Rasheed. You know that you and I aren't on good terms, and I'm pretty sure your family is not that happy about me keepin' Messiah away from them for so long."

"Don't worry about the rest of my family. This is about Nana. She wants to see Messiah. I have never asked you to do anything that you didn't wanna do," he said. Rasheed stopped before he opened old wounds. It wasn't about him anymore.

"Please, don't go there! Just let me just think about this. I need a day or so," Sierra pleaded.

Rasheed was getting impatient. He didn't understand why Sierra was being so difficult. He already told her that his grandmother wanted to see Messiah before she left this earth. What was her problem?

"Sierra, I'm beggin' you. I love my son and I do want to see him and have a relationship with him, but before I start doin' that, can you bring Messiah to my house tomorrow? A day or two to think about it may be too late." Sierra was silent. "Is it Lamont? Because if it is, he don't have to know your every move, does he?"

Sierra hesitated. "No, Rasheed. I just don't want to bring Messiah over there and you start givin' me problems. You know how you do."

Rasheed sat upright and pulled off from the corner. "Just bring Messiah to my house tomorrow."

He listened to Sierra sigh loudly. "Okay, okay. I'll be there."

"Thank you very much." They disconnected the call and Rasheed proceeded down the street. The anticipation of seeing his son had lightened his somber mood. Rasheed hadn't seen Messiah since he was six months old and couldn't wait to see how much his boy had grown.

As he waited for the light to change, he saw one of his old comrades from the neighborhood. He decided to pull over and ask the man about Anwar's whereabouts.

"Yo, Dino, what's good, son?" Rasheed got out of his truck and gave the well-dressed man a pound.

"What up, my dude? You chillin'?" Dino asked, smiling from ear to ear. "I thought you was in Atlanta. Looked like it did you some good, too."

"Yeah, yeah, I was down there, but I moved back to New York today." Rasheed looked around the block. "Have you seen Anwar around here anywhere, Dino?"

Dino shook his head. "He's not anywhere around here. Anwar is locked up."

Rasheed rubbed his goateed chin. "Get outta here! When did this transpire?"

"Um, like the other day. He was supposed to go to court for some bullshit but the judge remanded him and they still got the nigga in there. I think Anwar is doin' like ninety days for some suspended license shit or somethin' like that."

"Do you talk to him?" Rasheed asked.

"Yeah, as a matter of fact, he called me last night. Give me your math and let me give it to him. You got a New York area code, right?"

"Yeah, I got a 347 area code so he should be able to call me with this number." They exchanged numbers. "What buildin' is he in?" Dino told him the building and Rasheed shook his head.

"Oh, word?" Rasheed said. "That was my building when I was locked up on the Island a few years ago. He's probably in Five North, too." He shook his head. "Damn, I don't miss that jail shit."

Dino sucked his teeth. "It's not funny but we all have been in there. It's actually kind of sad. One thing I can say though was that Five North was the livest house in that fuckin' jail. We used to wreak havoc in there, too. I even had a few CO broads checkin' for me while I was in there."

Rasheed quickly changed the subject. He didn't want to engage in any conversation about correction officer women or being locked up.

"Look, Dee, I'm out. Make sure you give Anwar my number when he calls you."

They gave each other a pound and Rasheed climbed back in the Range Rover. He beeped his horn at Dino as he pulled off.

Rasheed thought about the situation he was about to be in. He had left New York almost three years ago to get away from the negativity, to clear his head and ease his mind. His Nana was on her deathbed and Sierra was already showing signs that she was going to give him problems with seeing Messiah. Now for some reason he knew he had come back home to pure drama, and he was sure that this was only the beginning.

Chapter 7

Sierra

Meanwhile, back in Queens, Sierra hung the phone from Rasheed and plopped down on her bed.

How the hell am I goin' to tell Lamont this shit? Sierra thought.

Rasheed had moved back to Brooklyn, and, according to him, it was Miss Carrie's dying wish to see her great-grandson. There was no way Sierra could say no to that. First of all, how she was going to pull it off without Lamont becoming suspicious of her whereabouts was her dilemma? Sierra just figured that it wouldn't be a good idea to even tell Lamont about Rasheed wanting to see Messiah. Not yet anyway. Rasheed was not a good conversation starter in their household.

When Sierra realized that she was going have to eventually tell Lamont that Rasheed was living back in Brooklyn, she felt sick to her stomach. How in the hell was she going to do that? She was fine with Rasheed living out of town. She was also fine with him not contacting her or her son.

Now that Rasheed was back, it had opened a big can of worms. Rasheed was still upset at her refusal to be with him and she didn't trust him. For some reason, she felt that he had something up his sleeve. She just didn't know how or when he was going to strike.

After cooking dinner and giving the children a bath, Sierra settled into bed for the night. It was her day off tomorrow and Lamont had to work in the morning. Since Trey was going to be in school, Sierra began thinking that maybe, just maybe, she could sneak Messiah over to Rasheed's house without Lamont knowing a thing. She hated to lie to him when he had been so good to her and her son.

"Everything was goin' so good in my life and now leave it to Rasheed to fuck it up for me," she whispered to herself. "That bastard!"

Unable to fall asleep right away, Sierra was still awake when she heard Lamont's truck pull up in the driveway around 11:00 p.m. He was home early. Sierra thought that he was going to work the 11:00 p.m. to 7:00 a.m. shift which would have worked out perfectly for her. She would have been out of the house before he came home in the morning, and she wouldn't have had to explain her whereabouts.

"Shit!" she said. Her heart skipped a beat. Lamont was going to see that she was still awake and probably would want to cuddle. Considering everything that was going on in her mind, Sierra was in no mood for any type of affection. When Lamont walked into the bedroom, she pretended to be asleep.

The next day, it was 5:30 a.m. on the dot when Sierra was awakened as Lamont got dressed for work. She didn't know he had to work the 7:00 a.m. to 3:00 p.m. shift that day. Everything was working in her favor after all.

"You was sleepin' hella hard, babe," said Lamont while buttoning up his shirt. "I was tryin' to get my spoon on last night and your ass started snorin' on me."

She laughed and stretched. "Yeah, baby, I was exhausted. You know these boys can wear a sister out."

"I know that. They wear a brother out. In a minute,

I should have that position as head of the facility's security. I will have a steady tour and then I can spend more time with you and the kids. Workin' these crazy hours is kickin' my ass!"

"You're goin' to go for that position? I thought you were retirin'when you hit your twenty years."

Lamont shrugged. "I dunno. I'm still up in the air about retirement." He looked at Sierra. "I know what it is. You want me to be home all the time, huh? You miss your man?"

Sierra smiled. "And you know this," she answered with a seductive smile on her face.

Lamont reached over and kissed Sierra on the lips. "You better miss me." He slid into his uniform pants and put on his boots. "What do you have planned for today?"

Sierra was stuck for a moment., Then she caught herself. "Oh, yeah, me and, um, Messiah might be goin' to the mall."

"No day care for Messiah today?" Lamont asked, looking back at Sierra.

"I don't know. It's up in the air. I don't know what I'm gonna do with Messiah yet."

Lamont stopped and turned all the way around to face Sierra. "Are you all right, babe? You're actin' like you might need to go back to sleep or somethin'."

"I'm okay. On second thought, maybe I do need to go back to sleep."

Lamont kissed her on the forehead. "Yeah, that's a good idea. Look, I'm gonna call you later. So you better have that phone charged up and ready to talk to your man, or else I'm gonna come home and spank that juicy behind of yours!"

Sierra laughed nervously. She couldn't wait for him to leave. "Okay, baby, I will. I love you."

"Love you too. Kiss my bad boys for me. I'm out."

Sierra heard the front door slam, breathed a sigh of relief, and lay back down in bed. She didn't know whether to laugh or cry. What was going on? All the feelings for Rasheed that she thought she had left behind were resurfacing, and here she was lying to the one man she knew loved her very much.

Now that Rasheed's grandmother was approaching what could possibly be her last days, she felt bad about not wanting Messiah to be a part of Rasheed's life. Even though he was being unreasonable with her at the time, Sierra felt that she should have taken the initiative and allowed her son to establish a relationship with his paternal side of the family.

The Gordon family was huge; something that Sierra yearned for when she was growing up, and Messiah was the only direct descendant of Rasheed Gordon. It was already very unfortunate that Messiah would never get a chance to meet his paternal grandmother, Lavon, and now he would never get a chance to know his great-grandmother, all because his parents couldn't get along.

Thinking about this, helped Sierra get out of bed. She needed to prepare Messiah for the visit to his father's home.

It was 9:00 in the morning when Sierra dropped Trey off to his preschool. Two-year-old Messiah was asleep in his car seat in the back of her BMW truck, looking extra cute in his Baby Gap outfit and his Nike sneakers. Sierra removed a purse-sized perfume bottle from her Marc Jacobs bag and sprayed it all over her body. Her hair was in bouncy curls and her Bobbi Brown makeup was immaculate. She didn't want to overdo it, but she knew that Rasheed was going to be checking her out, so she wanted to look good. Sierra smiled to herself and picked up her phone to call him.

"Hello?" he answered groggily. Rasheed was always a late sleeper. "Hello?"

"Hey, it's me, Sierra," she said. "I see that you were still asleep."

"Nah, I just dozed off. I was sittin' here in Nana's room, watchin' television," he replied, clearing the frog out of his throat. "Where are you?"

"I was on my way over there," she said, turning onto the Conduit.

Rasheed looked at his watch and saw that it was a little after 9:00 a.m. "This early in the mornin'?" He paused. "Oh, yeah, I forgot. You wouldn't want your man to get suspicious. You must be tryin' to be back in the house before he gets home from work."

"Are you finished?" she asked. Rasheed grunted. Sierra looked at her phone and rolled her eyes. "Anyway, I was on my way over this early so that maybe you can spend a little time with Messiah, or do you want me to just let him see Nana and keep it movin'?"

Rasheed changed his tune. "C'mon, Si, I was just playin' with you. Come through. Everyone is good over here. I'm dressed, Nana is awake. She's kind of weak today but she's still up and talkin'. My brother, Karim, is on his way from the airport, too. Maybe he'll get here in time for you to meet him."

Sierra felt butterflies in her stomach. She hadn't anticipated seeing the rest of the Gordon family. She just wanted to make a safe getaway with Messiah when their visit was over. Any other family members being there would just prolong their visit.

"That's cool," Sierra said, lying through her teeth. "I'll be there in a few."

As Sierra took the Conduit to Atlantic Avenue, she grappled with the decision she was about to make. Considering all of the things that she had been through with Rasheed, today was the day that she was going to make the choice to let him be a permanent part of Messiah's life. Out of respect, she had to discuss it with Lamont, of course, being that he was the only father figure Messiah had known since he'd been in the world. She felt that it was only fair that Messiah knew his biological father. Building a father-son relationship was going to be Rasheed's responsibility, though, not hers.

Sierra thought back to that day when she told Lamont that she was pregnant.

"Lamont, I have somethin' to tell you," Sierra said *while they were lying in his bed one night after making love.*

Lamont kissed Sierra softly. "What's up, baby girl?"

"Um, before I tell you, I just wanna let you know that I already made my decision."

Lamon sat up and rested his head on hand. "Decision? What is it, babe?"

"I'm pregnant, Lamont. I was pregnant when we first hooked back up with each other, and I didn't want to say anything because I wasn't sure of what I was goin' to do."

Lamont sat upright in his bed and turned on the light. "What do you mean, Sierra? Am I goin' to be a daddy? How far along are you?"

This time Sierra sat upright. "I'm fourteen weeks pregnant, but you're not the father of my baby, Lamont."

Lamont looked up and shook his head. "Are you tellin' me that you're pregnant by that nigga, Rasheed?" he asked with a disgusted look on his face.

Sierra shrugged. "I think so," she whispered, lowering her head in shame.

Lamont folded his arms. "What the fuck do you mean, you think so?"

"I mean, I think it's Rasheed's, but it could also be Tyquan's."

"That dead murderer nigga, Tyquan?"

"Yes, Lamont. The dead murderer nigga, Tyquan."

"But didn't Tyke want to kill you and Rasheed? How did this happen? When did it happen? What the fuck is goin' on with you? You're throwin' your pussy around like that?"

Sierra was beginning to get angry at Lamont's insensitivity. She thought that he would be more understanding considering he had had a baby on her during their previous attempt at a relationship.

"I don't believe that you of all people are actin' like this, Lamont. I'm tryin' to tell you what's goin' on and you're sittin' here disrespectin' me and actin' like I'm some ho! At least I'm bein' honest with you!"

"I'm disrespectin' you? Okay, so now it's my turn to be honest! You disrespected yourself! You're runnin' around here, givin' up raw pussy to these criminal-ass motherfuckers and you wanna talk about disrespect? Not to mention, you had these dudes about to kill each other over you!"

"You're buggin', Lamont! For your fuckin' information, they had beef with each other before I even knew that they both existed, and how are you goin' to judge me when you had a goddamn baby on me and you fucked your own sister!"

Lamont hopped out of the bed. *"I want you the fuck outta my house! Right now!"*

A blank expression came over Sierra's face. *"So you're kickin' me out because I told you the truth? If you're gonna throw some shit in my face, I'm gonna throw some shit right back in yours!"* She crossed her arms and refused to move. *"And I'm not goin' anywhere!"*

Lamont grabbed Sierra by her arms and pulled her out of his bed. She was butt naked on the bedroom floor, acting a fool and crying hysterically. She began kicking wildly and caught him in the upper thigh.

"You fuckin' cheatin', lyin' bastard! I tell you the truth and this is how you're treatin' me?"

Lamont threw clothes at the naked Sierra, and removed a robe from his closet to cover his own nakedness.

He hovered over her and pointed a finger in her face. "Guess what? You can't do what I do! I'm a fuckin' man! That's what we do!"

Sierra stayed down on the floor until she retrieved all of her clothing. She finally gathered up the strength to get up, and walked into the bathroom, locking herself inside. She continued to cry while sitting on the cold, marble floor while Lamont banged on the door from the outside.

"Sierra!" yelled Lamont through the closed door. "You're a bitch, do you know that? You're a real live bitch, Sierra! I told you that I love you and wanted to make a life with you and now you're gonna hit me with this shit? How am I supposed to deal with raisin' some crook's baby?" Sierra put her hands over her ears. "Huh? Do you hear me talkin' to you?"

Sierra's tears continued to flow. She sat on the bathroom floor for a few more minutes and then stood up to put her clothes on. She inspected herself in the mirror as she put a warm washcloth to her face. After she was fully dressed, she opened the door. Lamont was leaning against the wall. He had tears in his eyes too. He grabbed Sierra and hugged her tightly.

"You don't understand," he whispered in her ear. "I love you, Sierra. I love you so much, I swear I do. I just wanted you to have my baby."

Sierra wiped a tear from her eye thinking about that day. She glanced at Messiah in the rearview mirror and saw that he was wide awake. The chubby toddler giggled at his mother and Sierra smiled back, realizing that his happiness was more important than anything else.

Thirty minutes later, Sierra pulled up in front of the Gordon household. It was an early Thursday morning so the Halsey Street block was quiet. She sighed as she slowly climbed out of her driver's seat and walked around to the passenger rear to take Messiah out of his car seat. When she opened the door, he began flailing wildly and reached for his mother.

"Mommy, Mommy," chanted Messiah as she took him into her arms.

Sierra kissed his chubby cheeks. "Hi, mommy's big man! Love you, 'Siah! Mommy loves her big man! Yes, she does!" she cooed.

Messiah giggled as Sierra nuzzled his neck. After gathering his bag, she put him on the ground so that he could walk toward the house. When they turned around, Rasheed was standing at the door watching them. For a moment, it felt like déjà vu.

Oh, my goodness, the chemistry between me and Rasheed is still there, Sierra thought.

Rasheed ran down the outside stairs and scooped Messiah into his muscular arms. The toddler looked at Rasheed like he had never seen him a day in his life. After being out of his son's life for most of his two years, Messiah didn't know Rasheed.

"Hey, Messiah!" Rasheed said excitedly. "I'm your Daddy!"

Messiah looked at Sierra, as if he was looking for an explanation. Sierra smiled.

"Can we take this slow, Rasheed?" she asked. "He doesn't know you."

Rasheed looked at her and shook his head. Sierra knew his feelings were hurt when she said that, but it was the truth, and it was no one's fault but his own for staying away.

"How are you, Miss Howell, or should I say Mrs. Simmons?"

She rolled her eyes. "Can we please get through this day without all the fussin' and fightin'? Anyway, this day isn't just about you, Rasheed. It's about seein' your Nana and fulfillin' her request to see Messiah. That's why I'm here."

Rasheed kissed Messiah on the cheek and the baby laughed. "You're such a happy baby, aren't you?"

"Yeah, thanks to me," Sierra mumbled under her breath.

"What did you say?" Rasheed asked as they walked through the front door of the brownstone. "Why are you always talkin' shit?"

Sierra walked into the spacious living room with a smirk on her face, and sat on the rust-colored microfiber sofa.

She looked around the house like it was the first time she had been there. She remembered when she was so excited about coming there to be in the company of the man she was in love with at one time. Now, she just couldn't be in a relationship with him anymore. Sierra knew who and what was good for her, and it wasn't Mr. Gordon with his superiority complex.

Rasheed stood in the living room with Messiah still in his arms. "What are you sittin' in here for?"

"Because I'm waitin' for your Nana to see the baby. What else do you think I'm sittin' in here for?"

Rasheed sucked his teeth. "Stop actin' silly and come on down the hall with me. Okay, so Nana wants to see the baby, but you're Messiah's mother. Why wouldn't she want to see his mother too?"

Sierra sighed and stood up. She followed Rasheed down the foyer to his grandmother's room. As she did this, Sierra watched how Messiah immediately took to Rasheed. It was then that she realized that Messiah was beginning to look more and more like his father every day. This came as no surprise because she couldn't stand Rasheed throughout her entire pregnancy.

Rasheed opened the bedroom door and he walked in first with Messiah in his arms. Sierra slowly walked in behind him. She hesitated for a moment, almost not wanting to see Miss Carrie in the condition that she was in. She wasn't good with these types of situations.

Miss Carrie opened her eyes only to be greeted by Messiah's smiling face. Rasheed sat the toddler next to his great-grandmother.

"Oh, my Lord!" Miss Carrie announced, her voice feeble from sickness. "This is my great-grand, my first great-grand! He's so beautiful!"

Sierra looked at Rasheed. He looked back and winked. She didn't know that Messiah was the first great-grandchild. She had also forgotten that Rasheed and Karim were the oldest grandchildren.

Miss Carrie looked at Sierra and managed to smile. "Is that Miss Sierra?"

"Yes, ma'am. It's me. How are you feelin'?" Sierra asked.

"I'm managin', baby. Come over here and give me some sugar." Sierra kissed Miss Carrie's clammy cheek. She felt a lump in her throat. The once beautiful woman was now a skeleton of her old self. Miss Carrie was the matriarch of the Gordon clan, and if she passed, Sierra wondered what would happen to her children and grandchildren. Rasheed was already wandering aimlessly through life.

Miss Carrie held Sierra's hand. "I know that you and Rasheed haven't always gotten along, but I want to tell you that you and him have to got to get along for the sake of this beautiful baby." She kissed Messiah on the cheek. "You and my grandson have got to get along."

Sierra rolled her eyes at Rasheed, who wore a smug expression on his face. "Okay, Miss Carrie, we'll work on that," Sierra said, rolling her eyes at him.

Miss Carrie continued. "I think that you are still in love with him, aren't you?"

Sierra held her head down and shrugged. "I'm not—," she began. She wouldn't dare tell the sickly woman that her grandson was a bitter pain in her ass.

Miss Carrie held her hand up. "You don't have to answer that, baby. That's a question that I think I know the answer to already."

Sierra smiled sweetly because she had been asking herself the same thing. She really didn't know how she felt about Rasheed. Truthfully, she was afraid to even think about how she really felt about him.

They all sat there for the next hour, watching Messiah, amazed at how time had passed so quickly. Messiah entertained the adults with his antics and Miss Carrie loved every minute of it. When the visiting nurse came, Sierra said her good-byes and walked out of the bedroom behind Rasheed and Messiah. After they stayed for a few more hours, Sierra saw that it was 1:00 p.m. She told Rasheed that she had to go, and he walked them to the door.

"You be a good boy," Rasheed said to his son. He kissed him on the cheek. "I love you, little man."

Sierra took Messiah out of Rasheed's arms and put him down to walk. Rasheed looked at her with wonder in his eyes and she looked away. All the staring that he was doing was making her very uncomfortable; it was stirring up something in her that she'd thought was dormant.

"Well, Rasheed, I kept my end of the bargain. I brought your son here to see your Nana. Now do you think that you can give me a break?"

Rasheed leaned against the oak-stained door. "I'll give you a break when you let me see my boy on a regular basis."

Sierra put her hands on her wide hips. "I didn't have a problem with you seein' Messiah from the beginning."

"So you're gonna stand there and lie in my face? You

got back with this dude, Lamont, and that was it for me. I wasn't qualified to be a good father because I got a criminal background, right? But you're with some nigga who had a fuckin' baby on you while y'all was in a relationship with each other. Actin' like he all perfect and shit."

Sierra shook her head. "You see? That is what I'm talkin' about! You're too worried about Lamont."

"No, you're too worried about Lamont. I couldn't give less than a fuck about homie. I know that I made some fucked-up decisions in the past when it came to Messiah but I wanna rectify them. I want to be in his life for good."

As Sierra was about to protest, Rasheed grabbed her face and kissed her on the mouth. Sierra didn't resist. She had to admit that she was still a sucker for Rasheed's sweet kisses. His tongue explored her mouth and she kissed him back, while Messiah stood there, unable to understand what was going on.

"Don't leave me right now, Si," Rasheed whispered while holding Sierra in his muscular arms. "I need you so bad. That's what it is. I just need you real bad."

"Rah, I can't do that when I have Lamont."

"Please, Si, please! I miss you so much, baby. You just don't know."

Sierra knew that he missed her. His erection rubbing against her moist vagina said it all. She almost felt tempted to let Rasheed make love to her, but how could she do that? That would be entirely too selfish. Thinking about it had her feeling ashamed.

"Rasheed, I gotta go. We have to discuss all of this at a later date."

Rasheed looked disappointed, but surprisingly he didn't object to her leaving. It seemed as if he read her mind, because he looked down at Messiah too and shook his head.

"Okay, but don't be no stranger, Sierra. All I'm askin' is to be able to see my baby boy on the regular."

Who are you kiddin', Rasheed? Sierra thought. *That isn't all you're askin' for.*

"We'll see," she said as she stepped outside.

It felt as if Rasheed's leering eyes were burning a hole in her back as she walked to her truck. Even as she strapped Messiah into his car seat and pulled off, Sierra noticed that Rasheed was still standing in the doorway of his house, watching them.

When she got to a red light, she glanced at her cell phone. Lamont had called her a few times. She sighed, dreading the discussion that they would have when he arrived home from work.

Chapter 8

Lamont

It was approximately 5:00 p.m. when Lamont arrived home that evening. He walked into the kitchen and kissed Sierra while she slaved over the hot stove.

"What's up, babe?" Lamont greeted her. "I'm glad I didn't have to work that double tonight!" He stood behind Sierra and held her tightly around the waist. He watched as she added the finishing touches to their dinner. "That smells good."

Sierra smiled pleasantly, giving him a peck on the lips. "Hey, honey bunny. I made your favorite: chicken parmesan and pasta."

Lamont went into the refrigerator and grabbed something to drink. "Damn! You know that's my favorite dish! What's the occasion?"

"Nothin'. I just felt like makin' it for you."

"Where's the kids?" he asked.

"Watchin' TV in the family room."

While they were in the kitchen, Trey walked in, with Messiah following close behind him. The two boys walked straight to Lamont. He picked them both up at the same time and put one child on each knee.

"What's up with my big boys? Y'all watchin' the Nick channel?"

Trey shook his head. "Yeah, Daddy, we was watchin' *SpongeBob!* 'Siah likes that cartoon!"

Lamont looked at Messiah and kissed him on the

cheek. "You like *SpongeBob,* man?" The toddler nodded and smiled. They all began singing the *SpongeBob SquarePants* theme, while Sierra looked on and laughed.

"I should videotape this and send it to all your friends," she said with a chuckle. Watching the three of them together warmed her heart.

Lamont laughed too. "Yeah, put me on YouTube. That way we can show them deadbeats how a real father is supposed to act with his children." Lamont paused. "Where were you today? I called you a few times and your phone went straight to voice mail."

The children climbed off Lamont's lap and went back into the other room.

"I was in the mall and there was no reception in there."

Lamont frowned. They both had Verizon service and it worked almost anywhere. "Which mall did you go to, Green Acres or Roosevelt Field?" he asked with a suspicious look on his face.

"I went to Kings Plaza today."

"I don't understand. Why did you bypass all the malls in Long Island and Queens to go to Kings Plaza? What's out there? They were havin' a special sale or somethin'?" he asked.

Sierra turned around to face him. "Lamont, I have to talk to you about somethin'."

"Oh, boy. Can't it wait until after dinner? I'm starvin'."

"No, it can't wait."

He sighed. "What do you have to tell me, Si?"

"Rasheed is back in town." A blank expression came over Lamont's face. "He got in contact with me yesterday and he told me that his grandmother was dyin'. Her last request was to see Messiah. So I took Messiah to see his great-grandmother because she had never really had the opportunity to see him since he was born, and, yes, Rasheed was there, but nothin' happened between us, if that's what you're thinkin'. While we were there, he did suggest that he wanted to be a part of Messiah's life now that he has moved back to Brooklyn."

"So you're just now tellin' me this shit? How long has this dude been back in town?" He got up from the table and walked over to where Sierra was standing. "How long has he been back in town, Sierra?" he repeated.

Sierra shrugged. She looked nervous as hell. "I dunno, Lamont. I mean, he just called me, like, yesterday. I never asked him anything else."

Lamont rubbed his head. "So what the hell are you sayin', Si? Are you tellin' me that you're gonna allow this convict to come back into Messiah's life so that he could disappear on him again? Is it really that easy for him to come back and forth?" Sierra looked down into the pots that were on the stove. "Is this the type of man you want raisin' Messiah? A worthless, unstable street urchin who don't wanna take care of his responsibilities? He's no role model for Messiah!"

Sierra tried to say something but Lamont cut her off. "Listen, you got some decisions to make, homegirl, if you wanna be with me!"

"But, Lamont, I didn't say that I wanted to be with Rasheed. I just said that he wanted to be in Messiah's life."

"Wait a minute, let me finish. I told you that I wanted to adopt Messiah and raise him as my own son. I want him to see me as his father and as his daddy. I have been his daddy all of his life and I should be the only father he knows. Fuck Rasheed! If he was a real man, he should have been more concerned about bein' here for his son, instead of worryin' about who was screwin' you and runnin' the streets of New York and Atlanta."

Lamont's nose began to flare. "I'm not feelin' that shit, Sierra, not one bit, and if you take Messiah around this nigga again, I promise you, you're gonna have problems!"

Sierra began to get angry. "What kind of problems am I gonna have, Lamont? And why are you threatenin' me?"

"Because you keep forgettin' that I have a decent career, and I went and made a good life for myself, and that I am more of a man than Rasheed could ever be. I didn't have to kill nobody for a livin' or sell drugs or go to jail in order to prove somethin' to somebody. If you don't respect that, if you don't see me for what I am, then somebody else will!"

Sierra pouted. "I thought we had an honest and open relationship!"

"Yeah, we do, but don't take this relationship for granted, Si." Lamont sighed and walked away from her. "I'm goin' upstairs to take a shower and then I'm goin' out to hang with my dudes. I need a drink."

"What about my dinner? How are you goin' out? I made this dinner for you!"

"I don't have an appetite right now. I'll eat that shit tomorrow, man."

Lamont passed by the children, who were sitting back in the family room and playing with their toys. He went into the bedroom and shut the door. He couldn't believe Sierra. How could she even ask him that question after all the things that Rasheed had put her through? Not to mention, the rumors about Messiah being fathered by an inmate were still fresh in the minds of those peons at work, and his too.

He lay back on the bed and covered his eyes with his forearm. What the hell was wrong with women? They pushed and pushed their limits, not realizing that even the best men who were truly in love with them had boundaries.

This Rasheed dilemma was something that kept haunting him. He couldn't help but wonder why Sierra had even bothered to get back with him if she wanted Rasheed to be in Messiah's life. Part of their agreement was for Lamont to raise Messiah as his own, an agreement that he had kept. Now she was telling him that Rasheed wanted to be a part of Messiah's life, a part that any court in the land would let him have because, after all, Messiah Amir Howell was Rasheed Gordon's biological son.

Lamont jumped up and took off his uniform pants, throwing them in a heap in the corner of the bedroom. He wrapped a towel around his nude body and went into the bathroom to shower. Sierra walked in while he was washing up.

"Are you mad at me, Lamont?" she asked.

"Nope," he replied as he sloshed soapy water all over his body.

Sierra pulled the shower curtain back. Lamont wouldn't give her any eye contact. He was through with the conversation.

"Don't be mad at me, baby. Can we try to work this out?" she asked.

"Can you close the curtain, Si? I'm takin' a shower. I don't wanna talk about that shit no more."

Sierra gave Lamont a sad look and closed the shower curtain. Lamont rolled his eyes after hearing the bathroom door slam.

An hour later, Lamont pulled up to the Staxx pool hall. When he walked in, he spoke briefly with a few people he knew until he spotted his friend, Kaseem Brown, sitting at the bar.

"Yo, Kaseem!" screamed Lamont from across the pool hall. "What's up, man?"

Kaseem turned away from the flat-screen television that was mounted over the bartender's head. "Oh, shit! Looked who the cat dragged in! What's up, homie?" he said, giving Lamont a bear hug. "How did you know that we were over here?"

"I keep hearin' people at work talkin' about this spot so I decided to take a chance and come out tonight. Plus, I needed some fresh air."

Kaseem looked at him with a grin on his face. "What's the matter? Sierra's gettin' on your nerves or somethin'?"

Lamont smiled. "No, she's not. What makes you say that?" He wasn't about to tell Kaseem about the argument between him and Sierra.

"I think that because you haven't been out with the fellas in about a good six months! You know how many times me and Clemmons tried to get you to roll with us? The only thing that I heard was, 'Nah, man, I gotta go home to wifey and the kids' or 'I gotta ask wifey if it's okay to take my mouth off her titty!' You've been actin' like a little biatch and shit!"

Lamont laughed hysterically. "Man, fuck you! When was the last time you asked me to come out?"

"Man, you don't remember?" Kaseem said with a loud chuckle. "Then again, you probably don't. You're too pussy whipped to remember!"

As they talked trash to each other and played a few games of pool, Lamont didn't realize that he was being watched by two women—two women who would most likely change his life.

Chapter 9

India

The Staxx pool hall was located a few blocks from Rikers Island. It was where most correction officers came to unwind and get away from the stresses of the job. There were different cliques of officers who mingled with each other while shooting pool. What made it ironic was that even though they came to the pool hall to relax, the officers still managed to find time to talk about work.

The sounds of Ne-Yo boomed through the speakers as the Charles twins walked through the door of the pool hall. Although they were dressed very casually, they still looked like a million bucks. The men were leering at them and the women shot them a nasty look or two. Accustomed to all the hate they received from their peers and coworkers, the twins were unfazed by the attention. They were on a mission, and no one was going to stop them until their task was complete.

They copped a table and some pool sticks and instantly began playing pool, just the two of them.

Suddenly, India smiled. She had spotted her target from across the room.

"Just the man I wanted to see," India said. Asia looked in the same direction as her sister. It just happened to be a coincidence that Lamont Simmons, Sierra's man, was there. India couldn't believe her luck.

She tapped her sister excitedly. "Asia, Asia, look!

That's Sierra's man right over there! That's the guy I was tellin' you about!"

Asia shot one of the balls into the side pocket of the pool table. "Who, bitch? Who is it?" she asked with an exasperated look on her face. India had always been the more dramatic twin.

"Sierra's man! He's right over there," India said.

Asia's eyes widened as she took in the physical attributes of Lamont Simmons. "Damn, he looks good. I love his physique, even looks like he got a little swag about him."

India laughed. "Doesn't he? He's not the street guy we normally go for but he's seems so manly, you know what I'm sayin'?"

Asia couldn't take her eyes off Lamont. "You didn't tell me that he looks that good, though."

"Well, now you know," India replied with a look of satisfaction on her face. She was pleased that she got her sister's approval.

"So are you gonna holler at him or what?"

"Yes, I am!" India gave Asia a pound and swung her hair across her shoulders. From across the room, India found herself locking her eyes on the disturbingly handsome Lamont. She noticed that he had a fresh haircut and his goatee was trimmed up just right. She was instantly attracted to him.

The twins quickly made their way over to the bar, where Lamont and Kaseem were obviously headed.

"What's up, Deputy Simmons?" announced India, walking up behind him. "Hey, Captain Brown," she said, patting Kaseem on the shoulder. Kaseem nodded at her and smiled.

Lamont smiled. "What's up, sweetie? Um, where do I know you from?" he asked.

India rolled her eyes. "I work in the same facility as you do, sir!"

Lamont laughed and put his arm around India's shoulders. "Oh, I'm sorry, sweetie! I see so many people on a day-to-day basis; I don't know names, only faces. I don't even think I ever saw you around the jail. Are you on the wheel or somethin'?" he asked, referring to the nickname the Department of Correction used for a rotating schedule.

"Yeah, I am, but I have worked in the control room with you a few times. I see that you haven't noticed me," she said while pretending to sulk.

Lamont chuckled and India smiled as she watched his eyes roam all over her shapely frame. She smiled as she thought about how everything was definitely working in her favor.

Kaseem sat at the bar with his beer in his hand, staring at India and Asia. "So can we have some introductions, please? What's up with this young lady right here?" he asked, checking out Asia from head to toe.

"I'm sorry for being so rude. This is my twin sister, Asia Charles, and in case I haven't formerly introduced myself, I'm India Charles."

Kaseem shook his head approvingly. "Asia and India. Beautiful names for some beautiful sisters."

India smiled at Kaseem. "Thanks, Captain."

"You can call me Kaseem outside of the workplace, baby. I'm not a captain twenty-four seven. That's just my job title."

"And I'm Lamont. What brings you ladies out?"

India sighed. "It was a little boring at home so we decided to hang out tonight. You know, get a few drinks, have a good time, then go back home. It's very rare that we both have the day off at the same time."

"So, India, how do you like the job?" asked Lamont.

"Well, so far, so good. I don't have too many complaints about it," she replied.

Lamont was definitely checking her out. He seemed like he wanted to get to know her. She knew that it wouldn't take much to reel him in.

"That's good to hear. What else do you do on your days off?"

"Nothin'. I'm usually all work and no play," India replied with a smirk on her face.

Lamont licked his lips. "Oh, really? Why is that?"

India shrugged. "I hate the different shifts you have to work when you're on the wheel. I have to plan my life around my work schedule."

"I can't stand the wheel either," Asia agreed.

"You're a CO too? Wow. Were you ladies in the Academy together?" Lamont asked as Kaseem looked on.

"Yeah, we were," said India. Lamont and Kaseem looked at each other and nodded in approval

"That's what's up. What jail do you work in, Asia?" Lamont inquired.

"I work in C-95," she replied.

"How are they treatin' you in there?" Kaseem asked

"They're okay. Personally, I think that there are a lot of haters on this job. They hate without even knowin' you."

Lamont chuckled. "There is a lot of hate. Trust me, I've been goin' through the same thing for the last nineteen years on this job. The hate, the gossip, and the lies are endless."

"Some of those people revolve their lives around Corrections. Personally, I think they're pathetic," added India.

Lamont shook his head in agreement. "That they are, that they are." He looked at the bartender. "Ladies, I apologize for bein' rude. Would you ladies like somethin' to drink?"

India looked at Asia, who seemed impressed with

their chivalry. "Thanks, but we have our own money," India said.

Lamont waved her off. "Save your money, I got this. What y'all want? You want drinks? Appetizers? What?"

"Okay," India said as she slid on the bar stool next to Lamont. "I'll have an Apple Martini."

"What are you gettin', Asia?"

Asia sat next to Kaseem. "I'll have an Incredible Hulk."

Kaseem chimed in. "I got you, baby girl. Did you want anything to eat with that?" he asked.

"I'm okay for now," replied Asia, putting on a megawatt smile.

They sat at the bar for an hour or so and chatted with each other. Kaseem and Asia made small talk while Lamont and India were engrossed in their conversation.

"So, India, are you plannin' on makin' this job a career? Were you thinkin' about takin' promotional exams?"

India sighed. "I dunno. I haven't really had the chance to figure out how and what I'm gonna do yet. I think I'm just gonna go with the flow for a little while, you know, feel things out before I start thinkin' about takin' promotional tests."

Lamont reached over her to grab a napkin. India held her breath as his broad chest brushed against her arm. He was so sexy; he made her lower area tingle. It was funny, because she didn't even think that Lamont realized what he was doing to her.

All the undeservin' bitches like Sierra always get the good men, she thought.

After some hours had passed and the quartet had played a few pool games, it was time to call it a night. They all walked outside together to their respective cars, with Kaseem hopping in his Audi Q7 and pulling off first. Lamont took the liberty of walking the twins to Asia's Jeep Cherokee.

"You ladies seem like some real cool people."

India smirked. "You think so?"

Lamont laughed. "I know so. Is that more like it?" he asked, tipsy from the beers he drank.

"Thank you, Lamont," India replied.

They arrived at Asia's truck. She pressed the alarm and climbed into the driver's seat, giving Lamont and India a moment to themselves.

"Are you ladies gonna be all right on the drive home? Nobody's too drunk here, right, Asia?"

Asia chuckled. He didn't know that the twins were two lushes. They were able to drink most men under the table.

"I'm good, Lamont," she responded. "I only had one drink tonight."

India opened the passenger door. A wind passed through and her long hair blew into her face. Lamont stood there for a moment, as if he was mesmerized with her.

"Thank you, Lamont. Thanks for everything," she said.

"You're welcome, beautiful. I guess I will see you around the jail, huh?"

"Yeah, you will, so don't be a stranger," India added.

She was glad she wore the best fitting jeans in her closet, because Lamont was taking it all in with his roaming eyes. The tight Juicy Couture T-shirt she wore hugged her D-cup breasts and only made her even more of a threat to Lamont's beloved Sierra. India knew she looked good. The look on Lamont's face said it all.

"I won't, sweetheart, I won't," he said with a lustful look in his eyes.

India pulled Lamont back just as he was about to

walk away. "Wait! Don't you want my phone number? How are you goin' to keep in touch with me—outside of work?"

Lamont hesitantly reached into his pocket for his cell. He put India's number in the phone. He looked as if he didn't want to give out his number at all for fear that his whole spot would be blown up, so India just settled for giving him her phone number. Something was better than nothing.

After giving Lamont her digits, India gave him a nice kiss on the lips, even gave him a little tongue with it. A few seconds passed when Lamont stepped back, wiping India's lip gloss from his lips.

"Man, what did I do to deserve that?" he asked, smiling from ear to ear.

"Nothin'," replied India. "I just wanted to thank you for showin' us a good time."

Lamont hugged India again. She made sure she pressed her breasts against his chest.

"See ya, baby girl," he whispered in her ear.

India climbed into the Jeep and waved good-bye at the enamored Lamont, who stood there until they pulled off. Once they got to the corner of the block out of his sight, Asia and India began laughing hysterically. They gave each other high fives.

India looked back. "Do you think that Lamont is goin' to call me?" she asked.

"Sweetie, he's gonna do more than call you. He was actin' like he wanted to marry your ass!" replied Asia.

A feeling of redemption came over India as they drove home. Tamir's death wasn't going to be in vain after all.

Chapter 10

Anwar

The weekend had come and gone. It was a Monday morning in Five North. The cells that were being opened and closed awakened Anwar from his sleep. He reluctantly sat up on the bed inside of the dank cell and dragged himself to the cell window.

Looking out the small, rectangular cell window, everything that Anwar saw on the outside of his concrete box got under his skin. This was everything from the chipped paint on the walls to the inmates who walked around the tier of Five North, acting as if they were right at home. These types of detainees spent most of the days trying to convince everyone that they were the toughest dudes.

Anwar looked down on those inmates. They were posers, talking about things they never had or were ever going to get. Being locked up numerous times was like their sounding board but going to jail wasn't what made someone a "gangster." They had a perceived notion that extortion and gangbanging was the way to go, but the real gangsters had other inmates "offering" them commissary and contraband without saying one word or lifting a finger.

Then there were the inmates who resorted to begging. They were willing to accept scraps of cigarettes, food, and articles of clothing from other inmates.

Not Anwar. *Anwar ain't askin' none of these niggas for shit,* he thought.

If there was any way that someone could be locked up and walk around with a bourgeois attitude, Anwar made this very possible. A sociopath in his own right, it was highly unlikely that Anwar would make friends with any of the other cons during his skid bid anyway.

After standing at the window for quite some time, Anwar watched the female officer who was working in the housing area for the day. She was also the same pretty woman who Scooter had pointed out in Intake the day before. He claimed that she was Rasheed's baby's mother. Although Anwar was good friends with Rasheed, he never had the pleasure of meeting Sierra. Now that he saw her in the flesh, he could understand why his friend was so attracted to her.

Anwar quickly got his things together to take a shower. He decided at that moment that he was going to be the one to kill Scooter. Anwar wanted it to go smoothly when he did it. He knew that he needed the help of an officer, so who was better than Rasheed's baby's mother? After what Scooter had done to Rasheed, she should be more than happy to look out for him while he carried out his deed.

I'm real mad that Rasheed didn't kill this clown, Scooter, himself, Anwar thought.

After taking a refreshing shower, Anwar walked back to his cell to get dressed. He made his way downstairs toward the phone when the officer stopped him. She waved him over to her desk.

"Excuse me, I don't mean to bother you, but is your name Anwar Jones?" Sierra asked with a curious look on her face.

Anwar frowned. "Who wants to know?" he replied with an attitude.

Sierra sighed. She was unmoved. "I do, that's who."

Anwar smirked. "Well, why do you wanna know?"

I can see why Rasheed was feelin' this chick. She's a cutie, and feisty, too, thought Anwar.

"I'm not tryin' to do the back and forth thing with you, Mister. It's just that you looked familiar and I wanted to ask you your name."

"So why you just didn't say that then? I'm pretty sure that you already knew my name, and"—Anwar looked at Sierra's name tag—"now I know yours, Miss Howell!"

Sierra couldn't help but laugh at Anwar's antics. "You are so crazy! Anyway, I do know you. You do know that, right?"

He frowned again. "You don't know me, miss! Where you know me from?"

"You know Rasheed Gordon, right?" she asked, cocking her head to the side.

"Why?" Anwar replied, giving Sierra the runaround.

"Why the hell are you being so vague? I mean, damn, you're in jail, okay? If I wanna know anything about you, it ain't like I can't find out!"

"So if you can find out, why the hell are you askin' me a thousand and one questions?"

They paused for a moment and then began laughing again. "You are off the hook, Jones!" Sierra said, realizing that he had a good point.

"And you are nosey as hell, Miss Howell! Anyway, yeah, Rasheed is my man! Now, let me ask you a question—how do you know my dude? That's my man, fifty grand, right there."

Anwar already knew about Rasheed and Sierra's prior relationship. He just wanted her to confirm it.

Sierra was silent. Anwar looked at her and waited for her reply. "He's my son's father."

Anwar rubbed his chin. "Your son's father? Is that right?"

"Yeah, and that's not the only person I know you from," Sierra volunteered.

"I gotta hear this. Who's the other person you know me from?"

"Deja Sutton, your woman and my stepson's mother."
Anwar shook his head. Sierra was just telling it all.
"You're all in my business, aren't you? What's up with
your punk-ass man, you know, your stepson's father?"

Sierra flinched. "Why does he have to be a punk ass?
Does he have to be a punk because he has never been
locked up before and has a decent job?"

Anwar laughed at the fact that he had hit a nerve.
"Aw, that dude is a lame and you know that shit! You're
probably still in love with my boy anyway. Now that
you mentioned it, I remember him talkin' about you
every now and again. He was feelin' you too. He wasn't
gonna move to Atlanta until he found out that you was
talkin' to that bozo. Then he bounced."

"Oh, hell no! Don't put that shit on me! His brothers
were the ones who shipped his butt to Atlanta and I
moved on. Your boy still wanted to be a washed-up
gangster. I had no time for that."

"You still love that nigga, Rah. I know you do. I can
tell. Why else would you be up here tellin' me, a total
stranger and an inmate, all of your business, and you
know that's my man? What is it you really wanna say?"

Sierra put her head down. "Okay, okay. Even though
I think that I'm sharing a little too much information
with you, I do still love Rasheed, but it isn't my fault
that we aren't together; it's his. He was too out there,
and I had come too far and worked too hard to get to
where I am today to get caught up in his bullshit."

"I overstand, shorty. I overstand. But you knew what
you was gettin' yourself into when you started dealin'
with the nigga. So that was on you."

Sierra shrugged. "Yeah, I guess you're right. Ain't
nothin' I can say about that."

"I know I'm right. So what's up with your boo . . .
What's his name?"

Sierra twisted her lips. "My boo."

"I hear that," Anwar said.

"What's up with your 'boo,' Deja?" she asked.

"Nothin' is up. Why?"

"Are you guys still involved with each other?"

"Damn, you got the perfect job, man! You are too damn nosey!"

"Okay, I never said that I wasn't. So, what's up, are y'all still hollerin'? Weddin' bells, maybe?"

"I ain't tellin' you nothin' so you can run back and tell your man my business! You must think a nigga stupid!"

Sierra laughed. "Listen, Anwar Jones! Your 'business' is not that serious. Remember that. I have my own problems."

"Well, it must be that serious, Miss Howell, because you haven't stopped askin' me questions since I walked over here!" They both laughed. "And you better stop callin' out my government like that, girl, or else."

At the moment, the door to Five North opened and Lamont walked in. His white shirt was starched to a tee and his uniforms pants were neatly creased. The gold clovers on the collar of his shirt blinged in the sunlight that shined through the windows of Five North. He looked at Anwar, then Sierra.

"What's up?" Lamont asked with a suspicious look on his face. "What's goin' on here?"

Sierra swallowed and Anwar stood in the same spot. He wasn't about to scurry off because Lamont Simmons walked in.

"Nothin', sir," she replied.

"If nothin' is goin' on, why is this crook standin' near your desk?"

"Because he wanted to ask me somethin'."

Lamont looked at Anwar and Anwar gave him a dirty look. "What's your name, Mister?"

"Who wants to know?" Anwar sarcastically replied.

"I just asked you the question so that must mean I'm the one who wants to know."

"Yeah, but that don't mean I have to answer it. If you wanna know who I am, ask your chick." Anwar walked off, leaving Sierra standing there with her mouth wide open.

Lamont watched as Anwar walked away. Then he looked at Sierra. Anwar stood within earshot of the two because he wanted to hear their conversation. He pretended to use the phone while Lamont chastised Sierra.

"What does that crook mean by 'ask your chick'? I know that you're not in here tellin' these ignorant motherfuckers our business!" he said.

Sierra looked dumbfounded and didn't know what to say. After a brief silence, she just shrugged it off.

"I don't know what he's talkin' about, Lamont. You know how these guys in here feel that any male officer who walks on a female officer's post is her man," she said with a nervous chuckle. She glanced across the housing area at Anwar. He felt bad about putting her on the spot, but it served her right for getting too familiar with him just because he was Rasheed's friend.

Lamont's nose flared. "What is that inmate's name anyway?" he asked, signing her logbooks with his red Sharpie pen.

Sierra swallowed real hard. "I didn't ask him," she lied. It wasn't the time or place to tell Lamont that the inmate he'd addressed was his son's mother's man. Although he had never laid eyes on Anwar, Lamont hated that man more than he hated the inmate population, and Sierra knew this. He felt like Deja had given up on their son because of Anwar.

Lamont looked upset. He crossed his beefy arms. "Look, Si, you're here to do a job and you're a representation of me. You're my woman. You don't need to be talkin' to none of these assholes, and I damn sure don't wanna walk in here and see none of these crooks near your desk, is that understood?"

Sierra nodded. "You're right, Lamont, I apologize."

Lamont rested his hand on her shoulder. "Okay, baby. I'll talk to you later. I love you."

"I love you too."

Anwar watched as Lamont walked out of the housing area. Sierra sat at the desk and put her palm on her forehead, as if she had a headache.

Ten minutes after Lamont left, Anwar strolled over to Sierra's desk.

"Yo, Miss Howell, that's my bad," he said. "I didn't mean to put you out there like that, but that nigga called me a fuckin' crook. I am not no crook, man."

"Yeah, you did put me on blast. You have to understand that he is about his business and that he takes his position very serious."

"Yo, whatever! Fuck that nigga! I don't give a fuck about none of this shit in here, but fuck all that. I gotta talk to you about somethin' very serious."

"What is it?" Sierra asked with a frown on her face.

Anwar came close to Sierra so that only she could hear him. "The nigga who shot Rasheed is in here and I need to get at him. I'm gonna need your help."

"Where is he? Is he in here? Right now?" Sierra asked, glancing down the tier of cells.

"Yeah, he's in cell twenty-three, and I'm gonna body that nigga, right in here."

"What do you mean, 'body'? Are you askin' me to help you commit a murder?" she replied with a stunned look on her face.

"No, I'm not askin' you to get your hands dirty. I'm just askin' you to hold me down while I do it."

"But, Anwar, where is this comin' from? How can you ask me to help you do somethin' like that? I don't want no part of that shit, and your man, Rasheed, would never approve of me gettin' involved with no shit like that! And, besides, me and Rasheed aren't even together anymore!"

"Look, Miss, I don't give a shit about your personal feelings," he said through clenched teeth. He was so close to her that Sierra could see the veins protruding from his forehead. "This is on some straight revenge shit. I don't give a fuck what you do. Just do whatever it takes so that I can get the job done. Either way it's gonna go down. You're my last resort," Anwar added.

"You are crazy, nigga! That is conspiracy to murder! I am not gettin' involved in that shit! You got the wrong bitch!" Sierra whispered, staring Anwar right in his face.

"So I got the wrong bitch? No, I think I got the right bitch. Or maybe I should go ahead and just kill your boyfriend instead of Scooter, huh?"

Sierra began breathing heavily. "What?"

"Rasheed obviously didn't tell you about me. I'm nothin' to be fucked with in the hood, Miss Howell. I don't smile in nigga's faces and I definitely don't play with no bitches. I do what I do and keeps it movin'. This nigga violated your son's father, who is also my right-hand man, and you gonna sit your pretty ass on this post and take that shit lightly? What kind of baby mother are you? All I know is that I need to get at that dude and I have this little bullshit ninety day skid bid to do that."

Sierra shook her head and her eyes began to swell with tears. "I don't know why you're even tellin' me about this shit, Jones. I couldn't give less than a fuck about Scooter. I'm just happy that Rasheed survived the shootin'. That's all that matters to me."

Anwar stepped back and chuckled loudly. "Does it really matter to you? Do you really care about what happens to Rasheed? Scooter can get out tomorrow and finish Rasheed off! If that happens, whose fault will that be?"

Sierra's nose began to flare and tears formed in her

eyes. "What do you want from me, Anwar? Why do I have to be an accessory to this bullshit?" Sierra threw her hands up. "You know what, Jones? I don't give a fuck what you do to Scooter or anybody else in here for that matter. Just leave me and my man out of it, okay?"

Anwar shot her a disgusted look. "Yo, homegirl, I'm gettin' that dude, Scooter, whether you like it or not. And when it goes down—because you best believe that it is goin' down right here in Five North—I'd better not hear shit else about this from you or anybody else, you hear me? Or else you, your man, and Deja are all gonna die. That's three dead adults and two orphaned kids. You make the choice." Sierra gave Anwar the look of death. All he did was smile back at her.

"Well, here's the deal. You got until Friday to think about what you're goin' to say to them white shirts, and what kind of reports you're gonna write to cover your ass and mine when the shit hits the fan. You're gonna be falsifyin' documents like a motherfucker. Today is Monday and you got a good four and a half days to get your fuckin' mind right and keep this shit between us." Anwar began stepping away from the desk. "See ya, sweet pea," Anwar said, blowing the flustered Sierra a kiss as he walked back to his cell.

Chapter 11

Rasheed

While Sierra was going through it with Anwar on Rikers Island, Rasheed walked to the corner of his block, observing all the activity on the beautiful spring day. He had spent most of the morning doing errands for his grandmother, not being able to concentrate on anything else but her. Ever since he found out that she was sick, he couldn't bear to leave her side.

Rasheed hadn't heard from Sierra since she left his house that Thursday before. That was fine with him, because he had so many other things on his plate. The stress of his and Sierra's strained relationship had to be put on the back burner for now.

Rasheed thought about Nana, who had been the rock for all of them for as long as he could remember. Miss Carrie was the youngest of three sisters and two brothers, and they had passed a few years before her illness. The older generation was going to be extinct once she was gone. Miss Carrie was the last person to carry the torch, and there was no one who could ever fill her shoes, as far as Rasheed was concerned.

Rasheed walked into the bodega and gave a shout-out to Papi at the register. As he walked to the freezer to pick up a carton of Tropicana orange juice, he remembered that this store was the same place that he had crossed paths with Tyquan Williams, his deceased nemesis. All the years that he could have killed Tyke

and he waited until he got with Sierra to do it. He had
to ask himself, *Did he love Sierra that much to make
him want to kill over her? Or was she the fuel that
finalized the beef the two men already had?* Rasheed
never tried to figure it out, but when he found out that
Tyke had possibly killed Tamir, it was more than he
could handle.

Rasheed knew that if he would have personally
gotten a hold of Tyke, he would have probably burned
his eyelids closed, slit his throat, and thrown his body
into some hot acid. Born to a drug-addicted mother
and raised by his maternal grandmother, Tyke had no
real family, so it wasn't like anyone cared if Tyke was
gone, except his chickenhead wife, NeeNee. The kids
Tyke had "fathered" with his wife weren't really his
anyway, according to the hood, but Rasheed knew that
the menace just had to go.

Rasheed knew this, which made it easier for him to
carry out his plan to kill Tyke. Not to mention, by street
standards, Rasheed would have been less than a man if
he let Tyke's antics, which included murdering Tamir,
go over his head. Thanks to Lateef and Quan, his loyal
cronies, they made sure that Tyke was put down like a
dog. Rasheed didn't even have to get his hands dirty.

Now Rasheed had another problem on his hands. It
was Shamel Abrams, also known as Scooter.

The assistant district attorney tried to get Rasheed
to come to court to testify against the con, but he
would never admit that Scooter was the one who shot
him. He didn't care what the witnesses said; he wasn't
going to say a thing about it. He wanted to see Scooter
in the streets—he didn't want the man behind bars.
It was called "street justice," and this type of revenge
wasn't carried out by sitting on some witness stand in
a courtroom in front of a judge and jury. This type of
retribution was settled in the streets.

He was unsure of Scooter's whereabouts but the word on the streets was that he was locked up again. Rasheed secretly hoped that he was. The Scooter issue was something that he didn't want to deal with right now. There were too many things going on in Rasheed's life that were much more important than going to war with Scooter.

Rasheed paid for the orange juice and slowly walked back home, realizing how emotionally and physically exhausted he was. He hadn't had any rest since he got back from Atlanta.

After finding out Nana was sick, everyone was running around like chickens with their heads cut off, trying to make sure her last days were as comfortable as possible. But what's so comforting in knowing that his beloved Nana was approaching death? Rasheed couldn't answer that question, but anything he could do to make Nana happy while she was still alive, he was going to do it.

When Rasheed walked in the house, his immediate family members, including his little cousins, were there. Everyone had somber expressions on their faces. He knew what that meant. Rasheed put down the juice and made a mad dash for his Nana's bedroom. The visiting nurse was standing with her and Nana looked as if she was gasping for air. She held up her feeble hand and reached out to him. The nurse gave Rasheed a nod and backed away. He came over and softly grabbed Miss Carrie's hand. He knelt by the side of her bed.

"I love you, baby," Miss Carrie managed to say. "You were always my baby, my favorite, Rasheed. I want you to make Nana proud. Serve your God. Stay out of trouble. Raise your son right, find the love of your life, and get married, too. Okay, baby?" Tears of frustration poured from Rasheed's eyes, and fell onto Nana's 400-thread-count sheets.

"Yes, Nana, I will, I promise you," he replied. Rasheed began to weep a little louder.

All of a sudden, Miss Carrie began coughing and started wheezing, as if she was losing her breath. Rasheed jumped out of the nurse's way so that she could tend to his dying grandmother. He walked out of the room, calling 911 on his cell phone. Watching Rasheed, the other Gordon family members knew that it was over. They walked toward the bedroom. One by one, they slowly went inside, until everyone was standing around the bed. Carrie Ann Gordon, the beloved matriarch of their family, was dead at sixty-eight years old.

Three days later, after the funeral services for Miss Carrie, family and friends gathered at the Gordon home on Halsey Street. Rasheed didn't even notice the people who came in and out of the house, let alone the funeral services. His mind was in a blur as he thought about his grandmother and all the good times that they had.

Rasheed felt shame as he recalled all the times that he had gotten into trouble. He knew that she'd worried about him. Miss Carrie worried about all her children and grandchildren, especially after her oldest children, Peppy and Lavon, were murdered.

Kemp walked over and sat next to Rasheed on the chaise longue. Everyone was filing in and out of the living room, helping themselves to the delicious food that was being served in the kitchen. Rasheed didn't have the energy or the appetite to eat anything.

Kemp put his arm around Rasheed's broad shoulders. He knew that Rasheed would take the death the hardest. Miss Carrie had been instrumental in making sure that she made up for the loss of his mother. It was something that Rasheed would never forget.

"What's up, nephew?" Kemp said softly. "I know you're not okay, but I wanted to come over here and give you some kind of comfort."

Rasheed sighed and wiped a tear from his eye. "I know, Unc. Thanks, man."

"Damn, I'm gonna miss Ma, but you know what? She's not sufferin' anymore."

"Yeah, you're right. I know I wanted her to be here for my own selfish reasons, but she was too sick, Unc. She was fightin' it but she just couldn't do it anymore."

"Well, this house isn't gonna be the same." Kemp nodded at a few of his mother's friends. "By the way, Ma left us some money, but I don't even need that shit. You can have it."

Rasheed smiled. "Thanks, Unc, but I can't take that money."

"So you know what you do with it? Put it in a fund for Messiah. Sierra would appreciate that."

"That's cool, but I don't know what she appreciates anymore. Speakin' of Sierra, did she come to the funeral?"

Kemp shook his head. "I'm not sure. I didn't see her at the wake, either, but that doesn't mean that she didn't show up."

At that moment, the Charles twins, India and Asia, walked over to Rasheed. They looked good in their all-black attire. Kemp looked up at them and glanced at his nephew, who was emotionally drained. Kemp said hello, excused himself, and walked to the other side of the room. Asia sat beside Rasheed, and India sat on the other side of her sister.

"I wanted to come to you and give you my personal condolences," Asia began. Rasheed gave her the side eye. Her expensive Bvlgari perfume tickled his nose hair. "I haven't seen you in a minute, and when I heard about your Nana, me and my sister had to come and give you support."

Rasheed managed to smile. "Thanks, ladies. I'm just going through it right now, but y'all look good." He checked out their expensive threads. "I hope that y'all not still on that stolen credit card bullshit."

They both grinned. "Hell no," replied India with a smile. "You won't believe this, Rah, but we're correction officers now."

Rasheed's face lit up. "Damn. That's what's up. They must be givin' away shields if you two are COs."

India laughed. "That's what we said," she said. "But at least we're finally gettin' our shit together. We're gettin' older, and, one day, we both wanna settle down and even have kids and husbands. We don't need to have our kids doin' the same things that we did growing up."

"But how did y'all manage to get law enforcement jobs? Haven't you two been locked up before?"

"Man, we got our records expunged. It cost us some bread, but lucky for us they were all misdemeanors," said India.

Rasheed was impressed. And for some reason, Asia was unusually quiet and wouldn't stop staring at him. He made eye contact with her as well.

India sensed her sister's moment of opportunity and excused herself so that the two could be alone.

"I'm gonna go over here and talk to a few people," said India. "Hold your head, Rah."

"No doubt, India," Rasheed replied, giving her a nod. It was time to give his undivided attention to Asia. "So what's been up with you?" he asked.

Asia crossed her legs, exposing some French vanilla thigh, and smiled sweetly. "I'm fine. What's up with you, Rah?"

"Well, my Nana's passin' has got me down, but losin' my mind isn't goin' to change anything. I'm officially livin' back in Brooklyn so now I can see my son as much as possible. I need that balance, you know."

"What's your son's name again?"

"Messiah Amir Gordon. He's two years old."

"So how are you and his mother doin'? Are you two tryin' to work on the relationship?" she asked.

"We're not gettin' back together. She's moved on, and I guess I did too."

Asia shook her head. "I hear that, but do you and her still talk to each other? You do have a son together."

Rasheed shrugged, reluctant to give her any details about the relationship between him and Sierra. Even though she looked good as hell, he didn't want Asia all in his personal business.

"Yeah, we talk," Rasheed replied. "We're civil toward each other," he added.

She quickly changed the subject. "You do know that I always liked you, right, Rah?"

"You liked me?" he asked, pointing at his chest.

"Yeah, I liked you, but you ended up gettin' with Tamir. I was there the first day y'all started kickin' it with each other."

He smiled at the memory of that day. He remembered that Tamir was with a friend who was just as cute as she was. "That was you?"

Asia nodded. Rasheed got very quiet all of a sudden. He was grieving enough; he didn't need any more memories of his late ex-girlfriend, Tamir.

"You look real good, Asia. I'm definitely likin' what I see, for real."

She blushed. "I'm likin' what I see too. Look, I know you have a lot goin' on right now, so let's exchange numbers. When you feel up to it, call me."

They exchanged numbers and Asia kissed Rasheed on the cheek. Then she stood up to leave. "I'll be lookin' forward to hearin' from you," she said, blowing another kiss at him. Rasheed's eyes followed the silhouette of Asia's curvaceous body.

"You'll be hearin' from me real soon," he said to himself. He waved at India as she and Asia walked out the front door.

Twenty minutes later, Rasheed felt that he was composed enough to start making rounds. Just as he was about to do that, he heard a familiar voice in the foyer talking to his aunt, Sharee. When he walked over, Sierra was standing there, holding Messiah in her arms.

Chapter 12

Sierra

It was the night before Miss Carrie's funeral. When Sierra told Lamont that she was going to pay her respects, he didn't object to it at all.

"If that's what you feel you like you gotta do, then go ahead and do it," Lamont said with a loud sigh. She'd noticed that he had been sort of standoffish lately.

"So that's it," Sierra replied. "I'm not gonna hear about this later on?"

Lamont shook his head. "No, you're not. I'm done with it."

"Okay, well, the funeral is tomorrow. I'm not gonna be able to go to the services, but I would like to go to the house afterward. That's the least I can do." Sierra didn't see Lamont giving her a nasty look. "Well, thank you for understanding, babe," she added, kissing him on the lips.

"Good night, Sierra." Lamont turned off the light and climbed in the bed. He turned his back to her and was snoring in less than five minutes. Sierra lay in the dark with her eyes open. She wasn't able to get any sleep that night.

The day of the funeral, Sierra entered the Gordon home, and Rasheed's aunt, Sharee, was more than happy to welcome her inside. Rasheed immediately walked over to greet her and Messiah. He took the baby from Sierra and gave her a quick kiss on the cheek.

"What's up, Si? I didn't think that you would show up here," he said.

"I came to pay my respects. Miss Carrie was always very nice to me and I really cared about her. She was such a beautiful person," Sierra replied. "I would have liked to have been at the wake and the funeral but I couldn't make it."

"That's okay, Si. I'm just happy that you and Messiah were able to come out." Rasheed kissed Messiah's chubby cheeks. "Nana was beautiful, a good woman, a good everything. I just hate that she had to die like this and so soon."

"I know. It's so messed up when you lose a loved one. I lost my father when I was younger and I still cry sometimes. I am truly sorry for your loss."

"Thanks, sweetheart. I appreciate that," Rasheed said, giving Sierra a hug.

Kemp walked over to where Sierra and Rasheed were standing. He took Messiah out of Rasheed's arms.

"What's up, Miss Sierra?" Kemp said with a smile. He kissed her on the cheek. "I'm glad that you came. Rah is even happier now that you showed up! Look at him. He can't stop smilin'!"

Rasheed nudged Kemp's arm. He was smiling from ear to ear. He couldn't deny that he was happy to see Sierra and Messiah.

"Man, whatever!" Rasheed exclaimed. "I was real stressed out, but seein' you and Messiah made me feel better."

Sierra blushed. She hadn't expected this type of reception from the Gordon clan.

Everything is goin' good so far, she thought.

Sierra assumed they understood why she had stayed away from them for so long. She had to do what was best for her and her child.

Sierra followed Rasheed into the huge living room.

Most of people who had attended the funeral were standing around, drinking and talking. She figured that most of the people were relatives and some were ex-coworkers of Miss Carrie. Rasheed even introduced her to some of them.

When Sierra finally came face-to-face with Rasheed's uncles, Nayshawn and Shaka, they embraced her as well. Rasheed finally introduced his brother, Karim, to Sierra, and Kemp immediately passed Messiah to his proud uncle. Karim beamed with delight at the sight of his only nephew. This put Sierra at ease, but, unfortunately, that feeling would be short-lived.

"Well, well, well! Look who the wind blew in," said Rasheed's aunt, Carrie, who was visibly drunk. She took a sip of her drink and scowled at Sierra. "Never thought we would see you or my great-nephew again," she added.

Sierra shook her head. Coming there might have been a mistake after all. *I knew that it was too good to be true. Let me find out if I gotta whip some ass in here today,* Sierra thought.

Carrie Gordon, who was the most outspoken and obnoxious of the Gordons, was extremely upset by her mother's passing. She had had one too many cups of Hennessy Black and Coke that day.

"Well, I'm here now," Sierra sarcastically replied. She didn't want to have to tell anyone off while the family was grieving. She wondered if Carrie was still upset about the fracas that she and Tamir had in her beauty salon a few years before. There was some property damage and, of course, Carrie had not forgotten the mess.

"Hmph," said Carrie. "People think that they're too good to come around us! Personally, I think you should take your bougie ass back to wherever the hell you came from," she said, taking yet another sip of her drink.

Carrie's older brother, Shaka, grabbed her arm. "C'mon, Carrie! It's Ma's home goin' and I see you're tryin' to start some shit. This is not the time or place for this!" Shaka said through clenched teeth. "Pardon Carrie, Sierra. She just had too much to drink! It's the liquor talkin'.."

Rasheed intervened. Sierra could tell he was about to be pissed off. "Yo, Carrie, what the hell is wrong with you? You're embarrassin' everybody!"

Carrie gave Sierra the once-over, rolled her eyes at Rasheed, and then looked at Shaka.

"First of all, Shaka, I ain't no damn drunk, okay?" she yelled. "And ain't shit wrong with me but tryin' to figure out why is this bitch comin' around here all of a sudden! I still didn't get in your ass about fightin' Tamir in my fuckin' shop! As a matter of fact, didn't your little boyfriend, whatever the hell his name is, isn't he the one who killed Tamir? Yeah, mm-hmm, it's because of your ass that that girl is dead! You're a troublemaker and I don't want my nephew nowhere near you!"

Sierra sucked her teeth. She didn't come there for foolishness.

"I don't know what you're talkin' about, Carrie! Yeah, I had a fight with Tamir in your shop. I apologize for that, but I was defendin' myself! And as far as Rasheed is concerned, he wanted me here and that's why I'm not goin' anywhere!"

Carrie pointed her finger in Sierra's face while looking at her nephew. "Rah, why are you even fuckin' with this foul bitch?" she spat. "As a matter of fact, how do you know if this baby is even yours?"

"Whoa, Carrie! You're runnin' your mouth a little too much!" Rasheed yelled.

"Did you just say what I think you said?" Sierra shouted, stepping one inch closer to Carrie's face. She could smell the liquor on her breath. "It's one thing to fuck with me, but don't fuck with my child!"

The Gordon men attempted to quiet them down, but to no avail. At this point, Sierra had had enough. She was going through too much at home with Lamont just to be there for Rasheed. To have this type of disrespect directed at her from Carrie had put Sierra in a place that she never thought she would have to revisit.

Seeing what was about to go down, Rasheed stepped in between the two women. The other brothers were trying to talk to their sister, and Sharee attempted to keep Sierra calm.

Meanwhile, Carrie was still running her mouth. She must have figured that the petite Sierra was scared of her. Little did she know, Sierra was far from being a punk, or getting punked by anyone for that matter.

"Rasheed," Sierra said. "You don't have to stand in between us. I'm good."

Rasheed was hesitant to move. He glanced at his Aunt Carrie, who had a smirk on her face, and Sierra, who seemed as if she had calmed down a little.

"Are you sure?" he asked Sierra.

"I'm sure," she replied, tying her long hair into a knotted ponytail.

All of a sudden, Sierra reached around Rasheed and punched Carrie in the face. The two women began fighting right in the middle of the living room of the Gordon home. They were pulling hair and punching each other uncontrollably.

Children were crying and adults were yelling for someone to break it up. Furniture and food were falling all over the place as Sierra got the best of Carrie. She was beating her mercilessly as people who were not related to the Gordon family scrambled to get out the front door.

The relatives tried unsuccessfully to intervene in the fight between the two women. The wild catfight went on for a few minutes as Carrie's older brothers, Shaka and Nayshawn, tried to pull them apart, and Sharee attempted to pry Sierra's hands from Carrie's long hair. Their dresses were ripped and Sierra's left breast was almost exposed.

"Get off of me!" screamed Carrie. Sierra finally let Carrie's hair go and Sharee held her sister back. Rasheed held on to Sierra, whose hair was covering her face.

Everyone gathered around to see what was going to happen next. Karim walked up to Sierra, holding the crying Messiah in his arms. The toddler reached for his mother, but Kemp took him instead.

Rasheed was livid but Sierra didn't care. She felt that she'd had to prove to Carrie that she was no sucker.

"Give me my son, Kemp! We're outta here!" Sierra yelled, attempting to fix her ripped dress. "I don't need to be anywhere where I'm goin' to be disrespected!"

"So get the fuck out, bitch!" screamed Carrie, beaten up and in a drunken stupor. Her brothers were still trying to calm her down. Carrie's clothes were in disarray, and it looked like Sierra had done a number on her swollen mug.

Rasheed immediately helped Sierra gather up her things, and walked her outside to her truck. She was so humiliated, and she was pretty sure that Rasheed was too.

She began crying as soon as they got outside. "Rah, I'm so sorry! I hope you know that I didn't come here to start any trouble!"

Rasheed hugged her, with Messiah still in his arms. "It's not your fault. I know that she's upset about Nana, but I don't know what that has to do with you."

Sierra wiped her tearstained cheeks and opened her car door. "I don't know. Shit, I have never done anything to that woman! I barely even know Carrie, but, like I said, I'm not gonna sit around and let anybody disrespect me, I don't give a fuck who the person is!"

Rasheed put Messiah in his car seat and made sure that it was securely fastened. He gave his son a kiss and closed the rear door. Then he hugged Sierra and kissed her on the lips. Sierra blinked back her tears and kissed him too. They stood there silently for a few moments, just staring at each other.

"I gotta go, Rasheed. I shouldn't have come here."

"Please don't feel like that, and don't worry about Carrie. My grandmother's passin' is tearin' her apart right now, so she lashed out at you, but trust me, that shit won't happen anymore."

Sierra hugged Rasheed again before she climbed into her truck and pulled off. She watched in the rearview as he stood at the curb, waving at her.

When she arrived home, Lamont and Trey were not there. Sierra breathed a sigh of relief and undressed the sleeping Messiah, putting him in bed. After taking a nice shower and inspecting her minor injuries, she went into the family room to watch some television.

Then she picked up the house phone and called Lamont. He did not answer and the phone went to voice mail. Sierra found that to be strange because Lamont always answered her phone calls no matter where he was or what he was doing. Sierra figured that she would call Monique, Lamont's half sister, to see if she had heard from him.

Monique Phillips was not only Sierra's childhood friend, but Lamont's half sister from his father, Charles "Pops" Simmons. Pops was married to Lamont's mother when he had an affair with Monique's mother, Ann. Ann found out that she was pregnant, but a short time after that, she and Pops broke up with each other.

Years went by and Monique had no idea who her father was. She had no contact with her biological father at all growing up.

Her mother attempted to make up for her daughter's absentee father, but that didn't help. As time went on, Monique began acting out by resorting to promiscuity in order to replace her father's love. Unfortunately, she ended up pregnant at fifteen with her daughter, Destiny.

This risky behavior continued into Monique's adulthood, causing her to make irrational decisions. While at work, she flaunted herself to officers and inmates, but there was one incident that almost cost her her job as a correction officer. After having a sexual liaison with Shamel "Scooter" Abrams while he was an inmate, she was put on blast when some pictures of her were discovered in his cell during a search. They were headless shots, but the tattoos on her body were very prominent in the picture.

Due to Monique's professional experience in the Department of Correction, having worked with wardens and other brass, she didn't receive any immediate disciplinary action. Monique had to make some tough choices in order to save her job. She was backed into a corner when she made an agreement with the inspector general's office to rat out some of her coworkers in exchange for her shield. Needless to say, Monique gave up information about corrupt officers and her job was secured, under the premise that she would stay out of trouble as well. After complying with all the rules, she was instantly promoted to captain.

To add insult to injury, that wasn't end of the drama in Monique's life. Being the harlot she was, she had also slept with Lamont. Monique had pursued Lamont for years, knowing that Sierra, her childhood buddy turned nemesis at that time, had been in a previous relationship with him. Her mentality at that time was to "divide and conquer." So when Sierra and Lamont broke up, Monique jumped at the opportunity to have sex with the man she had been chasing for some years.

Lamont, on the other hand, had his own issues. He always wondered about the sister he had never met. This sister from another mother was the reason that his mother had left him and Pops, and, at one time, Lamont hated the child because of this.

Almost thirty years later, Lamont finally got the nerve to ask Pops about his half sister. To his surprise, Pops was more than happy to tell him about it. When he found out that his sister was a young woman named Monique Nichelle Phillips, Lamont was mortified. This was the same Monique he'd had sex with months earlier. He was disappointed in Pops, but most of all, he was disgusted with himself. It was then that he decided that his playing days were over.

After telling Monique that she was really his half sibling, naturally, she was shocked. But they both decided that they would carry on with their lives and put the memories of their sexual tryst behind them.

This incident caused Monique and Lamont to change their lives for the betterment of their families and themselves. It seemed to work because Monique was a new woman who was totally committed to her family and her career. Having casual sex with various men was not important to her anymore, and she finally valued herself. In the meantime, Sierra and Monique rekindled their childhood bond, making it a happy ending for everyone involved.

"Mo, where are you? I needed to talk to you," Sierra asked in a hurried tone.

"Hello, Miss Howell! How are you?" Monique replied with a chuckle. "What the hell is wrong with you this evenin'?"

"Girl, every damn thing! I took Messiah to Rasheed's house. You know that they buried his grandmother today."

"Wow! I know that had to be hard for him. How is he takin' it?"

"He's doin' much better, but that ain't the half. I went to the house after the services to pay my respects to the family, and ended up havin' a fight with his aunt, Carrie. You know, the one who owns the Cuttaz hair salon? That's the same salon that me and Tamir had our fight in a few years ago."

"How in the hell did you get into it with Rasheed's aunt?"

"I was there with Rasheed when Carrie walked in and began dissin' me. I mean, damn, I'm already gettin' enough heat at home with Lamont. She asked Rasheed why was I there, and said that Messiah might not even be his. After she said that, I just lost it."

Monique sighed. "Damn shame. That woman's mother wasn't even good in the ground yet and she was actin' like a fool!" They were silent for a few moments. "By the way, you know that Trey is over here with me and Destiny, right?" Monique volunteered. "Lamont called Destiny and asked if she could watch Trey while he made a run."

Sierra was quiet. She balled up in a fetal position on the couch. "What run did he have to make? Did he tell Destiny where he was goin'?"

"Now you know he didn't tell Destiny his whereabouts, and my baby is not about to ask her Uncle Monty anything. That man could do no wrong in her eyes."

Sierra sighed. "I just hope that Lamont isn't tryin' to step out on me, Mo. He was real upset that Rasheed is back in town and that he wants to be a part of Messiah's life. I don't understand why he's actin' this way when Messiah lives in this house with him. My baby absolutely adores Lamont."

"Now you know damn well Lamont can't stand Rasheed! Number one, Rasheed was an inmate—an inmate who you, the love of his life, had an affair with. Number two, you had a baby with this man, not with him. Number three, Lamont knows how you and Rasheed felt about each other. It's competition, boo."

"Yeah, but where the hell is my man now?"

Monique sighed. "I don't know, Si. I can't help you with that one."

Chapter 13

India

"Oh, yes, baby, eat this pussy," India moaned. His face was immersed between her legs, slurping up all of her goodness, and she loved every minute of it. He had already licked her asshole and sucked her toes, and now he was making his snake-like tongue flick in and out of her vagina. India grabbed his head, as if she wanted to push his whole body inside of her.

"Uhh, uhh, oh my . . . ohh," she moaned. He moaned too, and continued to perform cunnilingus on her. Suddenly, his head popped up and he pulled out a condom wrapped in a gold package. He ripped the package open with his teeth and put the Magnum condom on. India's eyes widened as she inspected his mammoth-sized manhood.

"Wow," she said, licking her lips. "You got the Magic Stick for real!"

He laughed. "Do you want it?"

"Yes, I want it!" India held her legs open so that he could enter her. He pushed his rod inside of her and she grimaced. She didn't realize that it was going to hurt the way it did. "Be careful, baby. Don't hurt me," she whispered in his ear. This only turned him on more.

As he ground her pussy, she felt like she was on cloud nine; no one had ever sexed her the way that he was. India grabbed his face and shoved her tongue in his mouth, giving him one of the best kisses that she'd ever given anyone in her life. She smacked her lips as she sampled the leftovers of her juices that were still on his face.

He turned her over and propped her ass in the air, exposing her box. He entered her from behind and she threw it back to him, making him moan loudly. He played with her clit while he pumped in and out of her. India felt an orgasm building, but she wanted to wait for him. She wanted them to cum together—and cum they did. He collapsed on top of her, and a smile of satisfaction appeared on her face. She turned around and kissed him. He reciprocated.

"That was so fuckin' good!" India said. "I loved every minute of it."

He sighed. "I loved it too, baby."

"I didn't know you had it like that. When you called me earlier, I was goin' to take a rain check, but I'm glad I didn't," India said, licking her succulent lips.

He kissed her on the forehead and insisted that he get cleaned up. Once he went inside of the bathroom, India wrapped a robe around her naked body. Her room reeked of sex. She immediately ran to her sister's bedroom and knocked on the door.

"Girl," India began. "He is the best that done it!" she said.

Asia laughed. "It must have been somethin' like that, because I could hear you moanin' in my room."

She sighed. "Okay, let me go back into my bedroom. I think he's about to leave in a few."

India walked into her bedroom, and there he was sitting on the bed, fully dressed and looking handsome as ever. She walked over and gave him a big kiss.

"Thanks, sweetie," he said. "I needed that." He pulled India onto his lap. "Listen, anything that we do is between me and you. I don't need anyone in my business because, well, you know my situation."

India smiled, but she wasn't too happy about the talk they'd had earlier. He had told her about his commitment to his family and his woman, yet he wanted to have sex with her. Everything that her mother had told her about men was fresh in her mind.

"I'm a grown woman. I know how to play my position," she said, although she was slightly annoyed.

He stood up and they shared a kiss with each other for a few minutes. He held her tightly, and India felt good being encased in the muscular arms of a real man.

She walked him to the door and he turned around to give her another kiss. It seemed as if he didn't want to leave, but he knew that he couldn't stay, either. After all, it was too soon for that.

"Later, beautiful," he said as India watched him walk down the hallway. When he disappeared, India closed the door and was in la-la land. She could tell that she really was going to enjoy herself with this man.

Asia appeared in the doorway of her bedroom. "So you really like this Lamont dude now?" she asked.

"Yeah, I mean, he's cool. He does have it goin' on in the bedroom."

"Now, India, keep in mind that he does have a family, and if you get too emotionally involved with this man, you're goin' to be the one who gets hurt."

India rolled her eyes at Asia. "Why do you think that I'm goin' to get hurt? I'm in this for one reason and one reason alone, and that is to make sure Sierra suffers some heartache. "

Asia agreed. "That's my point. Remember, you're on a mission right now and Lamont is just a pawn in your game!"

India grew angrier by the minute. "Asia, if I decide to take Sierra's man away from her, then I think that's my business!"

"But if you take her man, then whose arms do you

think she's goin' to run back to, huh? She's gonna run
back to Rasheed! After all, he is her son's father!"

"So that's what this is about? It's about you and
Rasheed!"

"No, you're takin' this the wrong way! It's not even
like that . . . I'm just lookin' out for the both of us! I'm
tryin' to keep you from getting your heart involved
in this, and I'm tryin' to save myself any additional
drama, because I do want Rasheed for myself."

India frowned. "Well, I'm sorry, Asia. If I decide that
I want Lamont for myself, I'm goin' for mine. I don't
give a fuck. And if Sierra goes back to Rasheed, that's
gonna be your problem, not mine!"

India walked into her bedroom and slammed the
door. Asia shook her head and fell back against the
fluffy pillows on her bed.

The next morning, India walked around the house
with an attitude. She thought that Asia had her back,
but it was obvious that she was just looking out for
herself. She was more concerned about Rasheed. On
the flip side, Lamont turned out to be more than what
she'd expected, and now she wanted him for herself.
Why should a grimy bitch like Sierra have such a good
man?

At home, Asia did her best to try to pacify her sister,
but it didn't work. That morning, India hurriedly got
dressed and walked out of the house without even
saying good-bye to her. After she left, Asia decided to
pick up the phone and call Rasheed. He had been on
her mind ever since the funeral.

"Hello, miss," Rasheed happily greeted her, answering on the first ring. "To what do I owe this phone call?"

"I just wanted to call you and see how you were
feelin'," Asia replied.

"Let's put it like this: my grandmother, my moms, my uncle, Peppy, aren't comin' back. I gotta move on with my life."

"Yeah, I feel you, Rah, I feel you," Asia replied. She didn't know that else to say. Getting excited from the sound of his voice, Asia slid her hand into her panties. She began masturbating while Rasheed was on the phone with her.

"Yo, what are you doin'?" he asked, listening to her heavy breathing.

"I'm touchin' myself. I just love the sound of your voice," she said. "Why don't you join me?"

"Whoa, whoa, whoa. What do you mean, 'you're touchin' yourself'? Why are you doin' that now?" Rasheed asked.

"Because I want you so bad. Wouldn't you like to come over here and help me out?" Asia whispered into the phone.

"I think that you're a cool chick, but I don't understand why you think I need to have phone sex with you."

"What happened, Rah?" Asia moaned. "Are you scared?"

Rasheed chuckled. "Scared? I'm never scared of any pussy, but I just buried my grandmother the other day, remember? I'm not thinkin' about nobody's pussy right now," he said. There was silence on Asia's end. "Hello? Are you still there?"

Asia immediately stopped what she was doing, embarrassed at his reaction. She cleared her throat. "I'm so sorry, Rah. I didn't mean to be disrespectful," Asia replied, apologizing for her selfishness. "You just buried your grandmother and here I am, thinkin' about myself. I'm so sorry—," she pleaded.

Rasheed cut her off. "Damn, I see that nothin' has changed at all," he replied with an attitude. "Look, I'm hangin' up. When you grow the fuck up, call me." Rasheed hung up the phone in Asia's ear.

Asia looked at her phone with tears welling up in her eyes. "Damn!" she said, and threw her phone on the bed in frustration.

Chapter 14

Lamont

After leaving India's apartment earlier that evening, Lamont felt like trash. He hadn't cheated on Sierra since they had been back together, but he had an excuse this time. It was the Rasheed issue again.

To Lamont, Rasheed was such a loser, in more ways than one. He had no job, although, according to Sierra, his family had old drug money and owned businesses. He had a criminal record, which was probably a block long, and, of course, he was not father material.

But even with all of Rasheed's negative attributes, Lamont was still insanely jealous when it came to him. He didn't have any evidence of Rasheed and Sierra being intimate with each other, but he was no fool. They had a baby together, and with Sierra interacting with Messiah's father the way that she was, he felt that them having sex with each other was inevitable.

Also, Lamont didn't want the crook to get too comfortable with the father-son situation. The next thing he knew, Rasheed was going to be trying to pick up Messiah at the front door of their home. Lamont was not having that. How would it look if Rasheed, a former inmate, came to his home to pick up his son?

Lamont didn't sign up for this when he and Sierra agreed to take their relationship to another level. In his mind, Lamont thought that Rasheed was completely out of the picture, and he was going to be the only father Messiah knew. He loved that little boy like he was his own, and it didn't matter what Rasheed said or Sierra thought, Messiah was going to always be his son and Trey's baby brother. He was willing to fight for a spot in Messiah's life.

As Lamont pulled into the driveway, his heart began beating a mile a minute. He had to come up with a lie and fast. Even though he did threaten her with infidelity, the last thing he wanted Sierra to think was that he was out creeping on her. He needed India for his backup reinforcements, just in case Sierra decided to step out on him with Rasheed. It would kill him to know that she was getting busy with Rasheed when he was being faithful to her. Lamont didn't want to be the fool.

Lamont got out of the truck and chuckled to himself. Then again, maybe it wasn't about Sierra and her baby's father. Maybe he was developing his old fetish for new pussy.

Lamont put the key in the door, and when he walked in the house it was unusually quiet. What made it so bad was that he was so wrapped up in his thoughts, he had forgotten to go by Monique's house and pick up Trey.

Damn, what the hell am I gonna say now? Lamont thought with a dumb expression on his face.

Sierra emerged from the kitchen. "Oh, I see that you finally made it home. Where have you been, Lamont?" she asked with her hand on her hip.

Lamont looked at Sierra and rolled his eyes up in his head. He was nervous as hell. He wondered if she could tell. "Out with the fellas," he replied.

Sierra smirked. "Really? Where did you and the fellas go?" she prodded.

Lamont was in no mood for the interrogation. "I was out with my people, and what is it with all the questions? Now all of a sudden, you of all people, is askin' where I disappeared to? Where were you the other day when you claimed you went to Kings Plaza mall?"

"First of all, we're talkin' about you. When you start movin' a certain way, how do you expect for me to act? Usually we call each other when we're out and we always answer our phones! Why didn't you answer your phone when I called, Lamont?"

Lamont threw his keys on the glass coffee table in the living room. "Because I didn't fuckin' want to answer my phone, that's why!" he shouted.

Sierra was unfazed by his sarcasm. "Oh, is that right? You didn't want to answer your phone because you didn't feel like it? Did I hear you correctly?"

"You heard me! A few days ago, you didn't want to answer the phone neither. Remember? I think it was that time that you took Messiah to see his so-called daddy behind my back."

"Oh, please, Lamont! I don't wanna hear nothin' else about Rasheed. We're talkin' about you. Now if we're goin' to have this issue—" she began.

Lamont pointed his finger at Sierra. He had to use reverse psychology on her to cover his infidelity. "Listen to me! I don't have to deal with this shit! That is the same reason I have full custody of my own son, because y'all CO broads wanna screw inmates, crooks, and common criminals! If you want to ruin your career, you go ahead. But Messiah? He shouldn't have to suffer because his mother doesn't know how to keep her legs closed!"

Suddenly, Sierra walked up to Lamont and slapped him. Lamont grabbed her hand and threw her on the couch. She tried to wrestle away from his strong grasp.

"Go ahead and try to hit me and I will kill your ass!" she whispered, for fear of waking Messiah up.

"Maybe you would feel more comfortable with that crook then! I'm pretty sure he done killed a few motherfuckers!"

Sierra's bottom lip began trembling. He needed her to feel as miserable as he did. His conscience was eating away at him, and belittling Sierra was helping him cope with that.

Lamont let her go and Sierra began to cry. "When I saw Rasheed, it was all about Messiah. Don't you know that I love you? I told you many times before that I don't want to be with Rasheed. He can't give me what you can give me!"

He turned his back, not wanting her to see him cry. "Just leave me the hell alone, Sierra! Sleep in the family room tonight! I don't even want you fuckin' near me!"

Lamont walked into their bedroom, closed the door, and locked it. He flopped across the bed and buried his face in a pillow. He knew that he was slowly regressing and becoming that man he used to be: a philandering, womanizing, cocky son of a bitch. The little boy in him, the one who cried for his absentee mother at night, the one he had managed to suppress for the last couple of years, was about to reemerge.

It was early Friday afternoon when Lamont was awakened by the ringing cordless phone on the nightstand. He looked at the clock and it said 12:07 p.m. He grabbed the phone and answered it.

"Hello?" he whispered.

"Lamont!" Monique yelled into the phone. "You didn't even pick up your son last night! Where were you?"

"Hey, Mo, I was exhausted. I didn't—" Lamont tried to explain, but Monique talked over him.

"You are lucky we have extra clothes over here for Trey. Destiny got him dressed this mornin' and I took him to school for you. What were you doin' that was so important that it made you forget about Trey?" There was a slight pause as Lamont got his thoughts together. "I'm listenin'!"

"C'mon, Monique, give me a break, girl. I was kinda caught up with the fellas."

Monique calmed down a bit. "For the record, Sierra called me last night after she couldn't get in contact with you. I don't know what you're out there doin' but you had better be careful. You're goin' to end up losin' Sierra."

"What about Messiah's father? What about her losin' me?" Lamont announced.

"What about him?" Monique asked.

"He's tryin' to move in on my family. He's tryin' to take Sierra and Messiah away from me."

"C'mon, man. I don't believe that shit for one minute. Sierra is through with Rasheed Gordon, but on another note, why don't you just let the man go ahead and be a father to his child, Monty? Why can't Messiah have two lovin' father figures in his life?"

Lamont sat up in the bed. "Lovin' father figure? This guy is in and out of jail and has no stability in his life. I have been here for Messiah from day one! I am the one who was there when he took his first steps, I am the one who changed his Pampers, I am the one he calls Da-Da, Mo!"

Monique sighed. "You know what? I can't talk to you when you're like this, and I'm gonna stay out of this mess. You and Sierra have to do some serious soul searchin' to do, because I don't see anything good comin' out of this shit. I'll talk to you later, okay?"

He didn't want to hang up with Monique. He needed someone to vent to.

"Okay," Lamont said, and reluctantly disconnected the call. After talking to Monique, Lamont finally gathered the strength to get out of bed. He walked out of the bedroom and down the hallway into the family room. For some reason, he half expected to smell some turkey bacon and home fries in the kitchen when he got up.

On his day off, he would take the boys to school. Monique had taken Trey, so he figured that Sierra had taken Messiah to his day care. After thinking about it for a moment, Lamont wondered how she could have done that when she had to stand roll call at five in the morning. Did Sierra take Messiah to Rasheed's house? Lamont plopped down on the couch and put his head in his hands. What was going on with them?

Chapter 15

Sierra

In the wee hours of Friday morning, Sierra arose from the couch after a night of tossing and turning. Lamont was being unreasonable, and, for some reason, her women's intuition had kicked in. Because of his insecurities about her and Rasheed, Sierra felt that Lamont had met someone. She couldn't put her finger on it yet, but her gut instinct was never wrong; she could sense trouble a mile away. It would be heart-wrenching to know that her man had no faith in her or their relationship. After thinking about it, did she have any faith in their relationship?

She loved Lamont with all her heart, but if he messed up, she felt that Rasheed would be there to pick up the pieces. She had to admit that when she called him at 3:30 that morning to drop Messiah off, Sierra knew that it was going to be hard to maintain a sexless relationship with him. The sexual chemistry between them was so strong.

"Hello?" Rasheed answered, his voice groggy from sleep. "Who is this?"

"It's Sierra, Rah," she replied. "Look, I need you to watch Messiah while I go to work. Lamont is . . . Well, he had to work an overnight shift," she lied.

"No problem. Are you on your way now?" he replied with a yawn.

"Yeah. I packed all his things."

"I was thinkin', why don't you let him spend the weekend over here? I got him."

Sierra hesitated. "Um, Rah, I don't know if that's a good idea just yet," Sierra said, getting herself prepared to walk out of the house. She was trying not to wake Lamont.

Rasheed was fully awake. "Yo, Si, what is your problem? I wanna spend time with my boy. He's gonna be okay, so stop worryin'."

Sierra nervously looked down the hallway at the closed door to her and Lamont's bedroom. "Can we talk about this some other time? I have to get ready to get out of here."

"Well, I hope it's soon. I need to spend time with my boy."

"Yeah, fine," Sierra responded, giving him the brush off. "Look, I'll see you in a few."

Sierra hung up the phone with an attitude, thinking about how much of an idiot she was for putting herself and her baby boy in a complicated situation like this.

Sierra arrived in front of the Gordon home around 4:00 a.m. She called Rasheed's cell and he came outside to help her with the sleeping Messiah. Sierra caught a whiff of Irish Spring coming from his freshly scrubbed skin. His gorgeous bronze complexion illuminated in the streetlight, and his toned body looked right in the tank that he was wearing.

Sierra grabbed Messiah's overnight bag and followed Rasheed into the house. He walked upstairs to his spacious bedroom and carefully laid Messiah down on his bed. Rasheed turned around to look at Sierra. She didn't know what to do next.

Rasheed grinned. "What the hell is wrong with you? Why are you just standin' there lookin' at me like that?"

"I don't know. I guess I'm just a little nervous."

"Why? I know how to take care of a baby," Rasheed said, clueless of what she was really thinking.

"That's not it, Rasheed." She shook her head and put her hands over her eyes.

Rasheed shrugged. "You be buggin' sometimes, I swear you do. You can turn nothin' into a whole lotta somethin'."

At that moment, Sierra was thinking about the old times with Rasheed, who was looking irresistibly sexy. He was turning her on without even really trying to.

Suddenly, Sierra had an urge to take off her clothes. Giving Rasheed a taste of her goodies wouldn't hurt. She took off her uniform pants and T-shirt to reveal her lacy bra and panties. Rasheed looked surprised.

"May I ask why you're takin' your clothes off?"

Suddenly, Sierra pushed him back on his bed, while Messiah lay fast asleep. She sat on top of him and smiled at the erection that was forming in his Ralph Lauren boxers. She began to grind slowly on it and, for a minute, Rasheed looked as if he were in heaven.

Then the unthinkable happened. Rasheed pushed her off him. Sierra sat on the edge of the bed with a stunned look on her face.

"I can't do this, Si," Rasheed said, shaking his head. "I told myself when my grandmother died that I was goin' to do things differently, and that included you," he said.

Sierra felt stupid. She couldn't believe that he didn't accept her advances.

She calmly got dressed. "Rasheed, you are so full of shit," Sierra said as her eyes filled up with tears. "When she was alive, I'm pretty sure you said the same thing, and you haven't done anything to change yet."

Rasheed chuckled. "So you're mad at me now? Aren't you the one who's always talkin' about how I can't be

with you and how Lamont is the better man for you?
Now who is the one full of shit?"

Sierra sucked her teeth. Stress had played a big part
in her judgment that night. She was kind of glad that
Rasheed had dissed her.

Rasheed stood up and pulled Sierra close to him.
"What's really wrong, Si?" he asked. He was always so
in tune with her feelings.

"It's a lot of things goin' on. You're pullin' me in this
direction because you wanna be in Messiah's life, and
Lamont is pullin' me over in this direction because he
doesn't want you to be a part of Messiah's life." All of
a sudden, a shocked look came over her face. "Oh, my
God. Today is Friday!" she exclaimed, putting her hand
to her mouth.

"Yeah, today is Friday. What's the matter?" he asked.

She gathered the rest of her things. "Forget it, it's
nothin'," she said with a loud sigh.

Rasheed kissed her on the cheek. "Go ahead and go
to work, girl. Everything is goin' to be okay. We're goin'
to get through this. Did you notice that I said 'we'?"

Sierra breathed a sigh of relief. "Thanks for havin'
my back." She looked at her watch. It was going on
4:25 a.m. "Oh, shit! I have to go. I'll call you later."

She sprinted down the stairs and ran out the front
door to her car. She had twenty minutes to get to
Rikers Island; she didn't want to be late for roll call.

While Sierra drove to work, she thought about the
other dilemma she had to face at work, and that was
Anwar Jones. She wanted to tell Rasheed what was
going on, but decided to keep it to herself for fear that
it would only bring more havoc to her already chaotic
life.

She also couldn't help but wonder if Rasheed knew
anything about Anwar's decision to kill Scooter. She
knew that Rasheed was no stranger to being a co-
conspirator to murder and mayhem.

***

An hour later, Sierra was sitting at her post in Five North, dreading to find out what Anwar's game plan was. She didn't understand why he was involving her in his quest to kill Scooter. She couldn't stand Scooter—no, she hated him—but revenge was so beneath her at this point. She had seen what getting revenge on a person can do. Tamir and Tyke had lost their lives because of it.

Anwar strolled out of his cell for breakfast. He walked over to Sierra's desk and just stood there, staring at her. His icy demeanor was intimidating. Sierra's palms began to sweat.

"So did you think about what I said?" he asked with a condescending look on his face. "As a matter of fact, there shouldn't be any thought to it. You are my man's baby's mama so it's your duty to hold me down."

Sierra frowned. "Does Rasheed know anything about this?"

Anwar laughed. "Rasheed don't have to know nothin' about this right now, because the only thing he's gonna do is try to talk me out of it."

"You don't have to tell Rasheed nothin' because I'm tellin' him!"

Anwar got serious and walked closer to Sierra's desk. "So you wanna start tellin' on niggas now? I don't think you wanna do that, Miss Lady. Remember, I know your whole card, so if you wanna start talkin', let me know. I done already told you that my bitch has the inspector general on speed dial!" Anwar paused and let the thought seep into Sierra's mind. "Still thinkin' about runnin' your mouth?"

Sierra sniffed. She didn't know who to turn to, because, after all, Anwar did have her backed into corner.

Scooter came out of his cell, and looked as if he was

hesitant about coming anywhere near the desk where Sierra was sitting.

"What's up, B?" Scooter said, calling Anwar over to where he was standing to give him a pound. Scooter shot Sierra a look from a distance. "What you up to over there?"

"Nothin', homie," replied Anwar, patting Scooter on the back. "Just talkin' to Miss Howell."

"How you doin', Miss H?" Scooter asked.

Sierra looked up and saw that both Scooter and Anwar were standing in front of her desk. She was disgusted, to say the least.

"Fine," she mumbled.

If she could have jumped out of her seat at that moment and beat Scooter down herself, she would have.

"So, Miss H, what's good with your boy, Rasheed?" Scooter asked in a sarcastic tone.

Sierra gave Scooter a dirty look. "I'm gonna need you to get away from my desk, Abrams."

Anwar chuckled and tugged on Scooter's arm. "Yo, Scooter, leave her alone. Let me talk to you for a minute," he said, winking at Sierra as they walked away.

Sierra rolled her eyes as she watched the two men closely. She couldn't have Scooter and Anwar moved out of Five North, because they were high-profile inmates and they were barred from every other jail on Rikers. Moving them anywhere else in the facility would not be recommended. They were a nuisance to other inmates and caused problems wherever they were housed. Sierra didn't know what to do. The pressure was on for real.

Sierra looked at her watch. Her meal relief would be there any minute. She knew that once her meal relief came, Scooter was as probably as good as dead. She checked every cell and even did a security inspection of the whole of Five North to try to take her mind off what was about to happen.

She felt Anwar watching her, and every time she turned around to look at him, he ran his finger across his throat. At this point, she didn't know if he was threatening her or talking about what he was going to do the naïve Scooter. Scooter stood there with Anwar, talking his head off, not realizing that he was about to be a victim in Five North again.

Exactly three years before, during a previous jail stint, Scooter was slashed in the face by two Bloods named Pretty and Valentine. Due to Scooter's penchant for lying and snitching, Rasheed recruited the young gangbangers to teach him a lesson for running his mouth. They had no problem handling Scooter for Rasheed because they had their own reasons for getting at him.

A pathological liar, Scooter was running around the jail, claiming to be a Blood. Unfortunately for him, it was revealed that he was a Crip member. This was going against the code. If another gang member, especially a Crip, was caught acting like he was a Blood or even being a comrade to a Blood member, this was an insult to both gangs.

Nevertheless, the two men made an example out of Scooter because of this, and, of course, carried out the hit that was orchestrated by Rasheed. Scooter was left to walk around with a nasty scar across his left cheek as a reminder.

The gate opened and Sierra's meal relief walked in.

"Hello," Sierra said, greeting the officer with a phony smile on her face. She relinquished her equipment to him and was on her way to meal. She figured that she would call her area captain and feign illness so that she could go to the clinic. That way, she wouldn't have to come back to Five North.

Within the next hour, Sierra was hoping that Anwar would complete the task, because part of her secretly wanted Scooter to pay for what he did to Rasheed. The other part just wanted to close that chapter and move on. She had entirely too much to lose.

Chapter 16

Anwar

The night before, Anwar had worked on the weapon until 3:00 a.m. He had managed to loosen a three-inch piece of metal in the vent of his cell. He couldn't believe his luck. Anwar scraped the piece of metal across the concrete floor until it had a very sharp point. He then ripped a piece of sheet and wrapped it around the weapon several times so he wouldn't cut himself when he used it.

"Yeah, I'm gonna stab a hole in this nigga with this shit right here," Anwar said to himself, kissing the weapon. He inspected it by stabbing a few holes in his mattress. Then he put it in a secret hiding place.

A smile of self-satisfaction came over Anwar that night while he dozed off to sleep. After tomorrow, he was finally going to be able to pay back the one person who had looked out for him, and that was Rasheed. It was the least he could do after what his friend had done for him.

Rasheed and Anwar grew up together in Bedford-Stuyvesant, knowing each other since they were nine and eleven years old. Their grandmothers were good friends and they also attended the same church, so it wasn't hard for the two rambunctious boys to have a bond with other.

Anwar seemed like a pretty normal child on the outside, but on the inside, he was in turmoil. He was a victim of child abuse at the hands of his stepfather, Russell. After enduring all of the emotional and physical abuse when he was younger, it was obvious that Anwar was borderline psychotic, and he owed all of it to Mr. and Mrs. Russell Jones.

Back in those days, he suppressed his pain. He didn't tell anyone for fear that no one would believe him. What his parents did was paint a rosy picture of a perfect family to others, but behind closed doors, it was a living hell for Anwar. When his little sister was born, he really went through it. It seemed as his mother and stepfather really wanted no part of him after that.

It was the summer of 1989. Rasheed would come on his block so that they could ride their bikes together. Of course, Anwar had a beat up hand-me-down bike from one of his family members, and Rasheed had a sparkling new one. They would ride back to his house, where Anwar would hop on another bike that was similar to the one that Rasheed had. Little did his parents know that the Gordon brothers, Rasheed's uncles, had bought Anwar a brand new Huffy that they hid at their house. They felt sorry for the kid.

In the meantime, Rasheed would always question Anwar's bumps and bruises and fractured limbs. Of course, Anwar would make up excuses and tell the suspicious Rasheed that it was just clumsiness on his part.

One day, they were sitting on the steps of Anwar's building when Rasheed just happened to question him again about a broken arm.

"Yo, why do you always seem to be fallin' and hurtin' yourself when I'm not around?" asked the twelve-year-old Rasheed. "I have never even seen you fall before, man."

Anwar's eyes darted all over the place. "What you talkin' about? You don't remember me trippin' the other day? That's how I broke this arm!" Anwar lied, looking at the cast on his arm.

Rasheed stared at Anwar. "Yo, man, I may be only twelve years old but I ain't stupid! You're way older than me so why is you lyin' to me, man?"

Fourteen-year-old Anwar laughed it off. "Nigga, I only got you by two years!" he replied.

"Is your pops beatin' you up or somethin', man?" asked Rasheed. "Is he hittin' on you?"

Anwar held his head down. He couldn't even look his best friend in the eye. "Nah, why you ask me that?"

"Yo, A, you're my homeboy! I know you like a book. You always have all these bruises and stuff. You can tell your grandmother that shit and she would probably believe you, but I don't. Who's hittin' on you? Is it your mother or Mr. Russell?"

Anwar began to cry. He continued to hold his head down, and wiped his tears with his good hand. Rasheed put his arm around his friend to comfort him.

"It's Russell," Anwar whispered, wiping his runny nose with his T-shirt.

"I figured it was him." Rasheed patted Anwar on the back. "You're gonna be all right, man. Don't cry. I know that this shit has been goin' on for a minute. I just never said nothin'. I did tell my uncles about what was goin' on, and they figured that it was him too. They even said if you want them to, they will kill that motherfucker for you. Why do you think they bought you the new bike? They feel your pain." Rasheed stood up to face Anwar. "Look, I got an idea."

Anwar wiped his nose again. "What is it?"

"Let's kill that nigga, Russell, ourself," Rasheed replied, with a smirk on his face.

Anwar's eyes widened. "What? What are you talkin' about?"

"You heard me. Let's kill that nigga ourself," he repeated. "I ain't stutter."

"You're buggin' out, Rah."

Anwar looked at the young Rasheed and saw that he was serious.

Anwar shrugged. "I dunno, man, I don't think that's a good idea. We could go to jail for that shit. I don't want to spend the rest of my teenage years in Spofford," he said, referring to the notorious juvenile detention center in the Bronx.

Rasheed watched Anwar walk into the door of his building. "Yo, kid, just think about what I said."

Later on that evening, Anwar sat in his bedroom, thinking about what he and Rasheed had talked about. He was tired of being a punching bag for Russell, so murder was something that he had to consider.

Suddenly, Russell opened the bedroom door. He stood in the doorway, looking for something to complain about. Russell was a slender man, but he was pure muscle. He worked for the Department of Sanitation, and had everyone who knew him thinking that he was a hardworking family man. Little did they know that Russell was a replica of his very own father, Russell Sr., who used to beat him ruthlessly. The elder Russell was also emotionally and verbally abusive to his wife and other children as well.

"You little dumb motherfucker," Russell said with bloodshot eyes. "Didn't I tell you to clean up this nasty-ass room?"

Anwar looked around his room and did not see one thing out of place. He couldn't imagine what Russell was talking about.

"My room is clean, Daddy, what you—"

Russell slapped Anwar so hard that he fell backward to the floor with a busted lip. Russell then grabbed Anwar by his shirt collar, lifting him from the floor, and threw him back onto the twin bed.

"Don't back talk me, boy! Don't you know that I will half kill your little ass in here?" Russell said through clenched teeth.

Anwar lifted his bad arm up to shield himself from the impending blows. Russell held the broken arm and proceeded to hit his son with eight consecutive slaps to the face. Anwar felt himself about to pass out. He was too weak and too small to fight Russell back.

"Sick of your black ass not listenin' to nobody!" Russell said while hitting the willowy Anwar. He grabbed the teen and pulled him close to him. "If your mother wasn't here, I would stick my dick down your throat. You know the routine," Russell whispered in his ear. Anwar began to cry.

A few seconds later, his mother, Antoinette, appeared in the doorway. She just shook her head and walked back out of the room. Russell had his wife so brainwashed that she had convinced herself that Anwar was always doing something to deserve the vicious beatings.

"Stupid little bastard! I told your mama she shoulda got a fuckin' abortion when she was pregnant with your little ass! Now get the fuck up and clean up this mess!" Russell shouted, throwing Anwar back to the floor and walking out of the room.

Anwar attempted to hold his head up. His left eye felt swollen and his head and lips were pounding. He was able to get a visual of his room with his one good eye. He saw that he had some blood splattered on the floor and on the comforter on his bed. Too weak to move, Anwar ended up passing out on his bed.

Two weeks had passed since Rasheed had come to Anwar with the idea of killing Russell. They rode their bikes to Fulton Street Park so that they could talk between each other. They didn't want to take a chance on anyone getting wind of their plans.

"It's been two weeks and I done got about five ass

whippings already," blurted Anwar. "When and how and where we gonna do this shit, my nigga? Russell is fuckin' me up bad!"

Rasheed frowned. He looked at Anwar's unhealed arm and sucked his teeth. Anwar had a small scar under his eye, and the swelling in his lip had finally gone down. Of all the beatings that he'd endured, no medical staff in Woodhull Hospital ever made note of. No Bureau of Child Welfare social worker ever knocked on their door. It was amazing how messed up the system was back then.

"Don't that nigga work at night?" asked Rasheed.

"Yeah, he does."

"What time does he leave for work?"

"Um, around ten o'clock. But how are we gonna do that? We're gonna have to take him down, and Russell is strong as shit!" replied the nervous Anwar.

Rasheed laughed. "Don't worry about that, man! You ain't gotta do nothin'. I'm doin' this shit all by myself. This one is on me!"

Anwar blinked in amazement. He wasn't so sure that he wanted Russell dead, but he could only imagine how much better life would be without him. Anwar smiled as he thought about how he would feel not having his abuser around.

Anwar ran his hands through his coarse afro. "How you're gonna do that shit by yourself? You're only twelve years old! You don't need my help?"

"Hell no! You can't do it, 'cause then everybody would really be suspicious! You gonna have to be in the crib when I murder this nigga!"

Anwar looked at Rasheed, who was about a good ten pounds lighter than he was, and they both were slim boys. Could Rasheed really put in work like that?

"So are you gonna stab him or shoot him?"

"Man, what does it matter? As long as that nigga is dead, you shouldn't care about what I do to him!"

"That's true. So what do we do now—wait?"

Rasheed looked at the streetlights coming on. It was midsummer and the streetlights usually came on around 8:45, when it began to get dark.

"Go home, right now," ordered the street-smart Rasheed. "Stay in the house. Don't come outside no more tonight, okay?"

Anwar nodded, and rode his Huffy back to Rasheed's house. He put the bike behind the locked gate, and walked down the block to his own house. He cleaned up, ate the dinner that his mother prepared, washed the dishes, and went straight to bed. Once he was in bed, Anwar cried himself to sleep.

It was 10:00 p.m. on the dot when Russell Jones walked to the front door of his apartment. Antoinette walked closely behind him.

"Maybe you should call in, Russell, 'cause something just don't feel right about tonight," she said. "I got butterflies in my stomach."

Russell kissed his wife on the lips. "Don't worry, baby, I'm gonna be all right." He looked in the direction of Anwar's closed bedroom door. "That little motherfucker is in there, right?" he asked with a scowl on his face.

"Yeah, he's in there," Antoinette replied with a shameful look.

Russell kissed her on the cheek, and walked out the door with his car keys and lunch bag in his hand. He ran downstairs to the lobby, then walked out the front door.

As Russell strolled down Halsey Street, he didn't notice that a few streetlights were out. He also didn't hear the footsteps behind him as he walked toward his parked car.

"Yo, Russell!" a voice called out from a darkened alleyway directly behind him. When Russell turned around to look, three shots rang out, and he fell backward to the ground, busting the back of his head on the concrete sidewalk. His left eye was completely gone and his mouth exposed his missing molars. Dogs barking and the pattering of running footsteps could be heard in the distance. A cool breeze came out of nowhere and rustled the leaves on the tree-lined street. Russell Jones was dead.

After Russell was killed, the days were actually worse for Anwar. Because his mother had never done anything to stop Russell's abuse, Anwar despised her. He began disrespecting his mother to no end, and she eventually threw him out of her house at sixteen years old.

Then Anwar moved in with Russell's mother, Miss Ruby. Miss Ruby died a few years later in 1993, and by then Anwar had already begun to make Rikers Island his home.

The night that Rasheed committed the murder, he snuck out the house with his Uncle Shaka's brand new 9 mm semi–automatic handgun. He stood in the alleyway of an abandoned house on their block near Russell's car and waited. Later on, Rasheed told Anwar that he wasn't the least bit afraid.

He told Anwar that all he had to do was pretend that Russell was his own abusive father, Jihad. Jihad had never touched him or his brother, Karim, but murdered his wife and Rasheed's mother, Lavon, then committed suicide. Jihad immediately turned the gun on himself, because he knew that if the Gordon brothers got to him, he would have been killed anway.

With the negative images of his own father running through his mind, twelve-year-old Rasheed was able to kill Russell in cold blood without one care in the world. It was just that easy for him.

***

Anwar woke up in a cold sweat and realized that he wasn't in his tiny bedroom in Bedford-Stuyvesant. He was on Rikers Island in a jail cell. He got up and snatched down the white towel that was covering the cell window. He wiped the sweat off his face and body, taking off his drenched wife beater. He threw it to the side and lay down on the sweaty sheets. Feeling uncomfortable, Anwar sucked his teeth, getting up to snatch the sheets off the mattress. He put a Department of Correction—issued blanket in the place of the sheet and lay back down.

Although Russell wasn't his biological father, he had been around since Anwar was in his mother's womb. Anwar always hoped that the abuse would stop, and that the man could love him the way a father should love a son. But with him not being his real father, it only made Anwar even angrier at his mother—angry that she would allow a "stranger" to come into their lives and do what he did to him.

It had been twenty years since Russell's death and, strangely enough, it still haunted him.

As Anwar looked up at the ceiling of the cell, he always wondered why the NYPD had never really investigated Russell's murder. He found that to be very strange. Even though he thought Russell deserved what he got, his death made Anwar realize that a black man's life wasn't worth shit.

When that Friday morning came, Anwar was prepared to commit the perfect murder. He walked around Five North with the concealed weapon tucked in his Calvin Klein boxer briefs.

Anwar studied Miss Howell's face. She looked nervous, and he knew that she had every right to be.

Scooter played Anwar close most of the day, which was what he wanted him to do. His thirst for Scooter's blood was making him more and more anxious. He wanted to kill Scooter so bad, he could taste it.

Anwar impatiently waited for Sierra to walk out of the housing area. Once those gates closed behind her, he knew that it was going to be time to make his move.

Scooter walked into his cell and Anwar lagged closely behind him.

"What's up, Scoot?" Anwar said, stepping inside of Scooter's cell. He looked around. "You got them short eyes for me, right?" he said, referring to some porno magazines that were laid out on the bed.

Scooter laughed and handed Anwar two *Black Tails* magazines. "Yo, B, you're crazy! You can have those 'cause I got a few more comin' to me."

Suddenly, Anwar wrapped his hand around Scooter's throat. "Yeah, you got somethin' else comin' to you all right," Anwar whispered as Scooter gasped for air. "Yeah, that's right! Remember the nigga you shot? That dude is my fam, son! While you was runnin' your fuckin' mouth, you didn't know that Rasheed is my right-hand man, now did you?" Scooter's eyes widened with fear as Anwar produced the murder weapon.

Scooter attempted to remove Anwar's hand from his throat, but his strength was incredible. Anwar wasn't going to allow that to happen. He had a job to do and he was going to finish it.

After struggling for a few seconds, Anwar managed to stab Scooter three times. The third time he stabbed him, it felt as if he hit a bone, and he panicked. After twisting and turning the weapon, Anwar was able to pull the weapon out of Scooter's rib cage.

Breathing a sigh of relief, he flung Scooter's lifeless body on the mattress in the cell. Anwar watched as the sticky blood seeped through Scooter's tan T-shirt.

Anwar washed his hands in the sink and managed to flush the murder weapon, like most inmates did when they wanted to get rid of the evidence. Anwar inspected himself in the mirror to see if he had any bloodstains on his face. There was nothing that he could see with the naked eye.

Anwar shifted Scooter's body so that he was lying on his side. The dead man's back was facing the cell window. If an officer looked into the cell, it would appear as if Scooter was asleep. He knew that some COs were lazy and didn't care anything about breathing bodies; they would just sign the count slip and that was it. Anwar was hoping for that same type of laid-back officer on the next shift. It was already 12:30 in the afternoon and the next shift didn't start until 3:30. That would be just enough time for rigor mortis to set in on Scooter's body and for him to get his mind right. It seemed as if everything was going according to plan.

"Yo, old timer," Anwar called out to an older inmate, who was walking toward the front of the housing area. The older guy looked up at Anwar, who was walking along the top tier. "Tell that CO to lock thirty-four cell."

The inmate did as he was told, and the CO at the desk informed the control room officer to close cell number thirty-four, the cell with the dead body of Inmate Shamel "Scooter" Abrams. Anwar went to back to his own cell and slept like a baby.

Chapter 17

Lamont

"Sir, I'm sorry to disturb you, but you have to report to Five North immediately," screamed the female officer, standing in front of Lamont's desk, looking wide-eyed and scared.

Lamont immediately jumped out of his seat, retrieved his radio, and ran out of his office. He sprinted down the long corridor, passing by officers who had confused looks on their faces.

When he arrived at Five North, the female supervisor was in hysterics, and a rookie male officer looked as if he was in shock. Sierra was nowhere in sight.

"Oh, my God!" said Captain Evans, holding on to Lamont's arm with her left hand, and covering her heart with her right one. "There's a dead body in cell thirty-four!"

"How do you know that the inmate is dead?" Lamont asked.

"Well, I came in here to sign the book and I went to make a tour. I walked around to everyone's cell to make sure that I had livin', breathin' bodies in my area. So when I arrived at cell thirty-four and I knocked, he didn't answer. I'm thinkin' that he's asleep. Somethin' told me to keep knockin'. When I started bangin' on the cell door and callin' out his name, he still didn't respond. I told the officer to open the cell door, and when I stepped inside, I noticed that he still didn't move. So when I got closer to the bed, I saw all the blood and . . ." Captain Evans was too upset to continue. Lamont comforted her.

By this time, the whole housing area was on lockdown in their cells. One could hear a pin drop as Captain Evans gestured for Lamont to follow her to the cell. They walked upstairs to the top tier, where cell thirty-four was cracked opened. Lamont pushed the door open and stepped inside.

"What is this inmate's name?" Lamont asked Captain Evans, looking at the body.

"His name is Shamel Abrams, sir," she replied, her voice quivering.

Lamont paused to think for a moment. If he remembered right, Shamel "Scooter" Abrams was the same inmate that Monique was rumored to have had dealings with. He also recalled Scooter being slashed a few years ago in the same housing area. Then Sierra told him that Abrams was the person who had shot Rasheed.

Why did this have to happen on my watch? Damn! Lamont thought.

Not wanting to touch anything, Lamont leaned over the body and saw that Scooter's blood was all over the white sheets. He stepped back and put his hand over his mouth. Lamont knew that heads were going to roll, including his. Again, he wondered why Sierra wasn't on post. She should have been back from meal by now.

"Deputy Simmons, he's really dead, isn't he?" Captain Evans asked with a worried look on her face, as if she didn't know that already.

Lamont held his head down. "From what it looks like, yes, he's dead, but that's for the doctor to determine." He looked around Five North. "I wonder who the hell done this shit?" he asked.

Captain Evans shook her head. "I don't even know.

Oh, Lord, what am I goin' to say to the warden, Deputy Simmons?"

Lamont put his hand on Captain Evans's shoulder. "Calm down, sweetie! You did your part. Everyone did their part. Things like this happen in jail." He looked at the door. "By the way, where's Howell? Why isn't she back from meal yet?" he asked.

"She called me on the radio and told me to call the clinic. She said that she didn't feel good, so I told her that I would have the meal relief officer hold down her post. She said something about feeling nauseated."

Lamont frowned. "Is that right?"

Captain Evans nodded. Lamont sucked his teeth, knowing that he would not be able to leave Five North. He wanted to go to the clinic to check on Sierra. Something about her absence just didn't sit right with him.

Lamont walked into the control room. He took a moment to look through the floor cards at the names of the inmates housed in Five North.

When the doctor and medical staff arrived at the door of Five North, Lamont followed them inside the housing area with the cards in his hand. He continued to look at the cards until he got to the name of one inmate: Anwar Jones. He stared at the mean mug in the picture, and checked to see what cell he was in. Lamont glanced at cell fifty and saw that Anwar was standing there, watching him.

"So that's who Sierra was talkin' to that day," Lamont said to no one in particular. He remembered the day that he walked into Five North and saw Anwar standing by Sierra's desk. Lamont had never laid eyes on Anwar before that day, but he knew that he was also the same man Deja, his son's mother, was so hung up on.

Lamont felt his chest tighten. Everything was coming together and Lamont didn't like what was going on. For

some reason, he had a strange feeling that Anwar had
something to do with Scooter's murder. He just had
to figure out what kind of connection they had to each
other. He watched as the medical staff worked on the
already dead man.

After standing around for a few moments, he saw
that the warden and deputy warden had walked into
Five North. If they were there, that meant the chief
of the department was on his way as well. As Lamont
walked downstairs to greet them, he saw that Anwar
was watching his every move. It made him very
uncomfortable.

"Good morning, sirs," said Lamont, greeting his
supervisors with a grim look on his face. "I apologize
ahead of time for this inconvenience—" he began.

The warden cut him off. "No, Simmons, this isn't
an inconvenience, trust me. Now, it's gonna be an
inconvenience for the person who obviously wasn't
doing his job! I wanna know what went on. Do you
have any reports from the officers?"

"No, sir. Not yet. The officer who was on post went
to the clinic. I think that he may be experiencing some
type of trauma. Captain Evans discovered the body
while she was touring the area."

The warden rubbed his chin. He looked at the deputy
warden. "A tactical search operation is definitely in
order for Five North. This housing area always seems
to have some type of problem and I'm sick of it! This
has been going on for the last five years!"

Lamont agreed. "Yeah, you are right, sir. It has
been off the hook in Five North. Actually, this inmate,
Abrams was slashed in this exact same housing area
about three years ago."

"Why was he back in here then?" asked the deputy
warden.

"Well, he couldn't go anywhere else in the facility,

and this housing area is for high classification and assaultive inmates," Lamont replied. "Captain Evans!" he called out to the area supervisor. "Can you come here for a moment, please?"

Captain Evans nervously walked toward the men. She saluted the warden and the deputy warden. They saluted back.

As Captain Evans described what she discovered, Lamont branched off and did his own tour of Five North. Lamont walked around, ignoring the questions of the inquisitive inmates as he passed by their cells. He walked straight to Anwar's cell door.

"What's good, Mr. Jones?" asked Lamont.

Anwar leaned against the door of his cell. "What's good? Who wants to know what's good?" he replied with a smirk on his face.

Lamont chuckled. "I want to know," he replied, sarcasm dripping off every word.

"I'm good, nigga."

"I ain't your nigga. Anyway, why are you in jail again?"

"What you mean, 'why am I in jail'? It don't matter why I'm in here."

Lamont came closer to the cell window so that only Anwar could hear him. "Look, 'nigga,' I know who the fuck you are, so let's cut the bullshit! You're the one who fucks with Deja."

Anwar waved Lamont off. "Man, if that's what you came to my cell to talk about, you might as well keep it movin'! I don't feel that we need to have a conversation about nothin' that is my business."

"Yeah, we shall see, my dude!" Lamont replied. "Ain't that how you lowlife crooks talk to each other, my dude? You probably had something to do with this body up in here, and if I find out you did, you know your ass is goin' up shit's creek!"

Anwar laughed. "Man, check out this fuckin' Uncle Tom nigga tellin' me I'm up shit's creek!" he exclaimed, looking Lamont up and down. "Damn, you're a fuckin' cornball! Nigga, you're lucky I don't take your other bitch away from you! The only thing that's stoppin' me from doin' that is that she got a seed by my man, Rasheed! So get the fuck away from my cell, motherfucker, before I spray some shit all over that icy white uniform shirt of yours!"

Lamont was pissed. He turned around and looked at the warden, who was engrossed in conversation with the chief. The chief must have walked in while he was talking to Anwar. Lamont immediately turned around on his heels and walked downstairs. He quickly saluted the chief and his subordinates.

Lamont stole a quick look at Anwar's cell, and the ornery criminal waved back at him with a wicked smile on his face.

After thirty minutes had passed, the medical staff notified the warden that Scooter was indeed dead, with multiple stab wounds to the chest. Emergency Medical Service was going to be coming through the door with a gurney, and the medical examiner would have to be called.

Fifteen minutes had passed since Scooter was declared dead by the facility medical staff. The medical examiner, EMS, and the inspector general's office swarmed Five North. The cell area was cordoned off with yellow crime scene tape by investigators. Five-star chiefs were on the post dicussing the incident with the warden of the facility. They talked about how much backlash the Department of Correction would have to endure because of the killing. The warden had a worried expression his face.

"We need a tactical search operation and we need it now! Search every fucking corner in this housing area and get those crooks out of their cells—*now!*" he shouted at his subordinates.

Lamont, Captain Evans, and the deputy warden immediately walked out of Five North to arrange a search. They all knew that it was about to go down.

Approximately an hour later, a tactical search operation was in full swing. Correction officers from every facility in the five boroughs were in Five North, searching and practically tearing the housing area apart. Annoyed inmates were being strip-searched by the male officers. Once the male inmates were dressed, the female correction officers would step into their cells and search it from top to bottom. The inmates silently protested the unfairness of the operation. Never did they stop to think that one of their very own had caused the fracas; they would rather blame the officers for doing their job.

Meanwhile, the special search team then proceeded to use tools to search the cracks and crevices of the housing area and anywhere an inmate was most likely to stash a weapon. Three weapons were retrieved from various places in Five North, and the warden's face turned beet red. Now he would really have some explaining to do to the chief of security.

Ten minutes later, Lamont paced up and down the tiers during the search, but kept his eyes on Anwar. He felt that Anwar was a 730: the penal code for a mentally disturbed person. This made Lamont want to reconsider his initial approach.

"Why are you back over here, man?" Anwar asked Lamont. The male officer holding his arm while his cell was being searched tightened his grip. Anwar rolled his eyes at him. He looked Lamont up and down. "I hope you ain't gonna start stalkin' me now. I ain't with that homo shit, Deputy Simmons!"

Lamont ignored Anwar's statement and walked inside of his cell while another officer was searching it. There were a lot of things in Anwar's cell that he wasn't supposed to have.

"How did you get these into this facility?" asked Lamont, holding up a pair of Anwar's pricey jeans.

"'Cause that's what I do! You know my bitch, Deja, got connections with the Department of Correction!" he replied with a smirk.

Lamont threw the jeans on the floor and walked all over them with his boots. He brushed past Anwar as he walked out of the dank cell. He didn't have time to play with inmates and Anwar was one of them.

After walking back downstairs to talk to some officers, Sierra ran across his mind. After the search was over, he made a mental note to go straight to the clinic to find out what was going on with her. She had some explaining to do.

Chapter 18

India

While the incident was going on in Five North, on the other side of the facility, India returned to her post after her meal period. She had the clinic post that day and she was happy for it. After all, she was having an affair with an assistant deputy warden. Why should she have to sit on a housing area post around smelly inmates for eight hours?

India walked into the clinic area and her meal relief immediately stood up to leave. "Uh-uh," India said, waving her finger at the officer. "I'm not back from meal yet. I have to get myself together," she said.

The relief officer sucked her teeth. She had three five-year stripes at the bottom of long-sleeved shirt, indicating that she had fifteen years on the job. "Look, little girl. I don't have time for games. You need to come and sit your rookie ass at this desk and do your own work! They have a dead body in Five North, so you would wanna get started on this paperwork."

India looked at the burly woman and grinned. "I ain't gotta do shit, do you know who I fuck with?"

"Who you fuck with?" The officer walked from behind the tattered desk and right up to India. "Damn, you rookie bitches are so stupid. You think givin' up your pussy to one of these supervisors in here is gonna make your job easier?" She laughed. "Trust me, honey, you are just one of many. When that new class comes

in, watch how fast you get tossed to the side for that
new piece of pussy! Your ass will be wheelin' in these
housin' areas so much, your head will be spinnin'!"

The relief officer threw the duty keys on the desk
and began to walk out of the clinic. At this point, India
began yelling loudly. She had to save face.

"You're just mad because nobody wanna talk to you,
you fat black bitch!"

The relief officer rushed back over to India and tried
to grab her. Sierra walked over just in time and stood
between India and the woman. "Whoa! You ladies need
to chill. What's goin' on?"

The meal relief officer looked at India with a sour
look on her face. "Ain't nothin' goin' on, Howell. You
better put this new jack ho on to me." She pointed her
finger in India's face. "Bitch, I've been on this job for
fifteen years, so if I beat the brakes off your ass, what
do you think they're gonna do to me? Nothin'!"

India tried to go around Sierra, but this time a male
officer stepped in and convinced the meal relief officer
to leave the clinic. Sierra took India in the back to calm
her down.

"Girl!" Sierra began, after getting India alone. "What
is wrong with you? Don't you know that you can lose
your job for fightin' up in here? Remember, you haven't
passed probation yet!"

India smirked. "Nah, Howell, I'm good! I'm dealin'
with this assistant deputy warden now, so, to be honest,
if anything goes down, I'm sure that he would have my
back!"

Sierra nodded. "You're dealin' with a who?"

"With an ADW! I know if anything goes down with
me, he will have my back!" she repeated.

"Wow. Okay. I am not mad at you for that but you
still have to chill out. If anything, you utilize this
person to help you get ahead in the department, not to
get you out of trouble."

Sierra wouldn't have guessed in a million years that the assistant deputy warden India was talking about was her very own Lamont. India smiled at the irony of it all.

India prepared to go back to her desk. "What are you doin' in here anyway?" she asked.

Sierra held her head down. "I'm not feelin' well, so I came to the clinic."

"Aren't you steady in Five North? Didn't I just hear someone say that there was a dead body in Five North? What was that about?"

Sierra shrugged. "I don't know. I didn't hear anyone say anything about a dead body," she lied.

"Where were you when that happened?" India asked.

Sierra looked at India strangely. "What do you mean where was I? I went to meal. I haven't been back to Five North since they found a dead body."

India shook her head. "Well, let me go assume this post before this bitch blows me up. Thanks for lookin' out for me, Howell—I appreciate that."

"That's no problem. You seem like you're a cool person. We have to exchange numbers one day and hang out."

India chuckled. "Yeah, let's do that," she said. *She is so stupid,* India thought.

Sierra and India walked back toward the front of the clinic. When they arrived at the desk, Lamont was standing there. India smirked and eased into the chair. Lamont looked as if he had seen a ghost. He hadn't expected for India and Sierra to be in the clinic at the same time.

"Good afternoon, Deputy Simmons!" India said cheerfully. "What brings you to these parts?"

"Good afternoon to you too, um, Officer Charles. Hello, Miss Howell." Sierra looked at him strangely. "Oh, um, Charles, did you see the doctor walk by with the paperwork for that Five North inmate?"

India smiled sweetly. "Actually, I didn't see the doctor come by. I just came back from meal. Did you want me to see if they have that paperwork ready for you, sir?"

Lamont was unable to look India in the face. "Yeah, that'll be good, um, Miss Charles."

India got up and walked away from the desk. She disappeared behind a wall, blocking herself from their view. She just had to eavesdrop on their conversation.

"Are you all right?" asked Sierra. "Why are you stumblin' over your words like that?"

India laughed to herself. Sierra seemed to have picked up on Lamont's nervousness. Her timing was perfect. She peeked from behind the wall and saw that Lamont was wiping the beads of sweat that had formed on his forehead. Sierra was standing in front of him with her arms folded.

"Nah, I guess that, um, I am a little tired. That dead body in Five North got me runnin' around like crazy! The warden is pissed, but enough of that. Anyway, why are you in the clinic and not on your post?" Lamont asked.

India watched as they slipped behind the desk and away from the inmates waiting to be seen by the facility medical staff. She stepped back a little further so that they wouldn't see her.

"I felt a little under the weather so I asked Captain Evans if I could go to the clinic. She had the meal relief officer stay there for me until three o'clock roll call. What's the problem?"

India peeked again and saw that this time Lamont had crossed his arms. He appeared to be angry with Sierra.

"Let me ask you a question. Why didn't you tell me that Anwar Jones was in Five North all this time? Wasn't he the same inmate I caught you talkin' to that day, and when I asked him his name, he had a sarcastic-ass answer for me?"

Sierra bit her lip. "I don't know why I didn't tell you sooner, Lamont, it's not like I have anything to hide. It just slipped my mind."

"It's just slipped your fuck . . . It slipped your mind?" Lamont looked around to see if anybody was looking or listening to their conversation. He grabbed Sierra's arm. "Don't lie to me, Sierra! What is goin' on with you and this Anwar guy?"

Sierra snatched her arm away from Lamont's strong grasp. "What the fuck do you mean, what's goin' on with me and Anwar? Ain't shit goin' on with me and Anwar! How dare you even accuse me of something like that!"

"Well, it's not like you haven't ever done it before, right? Now you're holdin' back information from me?"

Sierra looked as if she was about to cry. "I don't have anything to hide from you, Lamont! I didn't want to tell you because—," she said.

Lamont cut her off. "Because what?"

"I just have to wait to talk about this when we get home. I don't wanna talk about this here."

It sounded if Sierra was about to cry, and India loved every minute of it.

She watched as Lamont wiped his brow again and shook his head. He looked at Sierra and rolled his eyes like he was annoyed with her crocodile tears. India waited a few more seconds, then walked back to her desk just as Sierra was wiping the tears from her eyes.

"Miss Charles, do you have that paperwork so I could get outta here? I gotta get back to Five North," Lamont said.

India tried hard to contain her glee. Sierra stood there with a spaced-out look on her face, embarrassed from her display of emotion.

"I apologize, sir. I just remembered the paperwork that you needed was right here on the desk," India said smugly. She handed the papers to him. Lamont caught the attitude and snatched the papers out of her hand.

"Miss Charles, I will get back to you if I need anything else." He gestured for Sierra to follow him. It was confirmed that Lamont was pissed.

India shook her head as she watched Sierra follow Lamont out of the clinic. She continued to do her work.

Later on that night, Lamont came to pick up India from her house. He came straight from work and the jail smell was still lingering on his body. This did not stop Lamont from sexing India in the back of his truck, which was parked on a deserted street near the Brooklyn-Queens Expressway.

He had her legs bent back so far, her knees were rubbing against her ears. She loved every minute of it, as his dick rubbed against the walls of her smoldering hot pussy. He ground and hit every corner of her insides, and India screamed in ecstasy. She tightened up her vaginal muscles like she was trying to squeeze all of the life out of him, as Lamont's eyes rolled in the back of his head. The glare from a nearby streetlight gave her a visual of his fuck faces, and gazing into his bedroom eyes only had her more excited.

They ground to the tunes of Joe's "All The Things (Your Man Won't Do)," and India turned Lamont over to begin her ride. She moved her body in a circular motion as Lamont held on to her waist. He tried to contain himself, but couldn't resist the excitement of fucking some new, forbidden pussy.

Her hair framed his face as she watched his dick go in and out of her soaking wet box. Lamont moaned as he felt her wetness drown his dick, and the squishy sounds coming from her vagina were driving him up the wall. While R. Kelly's "12 Play" blared through the speakers, India kissed Lamont on the mouth, and they even stopped grinding for a moment.

"I can fuck you forever, baby," purred India. "Your lovin' is so good."

Lamont bit his bottom lip. "You got me open off this pussy, you know that?"

India began to grind on his dick again. "How open do I have you, daddy?"

"Real open, baby," he replied as he began humping back. "Don't stop givin' me this pussy, baby. Don't stop. Give your daddy all of this!"

India stuck Lamont's fingers in her mouth and proceeded to suck them one by one as she continued to sex him into oblivion. Lamont sat up in the backseat and pulled her body real close to him. As she bounced up and down on his dick, her ample breasts smacked Lamont in the face. He didn't mind it one bit.

Suddenly, India's body began to shake. She was having multiple orgasms. Lamont ejaculated shortly after, and they collapsed right in the backseat of his SUV.

After India and Lamont cleaned themselves up, Lamont discarded the used condom. Five minutes later, he announced that he was headed home.

"So soon?" asked India. "I thought we were goin' to chill tonight."

Lamont sighed. "I want to, but I gotta be there in the mornin' to help my peoples with the boys. She has to go to work and I don't, so I gotta take them to school."

India sucked her teeth and folded her arms. "But I wanna be with you tonight."

Lamont kissed India's gorgeous face. "I can't, baby, I'm so sorry."

India slid into the passenger seat and turned her body

toward the window as Lamont started up the truck. As they stopped at the light, suddenly India reached over and slapped Lamont in his face. He looked surprised and grabbed her by her neck, with one hand holding the steering wheel.

"Yo, what the fuck is wrong with you?" Lamont asked in annoyance.

"You think that it's that easy to get my pussy and go home to your bitch, huh?"

"Why are you actin' like this all of a sudden?"

"Because I want you to come home with me. Please just stay with me for a little while!"

Lamont drove his truck toward India's block. She whined the whole time, trying to get him to come upstairs with her. Finally, after some pleading from her, Lamont reluctantly gave in. He parked his vehicle and they went upstairs to India's apartment.

Once they were upstairs, Lamont picked India up. She wrapped her legs around him and he pounded into her while they stood against the wall. They both fell to the floor as Lamont continued to inflict pain and pleasure on her vaginal canal while she screamed his name out.

After pleasing her, India let Lamont leave with the promise that he would be back to see her the following evening. She didn't have enough energy to make him stay with her any longer. The passion was so intense between them that getting Sierra back was the furthest thing from India's mind. She was feeling Lamont, and now it was going to be more than revenge for her. It was a competition that she refused to lose.

Chapter 19

Rasheed

It was a Saturday morning at the Gordon house when Rasheed's cell phone rang. He looked at the caller ID and it read "UNKNOWN CALLER." Once he heard the operator, he knew exactly where the call was from.

"Yo, what's good, A?" Rasheed yelled into his cell phone. "You're on the Island, huh?" he asked.

"Yeah, man. I got this little punk-ass ninety days I have to do!" replied Anwar. "I'm in here with a bunch of busters. What's poppin', homie? You're in Brooklyn for good now? What's up with my favorite girl, Miss Carrie?"

Rasheed's mood changed. "Yeah, I'm back. I don't know if you heard, but my Nana died."

"Word? I came by to see her a few times when I heard that she was sick, but I didn't know that she had passed. Damn, Rah. I'm so sorry to hear that. Miss Carrie was my girl. I loved that woman." There was a brief pause between the childhood friends. "Damn! Why didn't Dino tell me?"

"Dino wasn't even in town when Nana passed. When did he give you my number?" Rasheed asked.

"Um, like last week. He was in, um, Miami, I think," Anwar replied.

"Yeah, we buried my Nana last week, A. Dino didn't know about it yet. He probably heard about it by now."

"Damn, I'm so sorry to hear that. Why did I have

to be locked up? You know I would have come to the funeral. Was my sister there?"

"Thank you, A. I know you would have been there. As for your sister, I don't know if she was there. My mind was so messed up that day. What's up with her, anyway?"

"My sister don't mess with me like that, son. Her and my moms are real tight. And you know I don't fuck with my moms like that. As a matter of fact, me and my baby sis got into it about that. She said that I should let go of the past and work on havin' a relationship with my mother. I kinda screamed on her and told her that she was too young to remember how fucked up Mom Dukes and Russell treated me. She's not talkin' to me right now, but I'll get back right with her when I get to the town. It is what it is."

Rasheed shook his head. "Same old A. You ain't changed one bit, son. You still have that I-don't-give-a-fuck attitude!"

"Hell, yeah! I'm me and me is I. I'm not changin' for none of these motherfuckers out here! I had to be this way in order to survive in these streets just to keep myself from goin' crazy, nah mean, Rah? You know how it was for me. You were there."

"Yeah, I was there, A. I was there. You went through a lot. But, seriously, I'm gonna come up there to see you."

"You're comin' to see me?" Anwar laughed. "I'll believe that when I see you on that visit floor. You hate Rikers Island!"

"I hate the Island with a passion, but, damn, I can't come see my brother?"

"A visit from you will make me real happy. Plus, I gotta talk to you about somethin' anyway. It's about some serious shit."

"Word? In regard to what?"

"I ain't gonna speak on it over the phone—just get your ass up here. I got a visit tomorrow. As a matter of fact, do you mind hittin' Deja up to tell her to give you some clothes for me?"

Rasheed sucked his teeth. "Yo, A, don't insult me like that. I can get you what you need. I'll go to the Avenue and get you some new threads, man! You need some sneakers, socks, drawers, T-shirts, and what else?"

Anwar laughed. "Yeah, son. Bring me all that you just named. I like my undergarments to be crispy fresh, no matter where I am. These bum-ass niggas be in here scrubbing the same drawers in the shower every fuckin' day! I ain't with that shit!"

Rasheed laughed. "A'ight, A, I got you, man!" The recording came on the phone. Their six-minute conversation was about to be up. "Keep your head up, A. I'll see you tomorrow."

"No doubt, Rah. One."

It was funny, but after talking to Anwar, Rasheed couldn't even fathom why he had wasted his young life doing time in jail.

His uncles were disappointed in him because they thought that their nephew wouldn't want to make the same mistakes that they did growing up. They saw then that their actions had a negative influence on Rasheed, but, by then, he was on his second jail bid. Unfortunately, he had to learn on his own. Fatherhood had changed Rasheed's attitude for the better, and he even considered doing something more with his time.

Rasheed looked at some toys that he'd purchased for Messiah. He smiled as he thought about his baby boy.

His cell phone began ringing again and Rasheed picked it up. He sighed when he saw Asia's number on his caller ID.

"What's up, Asia?" he answered nonchalantly. He was in no mood for sex talk.

"I didn't mean to bother you, but I just wanted to call you and apologize."

"For what?" he asked, even though he knew what she was talking about.

"For the other day. That was just pure selfishness on my part. Your Nana had just passed away and here I was thinkin' about myself. Do you accept my apology?"

"I accept your apology," Rasheed replied with a sigh.

"I appreciate that. I also wanted to know if I can take you out for dinner some time."

Rasheed frowned. "I'm goin' to have to think about that, Asia. I do appreciate the thought, though."

"I even bought you a gift. As a matter of fact, I bought a few gifts for you and your son."

"You know that you didn't have to do that, sweetie."

"I wanted to. I bought the gifts with my very own money. No more stolen credit cards over here!"

Rasheed laughed. "I should hope not! Aren't you a correction officer now?"

Asia giggled. "Yeah, and I came this far. I'm really not tryin' to mess up my life anymore."

"That's what's up." They both paused.

"Is it okay if I come over for a minute, you know, to bring the gifts? I'm not goin' to stay long."

"Sure, why not?" Rasheed replied.

An hour later, Asia called Rasheed to let him know that she was outside of his house. He went downstairs and out the front door to her parked Cherokee. Asia climbed out of the driver's seat and walked around to the passenger side of the truck. Rasheed smiled. He remembered how he used to be so turned off by Asia and her sister. He always felt that they were so loud and ignorant, and Tamir put so much effort into being like them.

Now that Rasheed was standing before the new and improved Asia, he definitely saw that her outer beauty was still intact. Her inner beauty was finally beginning to shine through as well. He just hoped that she wouldn't do anything to change his opinion of her.

Asia turned around to face Rasheed and smiled sweetly. She wore a long sundress and gladiator sandals, with a freshly done French pedicure. Her giant loop earrings and long ponytail added to her sex appeal. Her eyes enticed him as she wrapped her arms around his neck. Rasheed had to catch himself as he felt her body brush against his manhood. It was hard to believe that the woman he was embracing had been Tamir's best friend, the same woman he couldn't stand a couple of years ago.

"Hey, Rah," Asia said, and kissed him on the cheek. She took her two fingers and rubbed her Clinique lip gloss off his face.

"Hey, baby girl," Rasheed replied, inspecting her from head to toe. "You look real nice."

Asia spun around so that he could get a full visual of her. "You like?"

Rasheed licked his lips. "I love it."

Asia giggled. "You are too cute, Rah. I swear you are."

"So are you, Asia." He stood there, biting his bottom lip.

Asia smiled at the gesture and opened the passenger door. She pulled out two large shopping bags. One bag was from Prada and the other bag was from Louis Vuitton. Rasheed eyes widened with surprise.

"Yo, who is that for?" Rasheed asked, pointing at the bags.

Asia laughed. "These bags are for you and your son."

"Where did you get the money to get all this expensive shit from?"

"Rasheed, just take the bags! I do have a job now, remember? I bought your baby a few things from Prada, and there's a Bloomingdale's bag in there. I got him a couple of outfits. And you? Well, I got you a pair of sneakers from the Louis Vuitton store and a hat and a belt and a—," she said.

Rasheed stopped her. "Asia, you didn't have to do this. And how did you even know what size shoe I wear?"

"From Tamir, remember?" she said. "Size eleven."

Rasheed held his head down. Memories of Tamir's face flooded his memory.

"That's right. My Tamir," he mumbled under his breath. "Thanks for thinkin' about me and my boy."

He took the bags out of Asia's hands and kissed her softly on the lips.

"You're welcome. Enjoy. I hope your son can fit into those clothes. Or maybe he could grow into them, along with the sneakers."

"I appreciate this, but you don't have to buy me."

Asia started to inch toward her truck. Rasheed didn't want her to leave. "It was somethin' I wanted to do, Rasheed. When I called you that day, I was bein' insensitive. I felt like a fool." Asia started the engine. "Do you mind if I call you later?" she asked.

Rasheed stood there, holding the bags in his hand. "Call me later."

He stood by the curb and watched her pull off. Rasheed looked at the bags in his hand and went back inside the house. Once he was in his bedroom, he began emptying the contents on the bed.

"Damn, Asia must be really feelin' me to buy all this expensive stuff," he said aloud while looking at all the items sprawled on his bed.

For a brief moment, he couldn't help but wonder what Asia was up to. The apology, the gifts, the phone calls were suspect, but he didn't want to think negatively about her. She'd said that she was trying to change, and a part of him wanted to believe her. He felt that they were both at turning points in their lives, so he had to start somewhere, and that was learning to trust again.

The next day, Rasheed proceeded to Rikers Island to visit Anwar. He knew that it was going to be a long day, because he hated everything about Rikers. Even the visitor transport bus was a ride from hell. Rasheed looked around at the women on the bus, especially the ones with the crying babies. He had only been on the visitor side a few times in his life, and it was a shame to see that absolutely nothing had changed.

When they pulled up to the facility, an officer with a Smith & Wesson 9 mm strapped to his hip came outside and gave them the same boring speech about the items that weren't allowed in the facility. Rasheed double-checked his pockets to see if he had left everything in his truck, especially his cell phone. Seeing that he had taken care of everything, he sighed with relief and walked with the crowd toward the facility visit area to register.

After being searched, Rasheed sat around and waited for Anwar's name to be called. Some of the COs who milled around the visit area looked familiar, but he didn't attempt to say anything to any one of them. He didn't feel like reminiscing about his days spent behind those walls. One or two officers gave him a strange look, but Rasheed paid them no mind and proceeded to the visit seating area.

Once he was seated, Rasheed smiled as he thought about being on the other side of the knee-high table. It wasn't too long ago that he was wearing that god-forsaken gray Department of Correction–issued jumpsuit. He sighed as he anxiously waited for Anwar to come out on the visit floor.

The metal doors slid open, and Anwar walked out

looking like a lost scholar with his Montblanc spectacles
on. They gave each other a brotherly hug and sat in the
chairs directly across from each other. All they did was
smile at each other for a good five minutes.

"What's the deal, nigga?" Rasheed asked. "You look
good, boy!"

Anwar rubbed his goatee. "You think so?" Anwar
inspected his friend as well. "You don't look so bad
yourself! That Atlanta livin' did you good, homie!"

Rasheed laughed and waved him off. "Fuck Atlanta!
I wouldn't live there again if you gave me a million
dollars of tax-free money. I love New York too much,
son, for real."

"I ain't mad at you, but at least you can move wherever you like. I can't live anywhere but New York
anyway because I've been on parole half of my life."

"You can live wherever you want, A. You can just
transfer your parole to the state you're gonna live in."

"Man, them POs ain't transferrin' me nowhere! They
know how I do. Why would they put a nigga like me in
the custody of another state? After lookin' at my rap
sheet, they would probably ship my ass right back to
New York on the first thing smokin'."

Rasheed keeled over with laughter. "You ain't lyin'
about that!" Rasheed looked around. He just happened
to spot two female correction officers smiling and
giggling at them. Rasheed waved at the women and
they waved back.

"Yo, A, you know them?" Rasheed asked, checking
out a brown-skinned female officer with a pretty smile.
"I see that these chicks are still up to their old tricks."

Anwar looked at the officers and a scowl came over
his face. "Man, fuck them hoes! I don't pay these
po-lice broads no mind." He glanced at them again.
"Forget them bitches! I gotta tell you somethin' very
important."

Rasheed diverted his attention from the cute officer. "What do you have to tell me, nigga? It sounded hella important and that's part of the reason why I'm playin' myself by even bein' on this visit floor right now."

Anwar came closer to Rasheed. "Remember that nigga, Scooter? You know the one who shot you? Yeah, well, thanks to me, that dude is on ice."

Rasheed looked at Anwar strangely. "What do you mean Scooter is on ice?"

Anwar smirked and looked around the visit area. "Nigga, I put that dude on ice! I put that dog down."

Rasheed leaned closer to Anwar and whispered. "You put him down as in murdered the nigga? Are you serious?"

"Yeah, I did, and, yes, I'm serious."

Rasheed covered his mouth. "C'mon, son, what did you do? Where did this happen at? Did this happen in Five North?"

"Yeah, I ran up on him and stabbed the shit outta that dude right in his cell in Five North. Had homeboy laid out on his mattress like he was takin' a nice little nap. Your baby moms looked out for me, too."

Rasheed felt hot under the collar. "My baby moms? What do you mean, 'my baby moms looked out for you'?"

Anwar playfully tapped Rasheed on the arm. "Yo, I told her what I was gonna do and she was with it! You have you a real ride or die bitch for a baby moms, Rah!"

Rasheed shook his head. "Nah, son! That doesn't sound like the Sierra I know. I was the exception, but she don't play that shit when it comes to her job. She would have never put herself in a position like that. There has to be more to the story. What did you really say to her, A?"

Anwar chuckled. "Nigga, why don't you believe it when I say that she was with the program? It was all for you! You don't think she will hold you down like that?"

"I ain't sayin' that, I'm just sayin' that you shouldn't have put her in the middle of this shit, 'cause this wasn't her beef, son. That's my son's mother, and regardless of whatever may be goin' on with us, her and her man takes very good care of my son, I can't front about that."

Rasheed continued, "Now with you gettin' her involved with this shit right here, her damn job and her freedom could be on the line. If someone finds out that she knew what was goin' to happen and she didn't say anything, she could be charged with conspiracy. It's bad enough people are associatin' her with me, but now this? If she loses her job, it's like you're takin' food right out of my son's mouth. I was just gonna leave that Scooter shit alone anyway because I have too much to live for. I'm not tryin' to go back to jail for killin' nobody!"

"Look, nigga, I owe you!" whispered Anwar with a deranged look on his face. "You did that Russell shit for me and I've been waiting half of my life for the opportunity to repay you. As a matter of fact, what if I would have killed that nigga, Lamont, instead, huh? Would that have made you happier?"

Rasheed waved him off. "Man, you're buggin' out now! You done got yourself into somethin' that you, Sierra, and probably I can get in trouble for." Rasheed sighed. "Look, just leave Howell's man alone and leave her out of this! If she wants to be with him, that's fine with me. I ain't tryin' to have nobody's blood on my hands."

Anwar looked at Rasheed like he had two heads. "What the hell is wrong with you, Rah? Are you gettin' soft on me, son? We had shit that we needed to take care of!"

"It's not about gettin' soft. I have a son now. I love the hell outta my boy. Do you know how hard it was to get him back into life? I lost my Nana, my moms, and my Uncle Peppy, and I'm not about to lose my son, A. If I get locked up, who's gonna bring my boy to see me? Why would I want him to see me locked up?"

Rasheed went on. "Bein' in Messiah's life is goin' to make a difference because I'm gonna teach him to not be like me when he grows up. He's gonna make somethin' of himself if I have anything to with it. My son's mother is finally lettin' me build a relationship with him, and she's straight catchin' hell in her household and on this job just so that I'm able to do that. That's why I'm not goin' to let anyone fuck her up in this game, not even you."

Anwar leaned back in the seat and looked at Rasheed with contempt in his eyes.

"Damn, nigga! Where is your loyalty? You really feelin' this Sierra bitch, huh? You're puttin' this chick ahead of our bond, man! You put that bastard Russell to rest for me, so I felt that the least I could do is return the favor! This nigga, Scooter, almost took your life. Your son would have *never* known you if this dude would have killed you, but I wasn't about to let that shit ride, homie! I owed you and I paid my debt to you!"

Rasheed shook his head. "So what do you want me to say? Thank you for killin' this nondescript-ass nigga who was no threat to me? Okay, he shot me, but that's not the big picture. The big picture is that I'm still alive. I'm right here on this visit floor with you. I don't want to see you go to jail for a hundred years for no Scooter. Russell's life bein' taken was done to save your life. If I didn't kill him, you would have killed him and possibly yourself. I didn't want to lose you so he had to go. That's the difference between these killings. So you don't owe me anything."

Anwar sat there in silence for a moment. Without saying good-bye, he stood up and walked off the visit floor. Rasheed sat in his seat with a confused look on his face, not knowing what to do or say. The female officer with the pretty smile walked over and slipped him her phone number. Rasheed balled the paper up in his hand and put on a weak smile. He felt sick to his stomach after seeing the behavior that Anwar had displayed. He couldn't believe that this was the same man he had referred to as a brother. After a few seconds, Rasheed got up from the seat and walked out of the visit area.

Later that night, Rasheed made arrangements to see Asia at her place. She was more than willing to have some company, and invited him over for a much-needed nightcap. They were going to sip on some drinks and chat. He needed something to do after what Anwar had confessed to him.

When Rasheed arrived at Asia's apartment, they sat on the couch together and talked, while sipping on some Cîroc and lemonade and listening to Marsha Ambrosius of Floetry sing "Getting Late." They chatted about Tamir for a brief moment, laughing at the times they had shared with her. Rasheed and Asia even cried together as they recalled the day that they found out that she had been murdered.

"Tamir was a good person," Asia said. "I had love for her, I really did. But to be honest, me and my sister weren't good enough to her, I realize that. She didn't belong in our crowd, you know? She could have done so much better than what she was doin'."

Rasheed nodded. "You're right. She could have done better than me, too. She was young, she was beautiful, two-parent home, nice background, and there she was in love with a guy like me. I think she was more in love with the bad boy Rasheed, because when I told her that I was changin' my life, she got mad at me."

"But she loved you. I know sometimes you think

that she was just in love with what you represented, but I honestly think that it was deeper than that. Tamir was tryin' to be down, and if you would have changed your ways, she felt that she would have lost her street credibility. That's only because she didn't know any better. Guess she wasn't ready to change— that's probably why she was upset with you."

"Well, I just need somebody who's gonna love me, not idolize me. I'm just a regular dude from the Stuy, not no icon like Michael Jackson."

Asia smiled seductively. "So can I give you some groupie love, Rasheed?"

They both began feeling the effects of the Cîroc. They started touching each other, gently massaging each other's body parts. Rasheed rubbed his hand across Asia's round derriere while she stroked his rod.

"Nice," she cooed.

"Thank you, baby," he replied. "You can have it, if you want it. Where do you want it?"

Asia gave Rasheed a soft kiss on his lips. "I'm gonna start with my mouth first, baby. I wanna put in my mouth, baby."

Rasheed watched as Asia pulled out his well-endowed penis. She put the head in her mouth and licked with expertise. His eyes narrowed as he watched her treat his rod like a chocolate pudding pop. This went on for at least a half hour.

Suddenly, they heard a key in the door, and Rasheed quickly zipped his pants. Asia pulled herself together and plopped on the couch beside him. When India walked through the door, she wasn't alone. Rasheed was shocked, only it wasn't because of India. After all, she did live there. It was the person who walked in behind her that he didn't expect to see.

"Lamont?" Rasheed asked with a surprised look on his face. Lamont was quieter than a church mouse. Asia shook her head. India smiled from ear to ear.

Chapter 20

Lamont

Lamont stood in the middle of the living room and stared at Rasheed. He couldn't believe his eyes. Of all the places that this man could have seen him, why did it have to be in the home of a woman—a woman who was not Sierra? Lamont knew that Rasheed was going to run this in the ground. He wanted to kick himself for allowing the crook for having one up on him.

"What's up?" Lamont said dryly.

"What's up, Lamont? I can call you Lamont now, can't I?" Rasheed replied sarcastically, with a devious smile on his handsome face.

Lamont grimaced. He wanted to kill India. "Yeah, you can, I guess."

He could tell that the con was getting a kick out of him being uncomfortable in his presence.

"You guess? Well, I was gonna call you Lamont whether you wanted me to or not. What's up with my baby mother?"

Lamont gritted his teeth as he watched Asia and India tiptoe out of the living room. They left the two men alone. He had to wonder if this whole thing was planned. It was just too much of a concidence that Rasheed was there at the same time he was.

"She's good."

Rasheed shook his head. "Damn, nigga!" Rasheed announced. "You know that you're in a real fucked-up position right now, don't you?"

"What do you mean, 'I'm in a real fucked-up position'? India and I are just friends. I gave her a ride home today."

Rasheed stood up. His six-feet-four frame towered over Lamont. He felt a flicker of jealousy running through his veins as he took in Rasheed's physical attributes.

Jail preserved this motherfucker, Lamont thought.

"What I mean is that you know and I know that your ass ain't supposed to be in this apartment right now. Your real woman, Sierra, is at home, the same woman you fought so hard to get back with when I had her."

Lamont smirked. He wasn't about to let Rasheed talk down to him.

"It was no fight, homeboy! She wanted to be with me because she had had it with your shenanigans! And you moved to Atlanta, remember? Were you there when your son was born? No, because I was there. Were you there for his first two years? No, I don't think so!"

Rasheed narrowed his eyes. "Do me a favor and leave my son outta this shit! I'm here now and it ain't too late for me to be a father to Messiah. The real question is, why are you here with India? You are standin' here in another woman's home while my son's mother is bein' a good woman to you!"

Lamont's chest swelled up. "Is she really? That's funny, because since you moved back to Brooklyn, her whole attitude changed. Are y'all plottin' somethin' behind my back?"

Rasheed covered his mouth and laughed. "Do you think that I need to hear that right now? Nigga, Sierra didn't get caught in my house. You are the one who's plottin'."

Lamont sucked his teeth. "So what are you tryin' to say, Gordon? What do you want from me?"

"What do I want from you? Funny you ask that."

Rasheed paused. "I wanna be able to see my son whenever I feel like it without your input. I wanna be able to come and pick my son up, from your front door, whenever I feel like it."

"You are not comin' to my house, motherfucker!"

Rasheed shook his finger at Lamont. "Look, Mr. Simmons, you can't tell me nothin'. I got this now. I wanna be able to come to your front door and pick up my son. Or maybe Sierra can bring Messiah to my house, but I don't think that you would want that to happen too often, would you?"

Lamont was steaming hot. He knew that there was nothing that he could do—he had been caught red-handed. Once again, his dick had gotten him into trouble, and now, of all the people he could have been caught by, why did it have to be Rasheed Gordon?

Lamont waved his hands. "Fuck it, okay! Just come by the house to pick up Messiah! I'm just askin' you to do me a favor."

Rasheed frowned. "What?"

"Just leave Sierra out of this. Don't try to fuck with her. Please."

"What? I don't think I heard you right." Rasheed cupped his ear. "Don't try to do what?"

"Don't try to fuck with Sierra."

Rasheed was in hysterics. He began laughing so loud that Asia and India emerged from the back room.

"Whatever, man! The nerve of a nigga! I'm the least of your worries right now, my man. You need to be worried about your woman leavin' you."

Lamont looked at India with a humiliated expression on his face. "I'm out." He turned around to leave.

India stomped her foot. "Lamont! I don't see why you're leavin'. You stayed with me the other night!"

Lamont glanced at Rasheed's face. He was getting a kick out of the whole ordeal, and India was talking entirely too much. Lamont grabbed her hand and walked out the door. As they stood in the hallway waiting for the elevator, Lamont grabbed India by her hair. She winced with pain.

"What the fuck are you tryin' to do to me, India?" he asked, talking through clenched teeth. "Did you know that Rasheed was gonna be here tonight?"

India attempted to pull her hair from Lamont's grasp, but he wouldn't budge. "No, I didn't know that he was gonna be there! I really didn't!" Lamont finally let her hair go.

"I don't believe that. What are you tryin' to do to me, India? Why are you tryin' to put me out there? Who are you, anyway?"

India massaged her sore scalp. "What do you mean, 'who am I'? I'm India Charles!"

"I thought that you were a different person. I thought that you wanted to have a little fun, but the way this went down tonight, I'm not so sure anymore. There has to be some type of motive for what happened here tonight!"

"There's no motive, baby. I am really feelin' you! Rasheed bein' here has nothin' to do with me or with us. My sister just happened to invite him over."

"But how do you know this dude, Rasheed? Did you know him before you knew me? Did you know that he was Sierra's son's father?"

"I didn't know anything about him bein' her son's father. I mean, I just knew him from around the way, but we never really interacted with each other. I never really talked to him like that until now," India lied.

Lamont didn't know whether to believe India. He stared at her for a brief second. He wondered if there was any way possible that he could still deal with her and Sierra at the same time with Rasheed knowing about their relationship. He sighed and hugged India.

"This might cause a lot of problems for me now, and I don't wanna have to stop fuckin' with you."

India looked up at Lamont. "And what are you tryin' to say? I ain't worth the trouble?"

He kissed her on her forehead and wiped the hair from her face. He grabbed her by the back of her neck.

"You better be, baby. You better be."

Lamont kissed India one more time and got onto the elevator. He was so pissed, he punched the elevator wall. He fell back and put his hands over his face. He had messed up big time and he knew it.

After taking the long route home, Lamont pulled into his driveway. The house just had a few lights on and the kids' bedroom light was completely off. As he walked toward the side door, that twinge of guilt came back.

Everything that he had worked so hard for could possibly crumble because of his insatiable craving for new pussy. After all, India was just a jump-off. What Lamont was really in love with was the excitement, not India. The woman he adored and worshipped was his Sierra and no one else.

When Lamont walked in, Sierra was in the kitchen, making herself a sandwich. She saw him standing in the foyer and smiled.

"What's up, baby?" she asked while chewing on some turkey meat. "You want some of my sammich?" she joked.

Lamont laughed and playfully grabbed her by the waist. "Nah, I don't want no, 'sammich'! Are you okay, though?"

She sighed. "Yeah, I'm good, just hungry as hell." Lamont watched as the PINK nightshirt that Sierra was wearing slightly rose over her plump ass. He licked his lips.

"Where are you comin' from anyway?" she asked, shoving a piece of sandwich into her mouth.

"From Kaseem's crib. We had a few drinks, watched some ESPN, you know, we did things that guys do."

Sierra looked at Lamont strangely. He wondered if she could tell that he was lying, or if it was just his conscious messing with him.

"Um, okay." They both paused. "I hope that you thought about what I told you the other day," Sierra warned.

Lamont had forgotten about what they talked about. After seeing Rasheed at India's house, his memory was shot. He couldn't think about anything else but getting caught out there by Sierra's baby's father.

"What were we talkin' about again?" he asked, scratching his head.

"Lamont! Yesterday when they found the body in Five North, I talked to you about gettin' Anwar Jones out of the jail. I don't wanna go into work and have to look at his despicable face anymore!"

"Well, baby, that is a situation beyond my control! I have to speak to the warden, then he has to give instruction to the security captain. Jones is a high-profile inmate. We have to get permission from downtown to move him. He can't go but so many places on the Island, and he can't be housed in the borough jails. What's really goin' on?"

Sierra sulked. "He has to go. I don't want him there. He gives me the creeps and I just don't feel comfortable with him bein' there."

Lamont kissed Sierra on the cheek. "Look, babe, I'm gonna work on gettin' him outta there as soon as possible, or, as a matter of fact, how would you like to transfer to another facility?"

Sierra sipped her cup of juice. "Another facility? I don't wanna do that. I like the facility that I'm in now! I don't feel like startin' over."

"I think it's time you made a move. Get you a new start. How about the Queens House of Detention?"

Sierra sucked her teeth. "I don't know nobody in no Queens House! I don't wanna work there. I like Rikers Island," Sierra whined.

"But what about this Anwar situation? I just told you about all the red tape I would have to go through to get him moved. As far as we know, he hasn't gotten into any trouble yet."

Sierra sucked in some air. "Well, if you can't move him, then maybe it's best for me to go to another facility, but I have to think about it."

Lamont smiled. He hoped his idea would work. To get Sierra out of the jail and away from India Charles was a great idea. This way he could have the best of both worlds. The sad part was he couldn't understand why he was still scheming on how to have relations with India.

"And I've been doin' some thinkin', Si. I know that I've been against Rasheed bein' a father to Messiah. I just wanna let you know that it's okay for Messiah to spend some quality time with his father. Maybe Rasheed could even come get him from here if he has to."

Sierra looked at Lamont in amazement. "Are you serious?"

Lamont smiled. "Yes, I'm serious. Why do you ask that?"

Sierra hugged him. "Oh, thank God! I didn't want this to cause problems between me and you, baby." She gave him a kiss on the lips. "What brought on this sudden change?" she asked.

"I thought that I was bein' a little too hard on you and Messiah. It's gonna take some gettin' used to, but, hey, why can't Messiah have two daddies, right?"

Sierra hugged Lamont tightly while he did everything

he could to hold back his tears of frustration. Rasheed had him by the balls and he knew it.

The next day, Lamont was up early pacing back and forth. India kept calling his phone the night before, so much that he had to turn it off. Sierra got up at her usual time to get ready for work. A few hours later, Lamont woke up so that he could take the boys to school. Once he was in the house by himself, he called India back.

"Hey, sweetness," India said when she answered the phone. "Why didn't you call me back last night?"

"Where are you?" he asked.

"I'm workin' in visits today. I'm standin' outside talkin' to you. Why?"

"Listen, don't be in there runnin' your mouth about what we do in our spare time, you hear me?"

India laughed. "What the hell are you talkin' about, Lamont?"

"You know what I'm talkin' about, India! I don't want any of them people in my business! I already have enough drama to last me a lifetime."

"Hmm. Well, whose fault is that, sweetie? Your problems were there way before I was even in the picture."

"Just remember what I said."

India cut Lamont off to talk to someone. "Hey, Captain Phillips! How are you? I'm so sorry about the cell phone! I was just talkin' to..." India paused.

India was talking to Monique and Lamont was nervous as hell. He didn't want his sister to know anything about his fling with India. He would really be through. He thought about hanging up the phone, but that would only make the situation worse.

"You better not tell her I'm on the fuckin' phone, India! I'm not playin' with you!" Lamont instructed through clenched teeth.

"Um, I'm just talkin' to my . . ." India playfully stammered.

"I'm not playin' with you, India!"

"Grandmother. She's in the hospital."

Lamont could hear Monique in the background telling India to make it quick. Using a cell phone on post was unauthorized in the jails.

Lamont breathed a sigh of relief. Their affair was beginning to become a headache, but he couldn't stop himself. He was like a drug addict who had relapsed.

"Please, India, I'm beggin' you to just keep this between us two."

"Why are you beggin' me, Lamont? Do you know that a beggin'-ass man is so unattractive?"

"I don't give a fuck about all that. Just do that for me."

India paused again. This time it was to speak to Sierra. Lamont felt as if he was about to throw up his breakfast.

India began carrying on a conversation with Sierra. "Hey, Howell! Girl, what are you doin' over here in visits? For real? Girl, please, I'm just talkin' to—" was all that he heard India say when suddenly the phone went dead. Lamont attempted to call India's phone back but it kept going into voice mail. The only thing that he could do at that moment was sit at home and wonder if India was telling Sierra about them.

Chapter 21

Sierra

"Hey, Charles! What are you doin' over here, girl?" Sierra asked India. She had gone outside of the visit area to get some fresh air, and saw India using her cell phone.

India clicked the phone off. "Nothin' much. Just checkin' in with this guy I deal with."

"Go, Miss Thang! Seems like you like this man a lot. You're all smilin'and whatnot. Is this the assistant deputy warden you told me about?"

India blushed. "Yes, that's him, and I really do like him. He's a real man, you know? Somethin' that I'm so not used to, but there's one problem."

Sierra frowned. "What?"

"He has a girlfriend. They are havin' problems, though. He thinks that she is still messin' around with her baby's father."

"What? That's not good. Is he tryin' to leave this chick or what?"

"Truthfully, he's workin' on that now. I guess I'm just helpin' the process go a little faster, if you know what I mean."

Sierra laughed. "Do what you gotta do, girl, and get your man! Sounds like the woman already has someone else . . . and that's her baby father."

India nodded in agreement. "You're right, Howell. Now maybe I can get my man."

Sierra walked India to her post. They talked for a few moments more before Sierra left her to go to Monique's office. Monique Phillips was the captain in charge of visits. Sierra walked into the small office and closed the door behind her. Monique had her face screwed up when Sierra sat in a chair positioned in front of her desk.

"What is your face lookin' like that for?" Sierra asked. "Who got your panties in a bunch, girl?"

Monique leaned back in her seat and looked at Sierra. "I don't care for that little bitch."

Sierra was confused. "Um, Mo, what little bitch are you talkin' about?"

"The little bitch who was out there on her cell phone talkin' to God knows who about God knows what! How dare she come into my area and act like she got it like that!"

"Well, she did apologize to you, didn't she?"

"Who did she say she was on the phone with, Si?"

"Um, she told me she was on the phone with her new boyfriend."

"Mm-hmm! The bitch told me that she was on the phone with one of her family members. She said somethin' about her grandmother bein' sick. She's so full of shit!"

"Mo, what's up with you and Charles? You don't really know her like that, do you?"

"Nah, I don't know the trick, but there's somethin' about that heifer that I don't like!"

Sierra waved Monique off. "Mo, that chick is a new jack! She hasn't even been on the job for two years! Nobody ain't checkin' for her."

"Now you know I know a whore when I see one, Sierra. Don't you remember how I used to get down? I could sniff out a ho from a mile away and that officer, Charles, or whatever her damn name is, is a certified ho. She's sneaky and there's somethin' about her that I don't like. I just can't place my finger on it yet. If I was you, I wouldn't mess with that chick."

Sierra sighed. "Well, I'm not gonna jump the gun and say anything about a person I don't really know like that. She's pretty, and she has a little swag about her, so you know that people are goin' to hate on her."

"Are you tryin' to say that I'm hatin' on her?"

Sierra laughed. "Hell no! You just said that there's somethin' about her that you don't like!" Sierra looked at Monique. "Are you hatin' on her a little bit?"

Monique smirked. "I don't believe you asked me that, Sierra! Why do I have to hate on that woman? I have my own house, my late-model car, money in the bank, money in my pocket, the body, the clothes, the position, the post, and, most importantly, I'm right with God, I'm in good health, and my family is good. Are you serious?"

Sierra shrugged. "I just asked a question. Damn!"

"Well, that's a question that was not warranted. Just be careful with that ho. I wouldn't trust the slut as far as I can throw her."

Sierra smiled. "I hear you, Mo, I hear you."

As they sat in the office and talked for a few moments longer, someone knocked on the door. Monique rolled her eyes when India walked in.

"Yes, may I help you?" Monique asked with an attitude.

"Excuse me, Captain Phillips, but what time is my meal break?" India asked.

Sierra shot Monique a look, signaling for her to be nice. "I will let you know, how about that?"

India smiled sweetly. "No problem, Cap. Sorry to bother you. Oh, Howell, I will call you on your post." India looked at Monique with a smirk on her face and waved. "Bye, Captain Phillips."

When India stepped out of the office, Monique shuddered. "It's confirmed. I cannot stand that bitch!"

After leaving Monique's office, Sierra walked toward the locker room. She thought about her and Monique's conversation, and she couldn't pick up on anything that was wrong with India. It had been a long time since she had any outside acquaintances. She chose to keep her circle of friends very tight because it meant less confusion, less aggravation. But as of late, she was beginning to feel like she was out of the loop. India seemed like she was young and vibrant. Maybe she was the antidote that Sierra needed to add a little spice to her ordinary life.

After retrieving some personal items from her locker, Sierra exhaled and walked back to her post. It was almost time for the inmates to lock out and she had to be there. Unfortunately, she would have to come face-to-face with Anwar, which she had been trying to avoid since Scooter had been murdered. Now that Anwar had done his dirty deed, maybe he was finished with her and he would leave her alone.

When she arrived in the area, Sierra began the options for some inmates who wanted to come out of the cells. Of course, like clockwork, Anwar walked toward her desk.

"Good mornin', Miss Howell," Anwar greeted her with a self-righteous sneer on his face. "Haven't seen you in a month of Sundays."

"Hello, Jones," Sierra replied without looking up from her book. There was a moment of silence between the two, and, for a minute, Sierra thought that he had gone his way. Instead, when she looked up, Anwar was standing there, watching her.

"May I help you?" she asked.

"You are a gorgeous woman, you know that?" Anwar said. "You look like you have some good pussy, too. I would love to know what it tastes like."

Sierra felt like her blood was boiling. "What? What the fuck do you mean, 'how I taste'? If you don't get away from my desk with that bullshit, I will—" Sierra started to say.

"You will what? You can't do shit! I got you. I told you my bitch got IG on speed dial, and all it takes is for me to give her the green light and your job is a wrap."

Sierra felt her jaw tighten. "Why are you harassin' me, Jones? What did I ever do to you?"

"It's not what you did to me; it's what you did to Rasheed. You shitted on him to be with that other dude. Rasheed told me everything. Y'all broads are so foul and will do anything for a man. Remind me of my fuckin' mother, that sorry bitch!"

Sierra saw that Anwar had serious issues, issues that stemmed from his mother. Anwar reminded her of Lamont with their maternal problems.

"Well, I'm not a foul bitch and I damn sure ain't your mother! You're tryin' to get back at me when I didn't do anything to you. From day one I feel that I have done nothin' but treat you with respect."

"Fuck respect! You're gonna do what I say and give me what I want you to give me! I think you know what's next."

"I ain't givin' you shit! Fuck you, nigga!"

"Yeah, a'ight. Yes, you will, whether you voluntarily give it to me or if it's by force, because if you don't do what I say, your man is a goner and so is your job! I just need to get a taste of what my man, Rasheed, almost lost his mind over."

CO Crawford heard the argument between Sierra and Anwar, and walked on her post. His intimidating presence had inmates walking toward the back of the housing area in a hurry. Anwar stood off to the side and pretended to use the telephone. Sierra couldn't bear to look at Crawford, afraid that a tear may fall.

"Yo, Howell, you all right out here? I heard you arguin' with somebody!" he said, opening and closing his fists.

Sierra shook her head. "I'm good, Crawford. I'm just tellin' these guys what they had to do, that's all."

Crawford caught a glimpse of Anwar, gave him a nasty look, then looked at Sierra. "Well, if you need me, you holler. Don't hesitate. I'll knock a nigga head off for fuckin' with you!" He looked at Anwar again and walked out the door.

When the door closed behind Crawford, Anwar blew a kiss at Sierra and walked off. She shuddered with disgust as her tears blotted the ink on the pages of her logbook.

Chapter 22

Anwar

After harassing Sierra, Anwar walked back to his cell and fell on top of his mattress. He felt as if he was losing his mind and he hadn't even been there that long. Being in that concrete box made him think about what was really wrong with his life, which was everything.

The truth was that Anwar was still angry about his past and he couldn't let go. He was angry at his mother for not protecting him when he was younger, angry at Russell for not giving a hell about him, and angry at his sister for not having to go through the abuse that he did.

He was tired of the inmates in Five North; he was just tired of being an inmate. It had only been the story of his life for so many years. Being a menace to society was ingrained in him.

"Yo, Anwar," a voice at the cell door called out. Anwar turned around to see a young man standing at his cell. "Yo, son, Miss Howell wanted me to tell you that you have a counsel visit."

Anwar frowned. "A counsel visit?"

The young man shrugged. "That's what she said."

Anwar sat up. "Yeah, yeah. Thanks, shorty. I appreciate that."

The inmate walked away and Anwar got himself together. A counsel visit? He wondered what that was about. He didn't have any lawyer; he was doing his time already. What was going on?

Anwar walked toward the desk to retrieve a pass from Sierra. She had a nasty scowl on her face, which only made Anwar laugh. He didn't take her seriously. She practically threw him the pass and he chuckled.

"What's the matter, sweetheart? Why are you so mad at me?" he asked.

Sierra rolled her eyes. "Just go where you was goin' and don't worry about me."

"You didn't snitch me out to anybody, now did you?"

"What are you talkin' about?"

"That's my girl. Hold me down like the good bitch you are." Anwar blew another kiss at Sierra. "Later, baby."

Sierra jumped out of her seat with an attitude to make a tour around the housing area. As Anwar waited for the gate to open, he watched her walk away, mesmerized by her rear end. When the door finally opened, he strolled out of Five North with a smile on his face.

Anwar made his way down the empty corridor toward the intake area for his counsel visit. He walked through the magnetometer posted in the hallway and it beeped. The male CO pulled him to the side and used a handheld Tran frisker to search him. It still beeped.

"What's up, kid?" the officer asked. "What do you have on you that's makin' this thing beep?"

Anwar shrugged. "I ain't got shit on me, homie. I don't know why it's beepin'."

The CO sighed. He didn't feel like writing any reports, and he damn sure didn't feel like whipping an inmate's ass in the corridor. He had a good post and didn't need an asshole like Anwar ruining his day.

The officer held out his hand. "Look, 'homie,' just give it up and I won't report you. I know you wanna go where you gotta go but I wanna have an easy day. Now give it up."

Anwar sucked his teeth and gave the CO a razor that he had tucked in the waistband of his sweatpants. The officer grinned.

"What's wrong with you, man? You're lucky my supervisor wasn't standin' here with me or else this would have been some shit!" he announced. He put the razor in a paper towel and threw it in the garbage.

"Nah, nigga, you woulda been in some shit. Now can I go where I was goin'?"

The officer shooed him away and Anwar proceeded to his visit. Two minutes later, he walked in Intake and gave the COs who were sitting at the desk his pass from Five North.

"Hmm," said a short, pudgy CO with a comb-over. "So you're the notorious Anwar Jones, huh?"

Anwar wasn't going to entertain the officer. He had other things on his mind. He walked toward the back to meet with his "counsel." The officer opened the door. He followed Anwar inside and sat at a desk directly across from the people there to visit the convict. Anwar slowly walked around the brick wall to take a peek. It wasn't a lawyer; it was two men dressed in business suits.

Homicide detectives, he thought. *I can spot them motherfuckers anywhere.*

Anwar's heart skipped a beat when he saw two homicide detectives standing there, waiting for him. They were probably from 114th Precinct, waiting there to question him. One was a tall black man with a muscular physique, and the other detective was a shorter officer with a tough look on his face. He knew what they were there for, but he was ready. When Anwar approached them, they both stood up at the same time.

"Good morning, Mr. Jones," the African American detective said with a smile. The other officer looked serious. "I'm Mark Ashland and this is my partner, Anthony Piamelli. First off, this is not an interrogation. We are merely gathering information from witnesses in reference to the homicide that occurred in the Five North housing area last week. We are going to be interviewing everyone who was there that day. How are you today?"

Anwar looked the men up and down. "I'm good," he replied in a curt tone.

Detective Ashland looked at his partner. "Look, Mr. Jones. You were in Five North the day that Shamel Abrams was murdered, right?"

"Yeah, I was," Anwar reluctantly answered.

"Okay. Did you see anything strange occurring before his murder?"

"No, I didn't."

"Where were you at the time of the murder?"

"In my cell," Anwar lied. He managed to keep a straight face.

"Okay. Um, how would you say you and Mr. Abrams got along with each other?"

"We were cool."

Detective Ashland saw that he wasn't getting anything out of Anwar, so he nudged his partner.

"Hey, there, um, Jones. Listen, somebody in that housing area says that, um, they saw you coming out of Abrams's cell before he was found dead. Is this true?" asked Detective Piamelli.

Anwar frowned. "I thought y'all motherfuckers said this wasn't no interrogation. Why are you askin' me about somebody comin' out of Abrams's cell? I don't know what happened to that dude and that's that!"

Piamelli and Ashland looked at each other. They were veteran detectives and they knew guilty like the back of their hands. But they didn't have any hardcore evidence, so they would have to do more investigating before they could make their arrest.

The detectives stood up, and so did Anwar. "Well, we'll be seein' you around, Mr. Jones. Thanks for nothing."

"Yeah. Whatever." The men walked out the door and the counsel visit officer escorted Anwar to the door. Anwar walked out of Intake with his pass in his hand to head back to Five North.

When Anwar arrived at the door of Five North, Sierra was still sitting at the desk. He totally ignored her and walked toward the back of the housing area. Aggravated with the visit from the detectives, he was looking for someone to take his frustration out on.

"Might as well make the bitch work for her money," Anwar said to himself, referring to Sierra. One inmate everyone called Chopper made the mistake of looking at Anwar, and that was all he needed.

"What the fuck are you lookin' at?" Anwar asked. Chopper looked around at everyone else to see if Anwar was really talking to him.

"I'm lookin' at you, motherfucker! And what?" Chopper replied.

Anwar walked over to Chopper and punched him in the face. Suddenly, it was chaos in Five North. At least three inmate fights broke out at the same time, and Sierra was at her wits end. Anwar continuously beat Chopper in the face with his fists. Chopper tried to fight back, but he was no competition for Anwar's skills. The other fights were continuing, and soon there was bloodshed on the chairs and tables.

Crawford exited the control room and summoned Sierra to leave the post. She pressed the personal body alarm that she had attached to her belt. In minutes, two waves of responding officers came into Five North to break up the fights. Correction officers had to fight their way through the melee, with one or two actually getting hurt while trying to restrain the inmates. Anwar managed to bust Chopper's lip and come out of the brawl unscathed. He was immediately removed from the area with flexible cuffs secured tightly around his wrists.

When Anwar arrived in Intake, the officers threw him headfirst into the "Why Me?" pen. They locked the gate, leaving the tight plastic cuffs on his wrists. He managed to put his back against the wall and scoot upward so that he could stand upright. Anwar began yelling out of the cell, but quieted down once he saw that no one was paying him any attention. A few moments after he calmed down, an officer came to the pen with some wire cutters and cut the plastic flex cuffs off. Anwar rubbed his raw wrists and gave the man the evil eye. He lay on the hard bench in the pen and fell asleep.

It was 12:30 in the morning and Anwar was still in the "Why Me?" pen in Intake. The midnight officers were on duty and he cussed them all out so bad that they had to call their area supervisor. When the intake captain came to talk to him, Anwar tried to spit on him, and that was the end of that conversation. The assistant deputy warden was notified to come and talk to him.

"So if it isn't Mr. Jones again," said Lamont, walking toward the pen with a nasty look on his face. "What is your problem, bruh?"

Anwar looked at Lamont with a smirk on his face. "First of all, homeboy, I ain't your 'bruh,' and, yeah, it's me again. So what?"

Lamont sighed. "Look, you can't come up in here startin' a whole bunch of ruckus and you only got fuckin' ninety days to do. What is your function?"

"Fuck you mean, 'what is my function'? I don't wanna be here!" Anwar yelled.

Lamont looked around. "Yo, my man, I'm talkin' to you like an adult! Why are you makin' a spectacle of yourself?"

"Nah, you must mean why am I makin' a spectacle of you? I don't give a fuck about embarrassin' myself. I don't have nothin' to prove to any of these motherfuckers in here!"

Lamont ran his hands through his hair. "Do you still mess with Deja? Because you're actin' like a fool, and if she's your woman, you need to be low-key, don't you think?"

Anwar laughed. "Wow! Is this what this is about? Deja? Why do you wanna know if she's my woman? Ain't Miss Howell, Rasheed Gordon's baby's mother, your bitch?"

Anwar could see that Lamont's whole body stiffened at the mention of Sierra and Rasheed.

"Yeah, mm-hmm! You know that I know how it went down. Rasheed is my man from young and he told me everything. He told me about how you stole his woman, how much of a dick you really are. Did your woman tell you that she knew that I was goin' to kill Scooter? She didn't even tell you about it, now did she? But, yeah, I did it. He shot my man. He shot your lady's baby daddy. She was a little upset about that because she really does love Rasheed, and she wanted to make her point by gettin' that nigga, Scooter, outta Five North in a body bag."

"What are you talkin' about, Jones? I don't believe you."

"Okay, so when it happened, why do you think that she left the post? Of course, she didn't want to be held responsible for something that she helped plan, so she broke out and went to the clinic. Was she in Five North when all that shit happened that day?"

Lamont was silent. He stood there and watched Anwar for a moment without blinking. Anwar saw that he was starting to get to the man, and that was exactly what he wanted to do.

"Yeah, see? I know you remember her being off post and in the clinic." Anwar grinned. "Yo, I gave you a confession just now. I ain't tryin' to hear no more of this shit, 'cause if I do, I'm gonna make sure some heads roll. Your precious little Sierra? She will be gone, even if I have to make the fuckin' phone call myself. Your reputation, your position will be no more. Your baby mother, Deja? Well, I'll just kill that bitch off— she ain't no good anyway. You make the call, Deputy Simmons."

It looked as if Lamont's vein was about to pop out of his neck. "Nigga, I will kill you if you fuck with my family, Deja included! Who do you think you are?"

"I'm motherfuckin' Anwar Jones, Esquire, nigga! I don't give a fuck about you, your fam—shit, I don't give a fuck about myself! So if you want it to be on, try me! Now go scream on your bitch, or should I say, my accomplice?"

Anwar turned his back on Lamont and sat in the corner of the cell. He watched as Lamont practically ran out of Intake. Anwar lay back on the hard bench and looked up at the ceiling. An evil smile came across his face as he drifted into a deep slumber.

Chapter 23

India

Later that morning, India went to visit Sierra in Five North.

"Your homegirl is not feelin' me," India said to Sierra while standing on her post. She wanted to win Sierra's confidence so that she could really do some emotional damage.

Sierra looked up from writing an incident report about the fights that had occurred in Five North the day before. "Oh, you can't pay Captain Phillips any attention. She doesn't really deal with new officers. She has her reservations about them. She's been here for a while, and you know how some senior officers are with the new jacks."

India sucked her teeth. "Please! People take this damn job too serious. It shouldn't matter if you're a new jack or an old timer when it comes to these inmates. Shoot, I just may be the one to save her ass."

"You're right," Sierra agreed. "But don't worry about that, girl. She will be all right. I told her that you were cool with me so she's not gonna mess with you."

India sighed. "Thanks, Howell. Good lookin' out. All I wanna do is pass my probation and move on, you know?"

"Yeah, I know, but what's up with you and your ADW? The one with the girlfriend who's still messin' with her baby's father?"

India giggled. "Yeah, that's him."

"Really? Did y'all get a chance to hang out with each other yet?"

"Did we? We hung out in more ways than one."

Sierra laughed. "Woo wee! Sounds like some hot and heavy stuff went on! I am not mad at you. Does he work in this jail?"

India wasn't ready to reveal that much just yet. "Um, no, girl. He works in Brooklyn House," she said, referring to the Brooklyn House of Detention facility.

"Well, that's a good thing. It's less bullshit like that. Shoot, I'm surprised that I even talk to half of the people who work here. I am a perfect example of a person who comes to work and goes home. I've had enough chaos in here and in my personal life."

"Like what?"

Sierra looked at India. "I can't get into it. Let's just say that my choice of men had me fucked up in the game for a minute, but I'm okay now. I have a good person in my life and he treats me well."

"I know, I know. Deputy Simmons, right?"

Sierra blushed. "Yes, girl! That is my baby! I love him so much. He takes really good care of me, too."

India felt a twinge of jealousy run through her veins. "Oh, okay, I need to get me a guy like that. Shoot, I wanna be taken care of."

Sierra smiled. "Don't worry, Charles. As cool as you are, you are guaranteed to get a man like mine."

"Hmph. I know I will," India replied. Sierra had no clue that India meant every word she said.

Suddenly, the gates to Five North opened and Lamont walked in. He stopped in his tracks when he saw India talking to Sierra.

India saluted Lamont. "Wow, good mornin', sir. I was just talkin' to Howell for a minute."

Lamont smiled. India could tell that he was tense and didn't know what to expect.

"Um, Officer Charles, could you, um, excuse me and Howell for a moment?" he requested.

India folded her arms, secretly sending Lamont the message that she didn't like that one bit.

"Yeah, a'ight." India rolled her eyes at Lamont while Sierra focused on her paperwork. "I'll see you later, Howell. As a matter of fact, call me later, girl," India chirped. "I gotta tell you about that guy I'm seein', you know, the one with the girlfriend?"

Sierra smiled, clueless of what was going on. "No problem, sweetie. Talk to you later."

India walked out, purposely brushing against the worried Lamont. While standing at the end of the hallway, waiting for the gate to open, she saw Lamont forcefully grab Sierra out of her seat. India walked through the gate with a huge smile on her face.

Twenty minutes later, India was surprised to run into Lamont on her way back to her post. They bumped into each other in the stairwell.

"What's up with you, India? Why do you keep fuckin' with me?" he asked.

"I'm not playin' with you, Lamont. You fuck me, then when you get in front of your bitch, you wanna act as if you don't know me! I'm not havin' that!"

Lamont rubbed his head. "Well, I'm confused. If you couldn't handle my situation, why did you even pursue this?"

India laughed. "I pursued this? Now you gonna blame me for pursuin' you? Last time I checked you pushed up on me in that pool hall. Don't you remember?"

Lamont eyes darted all over the cement walls of the staircase. He grabbed India's face and they shared an intense kiss. Lamont gave India a final peck on her lips.

"Now, I'm gonna need you to be a good girl for

daddy. You wanna keep gettin' that good stuff I give
you, don't you?" he asked.

"Yes, I do," India replied. "But—" she started to say.

Lamont held up his hand and silenced her. "How my
relationship with Sierra is goin' should be none of your
concern. Just worry about me and you. Nobody else."

She rolled her eyes and hugged Lamont.

Later on the day, India's cell phone rang. She didn't
recognize the number. "Hello?" India said.

"Hey, Charles, it's me, Howell. I need a big favor
from you."

India frowned. "What's the matter?"

Sierra began to cry. "Could you please come and get
me? I'm at a pay phone on Nostrand and Lexington!
Me and Lamont had a fight and I took a cab over here
to Brooklyn!"

"Wow, okay, I'll be there."

India reluctantly got dressed and Asia emerged from
her bedroom. "Where are you goin'?"

"I'm goin' to get this chick from Nostrand Avenue."

"What chick?" Asia asked, a look of confusion coming
over her face.

"Sierra!" India replied.

"Sierra? You're gonna bring her here? Now?"

"Yes, I am! Asia, this is goin' even better than what I
thought. She said Lamont whooped her ass."

Asia began laughing. "For what?"

"Who knows? Who cares? I just wish that he would
dump the bitch for good and recognize that he got him
a good chick named India on his team. Fuck Sierra."

"So if that's how you feel, why in the hell are you
bringin' her here?"

India stopped in her tracks. "What are you waitin'
for? Are you goin' to call your man, Rasheed, over or
what?"

Asia smiled. "Sis, you are too much! I love it, I love it!" She ran into the room to grab her cell phone. "Hello? Rah? What are you doin'? Why don't you stop by for a minute? I really wanna see you."

Chapter 24

Sierra

In the meantime, Sierra stood on the corner next to the pay phone, waiting for India. She didn't want to call Monique, and she sure as hell didn't want to hear what her mother would have to say. Marjorie Howell thought that her future son-in-law could do no wrong, and Sierra wanted to keep her thinking that way. Meanwhile, her body was sore and her face felt as if it was about to crack.

Lamont was on a rampage when he came home from work. Earlier that day when he came to her post, he was full of accusations. He had grabbed her out of her seat and pulled her into the dayroom of Five North.

"What the fuck is this I hear that you helped Anwar with that murder?" Lamont whispered.

Sierra's heart began to beat a mile a minute. She felt as if she wanted to faint. "Lamont, what . . . I don't know what you're talkin' about."

He grabbed her face and pushed her head into the hard brick wall. Sierra's head began pounding.

"Don't lie to me, Sierra! Did you know about Anwar's plans to kill Abrams?"

Sierra began to choke up. The cat was out of the bag. "Yes, I did."

Lamont leaned his 200 pounds into her small frame. He was so heavy that it felt as if her chest was going to cave in.

"What the hell is wrong with you, woman? Do you know that this motherfucker means business? He's threatenin' your job and talkin' about if you tell anybody about what he did, he's goin' to kill you, me, Deja, and God knows who else! Why didn't you tell me about this?"

"I tried, I tried!" Sierra cried out. Lamont's strong hands had a hold of her face as she attempted to talk. She was beginning to taste blood on the insides of her cheeks. Lamont finally let her go. He paced around the dayroom with a sour look on his face. Sierra cowered in the corner, attempting to get herself together.

"I cannot believe this shit! What is wrong with you, Sierra? Why do you insist on cavortin' with these crooks? What is it, I'm not good enough for you? Or am I too good for you?"

Sierra shrugged. "Lamont, I didn't do anything wrong! I promise you that! Jones is lyin'!"

Lamont looked at Sierra with his arms folded. "How is he lyin' when everything that he told me is what happened that day? He told me that you left the post to go to the clinic, that you weren't present durin' the murder on purpose. Then he mentioned Rasheed. This Rasheed thing is really startin' to fuck with me! Every time I turn around, I'm hearin' this dude's name. Why?"

Sierra was speechless. There wasn't anything that she could say in her defense, because she had been set up and badly. Her thoughts at that moment were that Anwar should have been zipped up in a body bag alongside Scooter.

A radio transmission came through the radio on Lamont's hip. "I gotta go. I will see your ass at home." Lamont walked out of the dayroom, leaving Sierra standing alone in the dark.

***

When Lamont arrived home, Sierra tried to make herself scarce. He began packing a bag for Trey and Messiah.

"Where are they goin'?" she asked.

"To Pop's house for the night. He wanted to see his grandsons," Lamont said. "I'll be back in half an hour. If you so much leave this house, I'm gonna break your fuckin' neck, do you hear me?"

Tears ran down Sierra's face. "Yes," she replied.

Lamont stuffed Sierra's car keys into his pocket and shuffled the boys out of the house into his truck. Sierra sat on the sofa in the living room, rocking back and forth. Anwar had screwed her big time. There was no way to prove that she had nothing to do with Scooter's murder. It was Anwar's word against hers, and he had managed to get in Lamont's ear before she could.

An hour later, Lamont walked through the door. Sierra had fallen asleep on the couch, and it was a shock to feel her body being dragged off the sofa with her head hitting the hardwood floor. He pulled her up by her shirt, bringing her face close to his. Sierra smelled the Hennessy on his breath.

"You really think I'm some fool, huh?" Lamont said, grabbing her by the neck and shaking her violently. "This is my career, your career, our life! And you're about to let all of this go down the drain! You bitch!"

Lamont slapped Sierra so hard that she fell backward onto the coffee table. She didn't have the energy to fight back, so she just lay there and moaned.

Lamont pulled her up by her hair and shook her violently. "I'm sick of this shit!" He slapped her again so hard that she almost flipped over the back of the couch. She cried out for him to stop, but he was coming for her again. Sierra knew that she had to do something to defend herself before Lamont killed her in that house.

Even though her broken spirit was making her physically weak, Sierra managed to grab the metal poker from the fireplace and swing it at Lamont. Of course, it missed him and he took it from Sierra, almost breaking her arm in the process. She fell to the floor again.

"You put me through all this trouble to still deal with these fuckin' ingrates!" Lamont hissed. "These niggas are the scum of the earth but yet and still you're gonna let them come between us and what we worked so hard to build!"

Sierra scooted backward and tried to stand up. She wobbled until she finally gained the strength to hold on to the back of the couch.

"I am not lyin' to you!" Sierra screamed through her salty tears. "Ever since Rasheed's been back in town, you have been givin' me straight hell! If you want me to leave, say it, and I will leave you the fuck alone! I'm not gonna take this abuse from you anymore. I'm gettin' out of here tonight!"

Lamont looked as if it were the end of the world. Sierra moved past him and he tried to grab her, only this time he went to hug her.

"Don't touch me!" Sierra screamed. She pointed her finger at him. "You're a sick, demented son of a bitch! Don't think that it's okay to put your fuckin' hands on me and get away with it, Lamont! The only thing that is savin' your black ass from bein' arrested is Trey. Keep your job and your . . . your . . . fuckin' position! Me and my son are outta here!"

Sierra paced back and forth on Nostrand Avenue, not even remembering how she got there. Lamont had taken her car keys and hid them, so she took a cab. Her first intention was to go to Rasheed's house, which was how she ended up in Bed-Stuy in the first place. Then, at the last minute, she decided against it. Making that mistake would only bring more turmoil into her life.

Sierra caught a glance of the black, late-model Acura pulling up to the corner. She smiled when she saw India sitting in the driver's seat.

"Oh, my goodness!" Sierra announced. "Thank you so much, Charles! I didn't have anyone else to call, so I hope you don't mind just lettin' me chill for an hour or two. I just can't call any of my other friends right now. I'm not in the mood to hear all of their feedback."

India helped Sierra get into the truck after she packed her two overnight bags into the backseat. Sierra immediately looked at her face in the visor mirror. She had two black-and-blue marks on her cheeks, and her mouth looked swollen, but she was more messed up emotionally than she was physically.

"Look, Howell, you're gonna be okay. I'm real sorry that that happened to you. It happens to the best of us. Trust me, I know," India said.

Sierra looked at her. "So this happened to you before, huh?"

"Hell, yeah!" India replied while turning the corner. "I got my ass straight whooped a few times by different men. Girl, I was a mess back in the days! Always poppin' shit to a nigga like I could beat their ass, and you see how small I am, right?" Sierra nodded. "I was even smaller back then. Hmph, them brothers still did me a favor because they could have done some real serious damage to this pretty-ass face of mine! Thank God, I finally got myself together and left them types alone."

Sierra tried to smile, but her mouth was still too sore. Lamont had done a number on her.

They arrived in front of India's apartment building. India helped Sierra with her bags into the elevator.

"So," Sierra began. "Have you and your sister always lived together?"

India sighed. "Yeah, we have. We moved straight out of our mother's house and into our own. It's been goin' good so far because, for the most part, we're very close, like most twins are."

Sierra nodded. "That's cool. I wish that I had a sister to live with. That only child shit is for the birds."

"You have one son, right?" India asked, even though she already knew most of Sierra's background.

"Yeah, I do. I would like to have another baby, but after all of this bullshit that I'm goin' through with Lamont, I doubt if that's happenin' anytime soon."

They got off the elevator on the fourth floor and walked down the corridor to India's apartment. She pushed the door opened and Sierra walked straight into the living room. She took a quick glance of the apartment and immediately felt comfortable. It was very cozy.

"Nice place, Charles," Sierra complimented her.

"Girl, call me India, for Christ's sake," India suggested with a chuckle. "We're not at work!"

Sierra laughed too. "Yeah, you're right, India."

India went into the kitchen while Sierra plopped down on the cranberry red sofa. She was physically exhausted from tussling with Lamont, and her mind was all over the place. India came out of the kitchen with two champagne flutes and a bottle of Moscato.

"I just thought that maybe you could use a drink," India said. "Considerin' all the shit you've been through in the last few hours."

Sierra began to cry as India filled the flute in her hand up to the rim. "I'm sorry, India, I'm just goin' through so much right now! I can't believe this shit!"

India sat on the love seat across from Sierra and shook her head. After a few minutes, she got up from the love seat and sat beside her.

"You have to leave Lamont. He put his hands on you and that is unacceptable. You're a very beautiful person, inside and out. Shit, you can meet another man!"

Sierra looked up, like she was about to pray, then looked at India. "You don't understand, India. Lamont and I built this life together. We've been through so much in these past years and . . . Let's just put it like this: the man held me down like a real man is supposed to. He treats my son like his own. He is raisin' his own son. Why would I want to give that up? I'm just tryin' to understand what is happenin' to us."

India shrugged, and patted Sierra on her knee. "I dunno," India replied. She sighed. "I think that you should move on. If a man hits you, it's only gonna get worse."

Sierra sat back on the couch and sipped her Moscato. India was right. She had some serious decisions to make.

Chapter 25

India

Secretly, India was happy that Lamont and Sierra were having problems. She had convinced herself that Lamont was so into her that he despised Sierra for forcing him to be with her and the kids. This made it easier for her to persuade Sierra that Lamont was so wrong for her. What had started out as a plot to avenge Tamir's death had turned into India wanting the man for herself.

It wasn't enough that India was infatuated with Lamont. Being a glutton was the way that she and her twin lived most of their lives. They didn't want just a piece of something. They wanted it all, which was the main reason India and Asia began committing credit card fraud in the first place. They had to have what they thought everyone else would want. Right now, India knew that Sierra still loved Lamont. This made India want him like a child wanted a little doggie in the window of a pet store.

Now all India needed to know was if Sierra and Rasheed were still involved with each other. Not only would that information be beneficial to her, but it was going to benefit Asia as well. Lamont was vulnerable, now that he and Sierra were on the outs. This would be the best time, if any, for her to spring into action.

The downstairs intercom rang and India smiled. At this point, Asia came out of her bedroom, smelling good and looking like a million bucks.

"Oh, hello," Asia said, waving at Sierra. She pressed the door button on the intercom and smiled at Sierra. "Hello, I'm Asia, India's sister. And you are?"

Sierra held out her hand for Asia to shake it. "Oh, I'm Sierra Howell. I work with your sister."

Asia opened the apartment door and hugged someone. From where Sierra was sitting she wouldn't be able to see who it was until he appeared smack dab in the living room. As Sierra sipped from her flute, oblivious to what was about to happen, India stood up when Asia and Rasheed appeared in the doorway of their living room.

"What's up, Rasheed?" India said with a big smile on her face.

Sierra slowly turned around and looked as if she had seen a ghost. Rasheed frowned, surprised to see Sierra sitting in the living room of the Charles twins. She obviously didn't know who they really were.

Rasheed looked at the twins, who had blank expressions on their faces. "Yo," Rasheed said. "What the fuck is goin' on here?" he asked them.

Asia looked as if she had a halo around her head. "What are you talkin' about, Rah?"

Sierra was speechless. India chimed in. "Yeah, Rah, what's your problem?"

It appeared that Rasheed was growing angrier and angrier by the minute. For a moment, India was kind of nervous.

"Do y'all know who this is? I think y'all know who this is!" he yelled, pointing at Sierra.

India played it off. "She's my coworker!"

"Don't fuckin' play with me, India! Y'all motherfuckers know that Sierra is my son's mother!"

"We didn't know that!" Asia began to lie.

Rasheed pointed at her. "Shut the fuck up. Real talk, just shut the fuck up, Asia! I'm not with no bitches tryin' to play me for some fool, and I damn sure ain't gonna let y'all play her neither!"

Sierra finally found her voice. "Play me like what? How?" she asked, still surprised to see Rasheed standing in Asia's living room.

"Yo, Si, check this out, these bitches are Tamir's best friends. They knew who you were from the beginnin', I'm sure of that!"

"No, the fuck we did not!" screamed India. "I didn't know that she was your baby mother, I swear I didn't!"

Rasheed smirked. "Yeah? So why the hell am I here, then?"

"To see me, Rasheed," answered Asia.

Rasheed looked at Sierra. She looked like she had been beat down. Her hair was unkempt and her face looked swollen. India caught Rasheed giving Sierra a concerned look, and signaled her sister.

"Oh, hell no!" Asia yelled at Rasheed. "What the hell are you lookin' at her like that for? Are you tryin' to feel sorry for this chick now?"

Sierra straightened up. "What do you mean feel sorry for me?"

Asia looked at Sierra and pointed her finger in her face. "You heard what the fuck I said." She glared at Rasheed. "I said are you tryin' to feel sorry for this sorry-ass bitch?"

Sierra tried to reach over the couch and grab Asia by her throat. India stepped in and pulled Sierra back.

"Look, look," shouted India. "Y'all don't need to be fightin'!"

India was surprised at Rasheed's reaction to Sierra being there, which made her wonder if the two were still intimate with each other.

"You know what? Yo, Sierra, come on, man, I'm gettin' you outta here! I have a feelin' that these grimy bitches are tryin' to do you dirty!"

Sierra didn't seem like she knew what to do. "Why can't you just leave her alone, Rah?" yelled Asia. "Why the fuck do you have to take this bitch with you?"

"Because she's my child's mother, that's why!"

Asia shook her head. She was livid. She couldn't even bring herself to speak to anyone. She watched as Rasheed helped Sierra gather her bags.

"Damn, India. I thought you were a cool chick. You really had me fooled," Sierra said, shaking her head.

India rolled her eyes. "Whatever, Sierra. I don't owe you shit."

Sierra chuckled. She stopped in her tracks before walking out the door. "Now that I know who you stupid little bitches really are, Tyke is the one who committed that murder, not me. I would have never done anything to intentionally hurt Tamir or anyone else over anything, especially a fuckin' man," she said sarcastically as she walked out the door. Rasheed picked up Sierra's bags and walked out the door behind her.

The door slammed and Asia began screaming at India. "This is your fuckin' fault, India! Rasheed was not supposed to leave with that bitch! He was supposed to be with me!" she yelled.

India plopped down on the couch and shook her head. "Okay, he left with her! What do you want me to do, Asia?"

"I want you to fuckin' fix this shit! I want Rasheed back," Asia said, tears forming in her eyes. "You have Lamont and I have nobody. Rasheed and Sierra may even get back together now."

India attempted to calm her down. "Okay, okay, let me think of somethin'," she replied.

Asia's bottom lip began quivering and tears fell from her eyes. "After today, I'm done with all the grimy shit. I'm done with the connivin', underhanded games that you always have me caught up with, and I'm done with you, too."

Before India could say anything else to her, Asia had already slammed the door to her bedroom.

India felt bad for her sister, but as long as she and Lamont were still dealing with each other, she couldn't care less about Asia and Rasheed or even Sierra. And now that Sierra had left with Rasheed, she knew that Lamont was hers for the taking.

Chapter 26

Rasheed

Downstairs in front of the twins' building, Rasheed put Sierra's overnight bags in the backseat of his truck as she sat in the passenger seat and cried. When Rasheed slid into the driver's side, he immediately comforted Sierra by taking her into his arms.

"Stop cryin', baby," Rasheed said. He pulled out some tissues from the glove compartment and wiped the tears from her face. He waited until Sierra regained her composure to ask her questions. "Now, tell me what happened with you. How did you end up over here with the twins?"

Sierra blew her nose. "Well, Lamont sort of roughed me up," she explained.

Rasheed's jaw tightened. "What do you mean, 'he sort of roughed you up'? Why would he do that, and where was Messiah at the time?"

"He took the boys by his father's house. He came back home an hour later, drunk as hell, and put his hands on me."

Rasheed sighed. He didn't want to get involved in Sierra's domestic dispute, because, in his mind, she had dissed him to be with Lamont. But since he was trying to change his attitude, he figured that the least he could do was let her vent about the situation.

"What was his sorry-ass excuse for puttin' his hands on you?" Rasheed asked.

Sierra hesitated. "He thought that I was involved in somethin' at work."

"What, an affair with another nigga or somethin'? I don't get it. What do you mean he thought that you were involved with somethin' at work?" Rasheed asked as they pulled off.

"You know your boy is locked up in Five North, right?" she said, referring to Anwar.

"What does Anwar bein' locked up in Five North have to do with anything?" Rasheed asked, playing it off. He knew exactly what Sierra was talking about. He was just waiting to hear her side of the story.

"I'm gonna be real," Sierra began with a sigh. "When Anwar first came to Five North, I started this whole dialogue with him because I knew that he was your people. No sooner than I started the conversation did Anwar come back to me and tell me that he was goin' to kill Scooter."

Rasheed was silent for a moment. "So did he kill Scooter?"

"Yes, he did."

"Damn," he said. Sierra had no idea that he already knew about Scooter's death. "I don't see what you would have to do with him killin' Scooter. If he was goin' to do that, he could have just done it without involvin' you."

Sierra looked out the passenger window. "That's what I said. I didn't want to know anything about it, but he threatened my job with everything that he already knows about me, including the fact that I have a child with you."

"Were you on post when he killed Scooter? Did you see him do it?" Rasheed asked.

"No, I didn't see him do it. He waited until I was relieved for meal. After my forty-minute meal period was up, I couldn't bring myself to go back to Five

North. I was sick to my stomach. So I contacted my area supervisor and was given permission to go to the clinic. I just stayed there for the rest of my shift."

Rasheed was visibly upset. "So why didn't you tell me about this sooner, Sierra?"

"I didn't know how to tell you or Lamont about Anwar. I was scared shitless! Now, after the murder, Anwar makes it almost unbearable for me to come to that post. He says some disrespectful shit and makes lewd comments to me. He even threatened to kill me and Lamont, too, if I said anything to anybody about what he did."

Rasheed pulled over to collect his thoughts. He wasn't going to tell Sierra that he had come to visit Anwar and that he knew about the murder. He wanted to take care of Anwar himself.

"Yep, he's puttin' me through it and I don't know this dude from a hole in the wall. What is his problem?" she asked.

"Anwar had a real fucked-up childhood, even though that's no excuse for this kind of behavior," Rasheed replied. "When we were younger, I did something for him. Accordin' to him, I saved his life. Ever since then, this dude had this obsession with repayin' me. I never once made him feel like he had to do that. He's my friend, man, and that's what I do for my friends." Rasheed sighed. "I'm sorry that you even gotta go through this shit with him. I'm gonna take care of this. I promise you." Rasheed paused. "I know you regret the day you laid eyes on me, don't you?"

Sierra looked away. Rasheed needed to see her eyes, so he turned her face to his. He kissed her nose, her forehead, even her eyelids. Suddenly, they embraced each other passionately and exchanged an intense kiss. Rasheed felt himself getting excited, but it was more than just sexual.

After a few minutes of the display of affection, Sierra pulled away. She looked down and then looked at Rasheed.

"Do you think that we should really do this?" she asked.

Rasheed grabbed onto the steering wheel. "Honestly?" he said.

"Yeah, honestly."

"Yes, I do. Fuck that. I don't give a fuck about Lamont and I don't give a fuck about that dude, Anwar. This is gonna be about me and you and the love that we have for each other, and all the shit we've been through these past couple of years. I ain't here to shit on you, I'm not here to make you feel less than a woman for fuckin' with me, and that's real talk. I love you, baby, and even if I have to let you go back to that clown-ass dude, Lamont, know that I'm not goin' anywhere— ever."

When they arrived on his block, Rasheed got out of the truck with Sierra's bags in his hand. She followed him inside the house and upstairs to his bedroom. Once the door was closed, Sierra began slowly undressing and stood in the middle of the bedroom, naked as the day she was born. Rasheed removed his clothing to reveal a perfect frame that would put most men to shame.

As Sierra stood there, her body began to tremble. Rasheed kissed her tenderly and kneeled down until he was staring at Sierra's hairless crotch. He gingerly opened her legs and began tasting her juices that had been marinating ever since they had left the twins' apartment.

He slid his tongue in and out her box, sucked on her clit, and tickled her insides. Sierra held on to Rasheed's head to keep from collapsing on the floor, and his strong grip on her mocha-colored thighs held her in place. As her pussy juices dripped from his nose, Rasheed lifted Sierra in the air, putting her legs over both of his broad shoulders.

With his hands on her ass to keep her from falling back, he pulled her body into his face and continued to dine on her goodness. Still holding her in the air, Rasheed walked to his bed and gingerly laid her on his 450-thread-count sheets. He put on a condom and entered Sierra very slowly, making her moan with pleasure.

They created a sexual rhythm as their bodies united with each other. Sierra tightened her walls around Rasheed's rod, and it was his turn to call out her name. He had almost forgotten how good Sierra's pussy was and how he was so happy the first time they made love. He closed his eyes and reminisced, thinking about how excited he was that night.

Sierra was throwing it back and Rasheed was doing his best to hold on. He wanted the interlude to last as long as it could. But the excitement of illicit desire left them no choice. Rasheed slowly pushed his middle finger inside Sierra's back door and she began moaning even louder. She grabbed his muscled ass and wrapped her legs around his thirty-six-inch waist. Sierra shoved her tongue down his throat as she thrust herself onto his nine inches.

"Rah, I miss you so much," she whispered. "I know I'm not supposed to be . . ." She drifted off.

"What?" he whispered back while looking Sierra in the eye. "You're not supposed to be makin' love to me?" Rasheed stated as he sexed Sierra into ecstasy.

Suddenly, Sierra began flailing wildly and Rasheed could no longer take it. She came first, with her body going limp for a brief second. After a few seconds, Sierra found her momentum and turned Rasheed over. She straddled him and rode him like a mechanical horse.

"I love you, Sierra! I love you," cried Rasheed, as he shot a load of semen into the condom. Immediately after, a tear rolled down the side of Rasheed's face. Sierra kissed it away, and they instantly fell asleep in each other's arms.

Chapter 27

Lamont

Later that night, Lamont drove around Queens with nowhere to go. He was not in the mood to go to his house. Being home alone was not an option at that moment.

Earlier that evening, after dropping the boys off at Pops's house, Lamont went to have a few drinks to try to clear his head. He had so many things that contributed to his rage, he felt like a ticking time bomb. With the alcohol fueling his anger, he had gone back to the house and gotten into a physical altercation with Sierra. Immediately after the fight, Lamont needed someone to talk to, so he decided to go back to his father's house for some much-needed advice.

Lamont shook his head as he thought about the conversation that they had before he left Charles "Pops" Simmons's residence for the second time.

"I love my grandboys, but goddamn, Monty," Pops said to Lamont. "Where the hell are you goin' tonight? I see you done had you some drinks, but, shit, you and the boys may have to go home! Me and Ann got a date tonight."

Lamont watched as the boys pulled out some of their toys that Pops had in various places throughout his home.

"So you're goin' out with Miss Ann, you old fart?" Lamont joked.

Pops pointed to the ceiling with a sneaky smirk on his face. "Yup! I'm goin' right up there to that there bedroom! Got me a refill prescription of Viagra, and I was just about to pop me a pill and call her up until your bighead ass called me to watch my grandboys!"

Lamont laughed. "Aw, man! You didn't even call her yet. And I don't know why you actin' like you all hard up for some sex, Pops! You got women on speed dial!"

"Nah, Monty, you don't understand. I don't want them women. I love my Ann. I've always wanted to get back in that ass since 1970 something or another, a little after Monique was born, but she wouldn't let me. Before I leave this earth, I'm gonna get me some of that again." Pops glanced at the boys and smiled. "Those some handsome little devils, I swear. I love them, too. They keep me young."

"Yeah," Lamont agreed. Suddenly, he began to get choked up, and Pops took his attention off the children to tend to his son. Pops sat next to Lamont and began comforting him.

"What's the matter, Monty? Is somethin' goin' on or is it the liquor?"

Lamont wiped his face. "Everything is goin' on, Pops." Lamont paused. "Pops, I put my hands on Sierra today."

Pops paused. "You did what to who?" he asked, cupping his left ear as if he hadn't hear what Lamont said.

"I put my hands on Sierra today."

Pops stood up. He put the children in a spare bedroom so that he and Lamont could have a man-to-man talk. When Pops came back, he tapped Lamont on the shoulder. When Lamont looked up, Pops slapped him so hard; Lamont almost fell off the sofa.

"What the fuck is wrong with you, boy?" Pops said through clenched teeth. "I ain't never, ever hit your momma or any other woman, and you done went and put your mitts on Sierra? Are you out of your rabbit-ass mind?"

Lamont rubbed his face and looked at his upset father. "I don't know why I did it, Pops!"

"That's no excuse, Monty! I didn't raise you like that!" Pops put his hands on his hips and paced back and forth. "Let me ask you somethin' else: Are you fuckin' another woman?"

"Pops, I—" Lamont started to explain.

Pops held up his hand. "Yes or no, son, and don't lie to me!" Pops said.

Lamont held his head down. "Yeah, I am," Lamont replied shamefully.

"Why in the hell you can't just screw the broad, have a little fun, and go home to your family?"

Lamont began to get angry. "I don't believe that you sittin' up here, actin' all self-righteous when you cheated on my mother! You laid up with Miss Ann, who just happened to be a friend of Mommy's, and had a damn baby with her. The same baby who was the main cause of Mommy leavin' me here with you! Then, years later, I ended up screwin' this . . . this woman, who is really my sister and your daughter!" he said, referring to Monique.

Pops's jaw tightened. "Look, Monty, it ain't about what I did back in them days. Yes, I was young, dumb, and full of cum, but I never, ever put my hands on no woman. Regardless of whatever kinda of skirt chasin' I was doin' in the streets, I made sure that you and your mother had a decent place to live, I paid these bills, I was the *man* of my household. I slipped up, I admit that, but damn, you woulda thought your dumb ass would have learned from my mistakes and tried to do better than what the hell I did back in them days. The sad part is that I had youth on my side. What the hell is your excuse? You are a forty-something-year-old man and you're actin' like a fuckin' twenty-year-old right now!"

"For your information, I think that Sierra is screwin' Messiah's father," Lamont added.

Pops shook his head. "Monty, how stupid are you? If she wasn't fuckin' him before, shit, she damn sure fuckin' him now! I'm willin' to bet my whole retirement pension money for the month that she is fuckin' that man right now, thanks to your hand problem!"

Pops picked up the remote and turned on the television. He plopped down in his La-Z-Boy chair. "Monty, it sounds like you need to go get your household in order. You better man up, boy, 'cause Sierra got a baby by that gangster, and it won't be nothin' for her to pick up and leave you for him. You need to go make you a nice cup of coffee and get sober so that you can go find that girl. You better make it right, because you are about to lose your woman. Yep, you're about to lose your woman, because you have a hand problem and a fetish for floozies."

After that conversation with Pops, Lamont rode around Queens not knowing the first place to find Sierra. The alcohol had worn off and his insecurities were getting the best of him. Suddenly, the vibration of his phone startled him.

"Hello?" Lamont answered in a stern voice.

"'Sup, babes, it's India."

"What's up, India?" Lamont replied with a hint of disappointment in his voice.

"I'm fine, Lamont, and how are you?"

"I'm okay."

"I just called to let you know that your woman was over here earlier."

Lamont frowned and pulled his truck over. "What do you mean, 'she was over there earlier'?"

"Well, after you whipped her ass, she must have run out of the house, and she called me to come pick her up. So I did that and brought her here. Needless to say, that wasn't a good idea, because she ended up leavin' on a very bad note."

"A bad note? What are you talkin' about, India?"

"Well, my sister, Asia, has this guy she's really diggin' and he came over, you know, to see Asia. Just by coincidence, Sierra happened to know this guy extremely well and they ended up leavin' together. My sister was pissed about that, too, but hey, it is what it is." Lamont was not in mood for India's playfulness. "Who was the guy, India?"

"Well, Sierra left with Rasheed, who, if I'm not mistaken, is her son's father, right?"

Lamont was furious. Pops had called it, and now it was definitely confirmed that it was happening. Sierra and Rasheed were together.

"Yo, India, where does this Rasheed dude live? Does he live anywhere near you?"

"Rasheed lives on Halsey Street and Stuyvesant Avenue. It's the biggest house on the block, you can't miss it." India paused. "You're not goin' over there, are you?"

"Yes, I'm goin' over there! My fuckin' woman is over there!"

"But, Lamont, I never said that she was at his house, I just said that they left together!"

"Fuck that! Me and this nigga, Rasheed, got history. I'm sick of this shit! I'm goin' over there and that's that!"

Lamont disconnected the phone call and headed straight for the Conduit. He was going to do exactly what Pops had told him to do. He was going to get his woman.

Chapter 28

India

India stared at her cell phone. Her heart began beating a hundred miles a minute. What had she done? Rasheed was going to kill Lamont if that man came to his house with beef.

Asia walked out of her bedroom with her cell phone to her ear. She had been calling Rasheed's phone for the last two hours and there was still no answer. After the last attempt, she threw the phone on the sofa and plopped down next to it.

"This is your fault, India, I swear!" Asia said, still sulking. "Me and Rasheed could have been doin' us, havin' a good time, then you had to come here with this bitch! You know I had plans for me and him."

"Why in the hell are you still blamin' me for Rasheed leavin' with his son's mother? I didn't know it was gonna end up like this!"

Asia waved her sister off. "What do you mean, 'you didn't know'? What you mean to say is that you didn't care, India!" She paced back and forth. "Personally, I don't give a fuck about Sierra. I may have talked a little shit about the Tamir thing but I realized that gettin' her back wasn't as important as bein' with Rasheed. I really like him, India, don't you understand? Tamir was our friend, but she is not here anymore. Damn, we gotta move on from that shit."

India stood there with her arms crossed, trying

to convince herself that getting Sierra back was the right thing to do. Truthfully, she was the one who felt responsible for Tamir's death because she was the one who had persuaded Tamir to go out with Tyke in the first place. India began to get choked up as she recalled the conversation that she and Tamir had on the eve of her death.

The girls were discussing their favorite topics, men and money, when Tyke's name just happened to come up.

"Girl, you need to go ahead and fuck with that dude, Tyke. He is a cutie pie, okay?" India said to Tamir while they were standing outside in front of her house.

Tamir was hesitant. "Um, I don't know, India. I mean, I don't even know Tyke like that. But I did hear that he used to go out with that CO ho Rasheed fucks with."

India sucked her teeth. "So what? He don't know you neither! Shit, if anybody could make Rasheed jealous, it would be that nigga, Tyke. Word in the hood is that they do not like each other—no, they despise each other. He's perfect to get back at Rasheed and that bitch."

Tamir laughed. "India, you are always tryin' to get somebody back for somethin'! Remember homegirl who lives in the buildin' next to yours, the one who was tellin' everybody that the clothes that we were sellin' were fake just so people would only buy shit from her? You did that chick so dirty," Tamir recalled, shaking her head.

India laughed. "Aw, fuck her! It ain't my fault that cats won't touch her stank ass with a ten-foot pole! Nasty self!"

Tamir laughed again. "India, you told everybody around the way that the chick had herpes! Of course they didn't want to touch her!"

India chuckled. "I bet you she stopped runnin' that mouth, though. I set that ass straight, didn't I?"

Tamir shook her head and laughed. "Yes, you did. You are a certified mess. I love you, though." They both paused. "Well, I'm supposed to be hangin' out with Tyke tonight. I've been brushin' him off because, truthfully, I'm still in love with my Rasheed."

"Yeah, I feel you, but we can't forget about Sierra. Rah is not checkin' for you, boo. That's why I'm tellin' you that you need to move on and hang out with Tyke."

Tamir smiled. "Yeah, okay. I'm gonna do that. Let me go give him a call." She stood up to walk into her house. "See you later, girl. I'll call you tomorrow to let you know what happened."

India gave Tamir a pound. "No doubt, Tee! Have fun with Tyke."

That was the last time India saw Tamir, and her death had been heavy on her mind ever since. She didn't want to take responsibility for her friend's death when it was so much easier to blame someone else. That was why India had been so hell-bent on getting back at Sierra.

Asia interrupted India's thoughts by throwing her hands in the air. "India, we have been together, like, all of our lives. We have done everything together, all the negative shit, and, personally, I'm tired of it. I didn't become a correction officer and try to change my life to be involved in a whole bunch of mess. Now Sierra and Rasheed will probably get back together. You and Lamont may even hook up. So where the fuck does that leave me? Did you even care about that? All you care about is makin' Sierra miserable because you feel guilty about Tamir. You're the one who told Tamir to go out with Tyke that night, not Sierra!"

India plopped down on the couch. Her face was expressionless.

"I figured that you probably wouldn't give a hell about me, but I do have news for you, India. I'm movin' out. I'm gonna get as far away from you as I possibly can and finally do my own thing. It's long overdue."

India watched as her sister went back into her bedroom and slammed the door. She shrugged, and turned on the television. She was unmoved by her sister's ranting and raving. She was more concerned with what was happening with Lamont and Sierra.

At first, India had been skeptical about directing Lamont to Rasheed's door. Now she didn't think it was such a bad idea. She smiled as she thought about how Sierra was in for one hell of a surprise.

Chapter 29

Sierra

As Sierra and Rasheed lay in bed, holding each other, they shared intimate kisses. She wrapped her legs around Rasheed and he pulled her closer to him. Sierra sighed softly as she thought about how safe she felt with him. She closed her eyes as she imagined him protecting her from the big, bad Anwar and Lamont. A smile of contentment came over her face.

After a few minutes of daydreaming, Sierra sat up in Rasheed's bed and looked at him. He had a loving look in his eyes. She turned away from him as a wave of remorse came over her.

"I gotta go, Rasheed," she said, attempting to get out of bed. He pulled her back to him and laid her head on his chest. Sierra could hear how fast his heart beating. Rasheed ran his hands through her hair. She wanted to submit to his love, but she knew that they could never be the same again.

"Why are you leavin'?" he asked. "Can't you stay with me a little longer? Didn't you say that Messiah was at Lamont's father's house?"

Sierra swung her legs to the side of the bed. "That's my point. He's at *Lamont's* father's house."

Rasheed propped himself up. "So you're just gonna leave me now? We made love to each other, had a nice little nap, and now you wanna leave?"

Sierra shook her head. "Rasheed, I love you and will

always love you but . . . but too much shit has transpired between us. I mean, you're a good man, aside from all that you've been through, but we can't go down this road again. It's just . . . it's just too confusin'."

Rasheed lay back. Sierra expected him to contest her statement, but to her surprise, he didn't.

"I'm not arguin' with you, Si. I think you just might be right about us. You got a family with Lamont, with his son. Shit, this dude is raisin' Messiah like he's his own. I have to respect that."

Sierra managed to smile. She rubbed Rasheed's face. Looking at him, she could recall the days that they first began their affair. It was exciting, it was risqué. Sierra knew that she had been in too deep with Rasheed. She never wanted to admit it, but when he went to Atlanta, it was exactly what they both needed. Things could have been worse had he stayed in New York at that time. Not to mention, after he got shot, he needed to get out of town. Sierra also knew that Rasheed was involved in the murder of Tyke, but she never said anything. It wasn't like he would admit to it anyway.

Sierra walked away from the bed and was surprised when Rasheed grabbed her from behind. She could feel his manhood rising between her legs. As bad as she wanted to climb back into bed with him, the urge to do so had to be suppressed. It was definitely time to leave Rasheed's safe haven and go home to face the music.

"Si," Rasheed began, turning her around to face him. "I never loved any woman like I love you, you know that?"

"What about Tamir? You loved her, right?" Sierra asked.

"Yeah, I loved her, but not like I love you. You are an excellent mother who takes great care of my son. It's because of you that I want to be a great father. I don't have the urge to go out in the streets anymore and do the things I used to do because of you and my boy. All these years, I've been wildin' and shit, even my own Nana couldn't control me. But you and Messiah? That was the prescription I needed to get my life together, man, for real. My moms is gone, my Nana is gone, and even though I always have my extended family, I have my own family, and that's you and Messiah."

Rasheed stood up and Sierra held back tears as she hugged him. He lifted her off her feet, causing her to giggle.

"I love you too. You're my heart, I swear you are. I'm gonna promise that I will never keep your son away from you again."

"No matter what Lamont says?" he asked, putting her down.

"Fuck what Lamont says! Messiah is our son. If he doesn't like the idea of you bein' in Messiah's life, then he can keep it movin'. It's important that Messiah knows his father . . . his biological father."

Rasheed threw on a robe. "I don't have a problem with Lamont bein' a father figure. I just have a problem with him not wanting me to be a father to Messiah. I'm here willin' to share my seed with him and he has a problem sharin' my own seed with me."

Sierra slid into her clothes. "Well, Lamont doesn't have a voice anymore as far as I'm concerned. He killed that when he believed that lyin' ass Anwar and then put his hands on me."

"So you're goin' back over there tonight?"

Sierra paused. "I'm goin' to go home tonight and pack a few things. I'm goin' to my mother's house for a little while. I'll get Messiah in the mornin'. My mother and I need to have a long talk anyway."

"About what?"

"First of all, about you bein' Messiah's real father."

There was silence for a few seconds. "Damn, you

never even told your moms about me? I was that fucked up of a dude that you couldn't even tell your mother about me, huh?"

"Rah, you wasn't a fucked-up dude. It was me who was ashamed of us. I was ashamed of how and where we met each other. I felt like I was goin' against everything that I said I wanted to accomplish. I mean, fuck, I always had a soft spot for a nigga from the streets, but here I was a correction officer and I was emotionally involved with an inmate I met on Rikers Island. I didn't want to tell my mother that I was riskin' my career over some dick. "

"So all I was to you was dick?"

"At first, yeah, you were. I mean, I liked you as a person, too, but it was initially a sexual attraction."

"Well, it was love at first sight for me, plus you had a nice, little fatty back there," Rasheed added, patting Sierra on her butt.

She slapped his hand away and laughed. "Stop playin', Rasheed!" She threw her arms around his neck. "Rah, I treated you fucked up, too. I didn't want to reveal you to anyone, but after this situation with Lamont, I don't care anymore. If he ain't with the program, then he can bounce. Why should I have him in best interest when he doesn't have me in his?"

Sierra got dressed and fixed her hair in the full-length mirror. She looked at the time. It was almost twelve o'clock in the morning.

"So what's up with the Charles twins?" she asked while gathering her things.

"Yo, they're fucked up for havin' you over there."

"Yeah, they are. I didn't even know that they knew Tamir."

Rasheed shook his head. "Not only did they know Tamir, they were her best friends. You couldn't have thought that India was your friend, Sierra."

Sierra looked back at Rasheed. "I knew that she wasn't my friend. She was just a chick from work who seemed as if she was mad cool. I mean, it is a small world, just like you walked into their living room. That was purely coincidental."

"Could you be that naïve, girl? That shit wasn't no coincidental nothin', Sierra." Rasheed paused for a moment. "Look, I'm about to go against everything I stand for as a man, but you know what, I think that it's only right that you know this. You gotta protect your job, your rep, and, most importantly, your heart. Bein' that me and you are on some unconditional lovin' each other shit from here on in, I gotta put you on to somethin'."

Sierra squinted, and plopped down in a fluffy armchair. She exhaled because she knew that this was going to be some bad news.

"Oh, God! Go ahead, Rah, just tell me, man," she said, waving her hand.

Rasheed sighed, and slipped into a pair of basketball shorts and a tank top. "You gotta promise me this is for your information only. You gotta follow the rules of the street with this shit here, and that means *no snitchin'*."

Sierra was growing impatient. "Yeah, Rah, I got you, man, just tell me."

Suddenly, the bell rang. Rasheed looked at Sierra with a frown on his face. He wasn't expecting company so he didn't know what to think. His uncle, Kemp, was out on the town for the night.

"Damn!" Sierra screamed. "Who the fuck is that? Did Kemp lose his key or somethin'?"

Rasheed shrugged and slipped his feet into some Nike slippers. "You stay in here. I will be back."

"Hurry up! I wanna hear what you have to tell me."

Sierra sucked her teeth as Rasheed walked out of the bedroom, closing the door behind him.

Chapter 30

Rasheed

Rasheed walked down the stairs and peeped through the peephole of the heavy oak door. He couldn't make out who it was because he or she was standing to the side. He hesitated as he opened the door. He was shocked to see Lamont standing on the stoop.

"Where is she, Rasheed?" Lamont asked with his chest heaving up and down.

"No, nigga, the question is how the fuck do you know where I live and why are you on my doorstep?" Rasheed asked.

"Look, don't worry about all that. That ain't your business, but my woman is my business and she's in here, ain't she?"

Rasheed smirked. "You really are a nervy-ass dude, you know that? Nigga, this ain't the Department of Correction! You ain't the fuckin' boss over here!"

"I'm gonna ask you this one more time. Where is Sierra?"

"Yo, man. Get off my fuckin' stoop with this stupidity, nigga, for real, before I end up in jail tonight!"

Rasheed attempted to close the door, but Lamont put his body between the door and the frame.

"You ain't gonna close this door until Sierra comes with me!"

Rasheed looked Lamont up and down. "Homie, you're buggin'! Get out my doorway, son, I'm warnin' you!"

Lamont insisted on forcing his way into Rasheed's house, and Rasheed pushed him back out. Lamont rushed the door again, this time pushing his way into the foyer. Rasheed punched Lamont square in the jaw, and Lamont was able to clip Rasheed's chin with a left hook. This only made the ex-con angrier.

"Oh, you wanna fight for real, homie?"

Rasheed began pummeling Lamont with left and right hooks. Little did Sierra's man know that Rasheed was known for his fighting skills in his Bed-Stuy neighborhood.

Sierra heard the commotion, and ran out of Rasheed's bedroom and down the stairs. She began yelling for the men to stop, but did not realize that the man Rasheed was fighting was Lamont.

"Stop, Rah, stop!" she screamed. Rasheed stepped back and Lamont clumsily swung a punch at his face. He missed by a few inches and fell to the floor.

Sierra froze. She knelt over Lamont. "What are you doin' here, Lamont?"

Lamont attempted to get up but appeared to be in too much pain to move. His right eye looked swollen and his lip was bleeding. Rasheed was pacing back and forth with his hands on his hips.

"This motherfucker barges in my damn house . . . Who the fuck does he think he is?" yelled Rasheed. "Get the hell up, nigga, so that I can finish beatin' your ass!"

Sierra stood up and pushed Rasheed back. "Rah, you did enough damage! Be easy before this shit gets outta control!"

Lamont stood up. He was wobbly, but managed to get himself together. He looked at Rasheed then Sierra.

"You're fucked up! I knew that you were here!" Lamont snarled, spitting out blood on the parquet floors. "How could you be with this . . . this lowlife—" he began.

Rasheed tried to charge him again, but Sierra held him back. "You got the nerve to have a problem with Sierra bein' here with me after what you did to her?"

Sierra frowned. "Rah, listen, don't bring up that again," she warned, thinking that he was talking about her and Lamont's fight.

"Nah, I ain't talkin' about y'all little bullshit scuffle. Uh-uh. Lamont here knows what I'm talkin' about, don't you, man?"

Lamont leaned against the wall. "Fuck you, you crook! You ain't shit and ain't gonna ever be shit! I'm the law! I'm one of the Boldest! I should get your ass locked up for assaultin' me!" he yelled.

Sierra covered her mouth. Rasheed knew that she was upset, but she had to know about Lamont; it was now or never. Everything was all good until Lamont decided that he wanted to get stupid in his house.

"Sierra, I have a lotta love and respect for you. I know I hurt you, but me and you had a different relationship than you and this dude." Rasheed glanced at Lamont. "The twins are some foul bitches, Si. The reason I was so angry today is because that chick, India, is really playin' you, hard. She and—" Rasheed was cut off by a gunshot to the wall. His eyes looked at the small hole by the doorway leading to the living room. Then he looked at Lamont, standing there with a Sig Pro 9 mm handgun in his right hand.

"What are you gonna do with that gun, man?" asked Rasheed with a sly grin on his face. "Oh, so you're gonna shoot me now? You're gonna shoot this crook?"

Lamont's eyes were bugging out of his head and he had a crazy look to him. "Yeah, I should just go ahead and shoot me a crook! That's what the fuck it's for! You know what it is!"

Sierra had her hands up. "Lamont, what are you doin'?" she screamed.

"Shut up!" Lamont screamed at her, pointing the gun in her direction. "Shut the hell up! The question is what are you doin' in this nigga's house? What are you doin' here, Sierra? Huh?"

Sierra began to stutter, and Rasheed's jaw was flexing from clenching his teeth. He wanted to get his own gun and pistol whip the lovelorn Lamont.

"You put your hands on me, Lamont, remember? I didn't have anywhere else to go!"

"So you had to come to your baby daddy's house?" he asked.

Rasheed took a step forward and Lamont bust another shot, this time barely missing Rasheed's head.

"Yo, Lamont, you're about to get murdered in here! Put that gun down, yo!" Rasheed ordered.

Lamont would have none of that. Sierra stood there, scared shitless, and Rasheed was pissed. He'd had many guns pointed in face in his day, but behind those guns were gangsters, certified killers. All Lamont was to Rasheed was a working stiff with a permit to carry a gun; that was it. It wasn't like he was going to use it. Rasheed figured that with the way that Lamont loved his career, he wouldn't dare risk his position to kill him.

Sierra began to sob loudly. "Lamont, please, baby, put down the gun! I will leave with you. You don't have to use that on anybody!"

Lamont pointed the gun at Rasheed's face. Rasheed's body stiffened. "Yeah, Gordon, you see me? I'm the real gangster! I'm the one who gets up in the mornin' and goes to work every day. I'm the one who takes care of his children and his lady like a real man is supposed to. I'm the one who pays the bills and makes sure my family has everything that they need. I'm the one who provides for your son, your baby boy. The same son you left when you moved down south. The same son you didn't want to try to be a father to unless you were fuckin' his mother!"

Rasheed's face began to flinch, and Sierra was standing there, horrified. "Lamont, please put the gun down! I'm comin' home with you. I'm gonna make it right. Just put the gun down, baby, please!" she pleaded.

Lamont hands began shaking. After about ten seconds had passed, he began lowering the gun. He put it back in his holster, and stepped back from Rasheed.

"I'm gonna be in the car, Sierra, and if you're not out there in ten minutes, I'm callin' the cops on this nigga and tell them that he assaulted me!" Lamont exclaimed.

Rasheed spit on the floor. "You's a bitch-ass dude! You would really call the cops on me after shootin' bullets into my fuckin' walls?"

"Yeah, I would call the cops and tell them that I was bein' assaulted!"

"But you're in my house, man! You forced yourself into my house!"

"Maybe I did that because you were holdin' my girl against her will! Who do you think that they'll believe? Me or some ex-convict like yourself?" Lamont walked out the door with a smirk on his face. Rasheed stopped because he knew that Lamont was right. There was nothing that he could do, thanks to the extensive rap sheet he had acquired over the years. When Lamont walked out the door, Rasheed punched the wall. His hand began hurting him immediately, but not as much as the pain he felt in his heart. He had to tell Sierra before she got into that car with Lamont.

Rasheed walked upstairs into the bedroom and helped Sierra with her bags. She had a pathetic look on her face, as if she didn't want to leave.

"Yo, Si," Rasheed said. "If you don't wanna leave, you don't have to. Fuck Lamont!"

Sierra sighed. "I have to leave, Rah. You heard what

he said. He said that he was gonna call the cops on your ass if I'm not out of here. I don't want you to get into any trouble."

Rasheed shook his head. "Look, Si, I wanted to tell you to watch yourself, man. I'm not sayin' that Lamont don't love you, but he's a sloppy dude."

Sierra walked down the stairs to the front door, and Rasheed followed closely behind her with her bags in his hand.

"I gotta go, Rah, so you gotta tell me what you mean! Make it quick!" yelled Sierra as she kept looking out the door.

Rasheed inhaled. "Lamont and India were fuckin' with each other. I caught Lamont over there with her a few weeks back. He made a deal with me by saying that I could see Messiah as much as I wanted if I didn't say anything to you."

Sierra froze, and Rasheed watched as her face became distorted. "This bastard! That little bitch! I can't believe that. You know what, Rah? I appreciate you tellin' me this." Sierra began crying.

"And Anwar? You don't have to worry about him, okay?" Rasheed said, wiping tears from her left cheek.

"Okay," she said in a barely audible whisper. He kissed her on the forehead before she opened the door. He watched her until she disappeared into Lamont's truck. Rasheed slammed the door shut. He went into the bathroom to look at his bruised face. But Rasheed didn't have any time to feel sorry for himself. He had to get some sleep. He had some plans to make.

Chapter 31

Anwar

Two days later, in Five North, Anwar looked outside the small window of his cell. The rain made a thumping noise against the glass as he looked across the river and sighed. Anwar was thinking about his freedom. He had done a few bids in jail, but the ninety-day bid he was sentenced to probably was one of the hardest that he ever had to do.

Although he knew that he was going home soon, he still felt empty inside. He thought about not having the ability to love or trust anyone. He had no children, no close relationship with his family, and definitely had no one woman he could say that he even cared about. Deja, Lamont's son's mother, was a good person, but he walked all over her. Anwar knew that Deja was the type of woman who would try to run over a man if she could. He saw how she treated Lamont. So he took control. He took control of her money, monopolized her time, and manipulated his way into her life.

After an hour or so, Anwar collected his thoughts and managed to gather enough strength to walk downstairs to the phone. He hadn't been feeling like himself lately, figuring that maybe he was coming down with a cold. As he made his way toward the telephones, he eyed the inmates that were using them at the time. One of the guys immediately hung up the phone when he saw Anwar, and walked towards the back of the housing

area. The inmate knew that Anwar was nobody to mess
with.

He picked up the phone and dialed Rasheed's number. After about three rings, Rasheed picked up.

"Yo, what's up with you?" Anwar said. "You can't
come see a nigga no more?" he asked, getting straight
to the point.

"Man, I hate comin' to Rikers Island," replied Rasheed
with an attitude.

"But I need you to come up here! You know my
broad can't come through. She could only send me
packages and commissary money and what not. What
I need is a visit. I have to get outta Five North for a few
hours! This shit is drivin' me crazy!"

Rasheed sighed and moved on to another topic.
"Fuck all of that. Let's talk about you. I thought you
were my peoples, man."

A look of confusion came over Anwar's face, and
he looked at the phone. "What are you talkin' about,
homie? You're my nigga and I'm yours."

"It may be a bad time to get into this shit right now,
but do you have a problem with me, man?"

Anwar began to get impatient. "Nigga, what are you
talkin' about? I don't have no fuckin' problem with
you!"

Rasheed's voice went up a few notches. "Man, you
know what—" he said, catching himself. "Well, I think
you do. You have problem with me because you keep
fuckin' with my son's mother!"

Anwar began laughing hysterically. "Oh, so the bitch
went back and told you some shit about me, huh? She's
lyin', homie."

Rasheed sucked his teeth. "Yo, watch your fuckin'
mouth! That woman don't have no reason to lie on you,
A. Why are you fuckin' with her?"

"'Cause the bitch has no loyalty!" screamed Anwar.

Some of the inmates looked in his direction, trying to figure out what was going on.

"'Cause that bitch has no loyalty," Anwar repeated in a softer tone. "She was supposed to be with you, not that other dude. You, her, and the baby was supposed to be a happy family. You can't tell me you want another man raisin' your baby, Rah! You seen what Russell was doin' to me all them years, didn't you?"

"I don't need you to be in my business, man. She's good with me. She's gonna be my son's mother forever. Don't worry about her loyalty to me and don't worry about who she fucks with. Just stay out of our business. Do your time, come home, and get your life together. Like, I'm dead serious right now."

"I'm sayin', Rah, sounds like you got a little beef with me! I thought that I would be doin' you a favor by puttin' these people in their place and I see you ain't respectin' that!"

"I respect that you wanna repay me, but, A, we were kids then. I did what I did because you were in trouble, man."

Anwar rubbed his face like he wanted to peel the skin off. "I don't appreciate this chick lyin' on me, man."

"She don't have no reason to lie on you. She don't have nothin' to do with—" Anwar slammed the receiver down before Rasheed could finish his sentence.

Anwar looked at the clock on the wall and paced back and forth. He didn't know what to do or how to feel. He was really losing it. His body felt as if someone was dripping hot wax all over him. Or maybe he was just that pissed off.

The next morning, Anwar arose from his bed after a night of tossing and turning. His eyes were bloodshot from madness and lack of sleep. He waited impatiently for Sierra to come to post. It was a weekend and normally, on the weekend there wasn't as much inmate movement as there was on a weekday. During this time, inmates didn't come out their cells until the early afternoon. This would only help Anwar carry out his next mission.

Anwar looked out his cell window and he observed Sierra walking into Five North looking a bit frazzled. Anwar studied her for a moment just to see what kind of mood she was in. She didn't look too happy. Anwar smiled to himself. He couldn't wait for breakfast to be served so that he could come out of his cell.

About an hour later, the pantry workers of Five North had breakfast prepared and ready to serve. Sierra instructed the officer in the control room to open the cells.

While inmates were filing in and out of the pantry, not paying attention to anything except the watery oatmeal on their trays, Anwar exited his cell. He waited until everyone was settled in the back of the housing area to eat their food and watch some television before he sprung into action.

As Sierra walked into the dark dayroom to get a chair for her desk, Anwar slowly crept up behind her and closed the door. To prevent her from screaming, Anwar put his hand over her mouth. She began to cry but Anwar was unfazed. He proceeded to put the homemade weapon he had in his possession to her neck.

"Shut the fuck up!" Anwar whispered, his saliva sprinkling her face. "What did I tell you would happen if you ran your mouth to anybody about me, huh?" Anwar licked her ear, and he could feel Sierra cringe. "Yo, lock this dayroom door and you better not try nothin' stupid," he whispered through clenched teeth. Still holding the weapon to the throat, Sierra removed the large Folgers key from the waistband of her uniform pants and did as she was told.

"Throw the keys on the floor," he ordered. Sierra dropped the keys and Anwar kicked them into the corner. "I'm gonna take my hand off your mouth, but if you scream, I swear, I will cut your fuckin' throat right here in this dayroom."

He slowly removed his hand from her mouth. "Now pull off them fuckin' uniform pants."

Sierra began to cry even harder. "Why are you—" she said, contesting his demands. Anwar grabbed her by the throat with his free hand and pushed her against the wall. He put the shank up to her left eye.

"See, it's bitches like you that make me sick to my stomach! You're a fuckin' needy bitch, got another nigga raisin' Rasheed's son! That nigga Lamont probably be beatin' the shit out your son when you're not around, and all because you need a man, you'll let that go down! You're a piece of shit just like my mother was!" He could feel her body shaking. Her obvious fear of him was turning him on. Sierra's reaction was the same effect Russell had on him when he was a boy. Now someone was afraid of him. Anwar always felt a rush when he knew that he had put panic in someone's heart. It gave him the power that he needed to carry out incorrigible acts.

He forcibly unbuttoned Sierra's uniform pants while she stood there, crying and pleading with him. She began struggling with him, which he found to be amusing. They both knew that she was in a compromising position. What female correction officer would want to be caught in a dark dayroom with a male inmate? Even if she wasn't guilty, she would still look like she was. On that job, reputation meant everything, and Sierra's man was an assistant deputy warden. Anwar smiled just thinking about it.

As Sierra's pants dropped to her ankles, Anwar tugged at her lacy panties and ripped them off in one pull. He stuffed the ripped undergarment into the pocket of his sweats. Still holding the cold metal against Sierra's throat, he pulled down his sweats. He was aroused from musky scent of Sierra's body. He forcibly kissed her on the lips. Sierra turned her head in disgust.

"Damn, you taste good, bitch," Anwar said in a hoarse whisper. "Fuckin' bitches. All of y'all broads." Anwar rubbed on Sierra's exposed vagina. "Didn't I tell you that I was gonna get this pussy?"

Sierra whimpered and her body went limp. Anwar entered her from the front, forcing his manhood inside of her dry vagina. Anwar didn't want doggie-style sex. He wanted to feel the warmth of her minty smelling breath on his face. He ground and ground inside of Sierra, causing her to squeal with pain. It was dark in the dayroom but he could imagine her expression. Her fear of him was what was giving him the most pleasure as he pummeled Sierra's vagina with his penis.

"Ooh, shit," Anwar moaned with pleasure. "This pussy is so good, bitch. This pussy is so good. I can see why Rasheed wanted you so bad. Ooh, I love this pussy."

"I hate you, Anwar, I hope you die," Sierra managed to say through clenched teeth and tears. Anwar put the shank near her throat again. He began poking her in the neck with the pointy end of the weapon as he continued to grind inside of her.

"This pussy is so moist. You been wantin' me too, huh?" Anwar asked. Sierra cried even harder as the point on the shank kept poking her in the side of her neck. One wrong move and she was a goner.

Anwar didn't care. He was in pain too: emotional and psychological pain. The physical scars from his abuse were long gone, but there were other unseen scars that were still there.

Anwar felt as if he was about to explode. He took his rod out of her and forced Sierra to get on her knees. Once she did that, Anwar grabbed her by hair and forced his penis into her mouth. He chuckled as he listened to her gag. He then pulled it out and began to jerk off in Sierra's face.

"Bitch, open your mouth so that you can swallow this nut!" he whispered.

Sierra resisted and Anwar slapped her. She cried softly but she did what she was told. Suddenly, Anwar let out a load of semen in her face. He was satisfied as he listened to her moan in horror. She immediately began choking.

Anwar's legs were weak from ejaculating, almost stumbling over Sierra as she sat on the cold floor and whimpered softly. She made no attempt to put her pants back on as Anwar got himself together. Losing patience with her display of emotion, he lifted Sierra to her feet with one hand.

"Shut the fuck up and put them fuckin' pants back on!" he whispered while listening to the cell doors closing. Fifteen minutes had passed and it was time to lock in. "You don't wanna get caught like this, do you? The only thing that I'm gonna say is that you gave it up willingly, and who do you think they're gonna believe?"

Sierra wiped her face and mouth with the bottom of her dark blue uniform shirt. Anwar went into his pocket, fishing for the panties that he ripped from Sierra's petite frame. He pulled them out and sniffed them.

"I'm gonna keep these ripped panties as evidence. So tell somebody somethin' else if you want. I will give these panties to your man Lamont." Sierra was silent as she slid into her pants. "Fuckin' whore! Hurry up and open this door before I kill your ass. Make it quick because they need you on this post out here." Sierra crawled around the floor until she found the keys. She hurried to open the door.

Anwar shoved the ripped panties into his pocket and walked back to his cell. Once he was inside and his cell door was locked, he laid back on the mattress, not even attempting to wash the stench of Sierra's vagina off his lower region. He sniffed Sierra's panties and sighed heavily. Having some regrets about what he had done, he thought about his stepfather, Russell Jones, and what he used to make the young Anwar do to him.

"Get on your knees, boy!" ordered Russell. "Suck this big black dick before your mama gets home."

The twelve-year-old Anwar was frozen with fear and disgust. He began to cry. "I don't wanna! I ain't no fag," said Anwar. All of a sudden, Russell slapped him so hard, his nose began to bleed.

"Do what I say, little nigga! Or else I'm gonna stomp a mudhole in your ass!"

Anwar hesitated.

"Now!" Russell screamed.

Anwar wiped the blood from his nose and reluctantly got on his knees. Russell pulled out his grown man's penis and had sex with Anwar's mouth. Russell's eyes rolled in his head while his stepson gagged. As Anwar wiped his tears and drool, Russell pulled out and ejaculated all over his face and clothing.

"Now get out my face and go clean yourself up!" Russell said to him, obviously ashamed of what he had his stepson do to him.

Although the physical abuse was evident, Anwar never told one single soul about Russell's sexual abuse, not even Rasheed. He sat upright and held his head in his hands. Anwar realized that he was no better than his abuser, Russell Jones. He wreaked havoc wherever he went. Now he had violated his one true friend, Rasheed, in the worst way, by forcing himself on the mother of his child. It was that moment when Anwar realized that maybe Rasheed should have killed him instead of Russell.

Chapter 32

Sierra

A half hour after the run-in with Anwar, Sierra couldn't bear to leave the dayroom. Humiliated and afraid, she was still sitting on the cold floor of the dayroom. She couldn't believe what had just happened to her.

I've been raped, she thought. I can't believe that he raped me.

She didn't know what to do or who to tell. With the rumors floating around about her and Rasheed, she was hesitant to say anything to anyone. How does a female correction officer get raped on Rikers Island? The department was so sexist that she would be looked upon as the bad guy. Anwar was an inmate, but he was a man and she was a woman. No one would believe her. Sierra knew that she couldn't afford to lose her job now, especially after she had seemingly got away with the Rasheed situation. This would have to be a secret.

Sierra finally got the strength to stand up and pull herself together. It was still early in the morning and 7:00 a.m. roll call was about to start in a half an hour. The inmates were locked in and she walked off post to go to the bathroom. The control room officer was too busy yapping on the phone to even notice that Sierra's clothing and hair were in disarray.

Sierra closed the bathroom door and looked in the mirror. She began crying softly as she wet some paper towels and wiped the dried cum stains from her face. Her hand went to her neck, which had been scraped up by the point on Anwar's shank. The skin was bruised but not broken. Her uniform collar was irritating it, and she felt as if she wanted to rip the skin off her body. She was so disgusted with herself, with the people that she was involved with, and with life as she knew it. What was she doing so wrong to deserve all of this bad luck?

After being in the bathroom for ten minutes, her coworker tapped on the door.

"Howell, are you okay in there, girl?" the female officer asked.

Sierra pulled herself together. "Oh, yeah, Banks, I'm good! Just needed a moment to myself to meditate, that's all," she replied.

"Oh, okay. For a minute there, it sounded like you were cryin'."

"Nah, I'm good." Sierra rolled her eyes and looked in the mirror. "So damn nosey!" she said under her breath. "Where the fuck was she when I needed her to be nosey?"

After a few more minutes passed, Sierra finally found the energy to freshen up. Her world was crumbling around her, and she didn't know what to do. All she knew was that she wanted Anwar to die, and she had never wished death on anyone.

Sierra came out of the bathroom and rushed back onto her post, avoiding any eye contact with Banks. She attempted to write in her logbook, but it was going to be impossible to concentrate on anything else after what Anwar had done to her.

She thought back to other night at Rasheed's house. She didn't know who Rasheed had been fighting at first, but when she saw that it was Lamont, she knew that there was going to be trouble among the three of them. Their relationship had already been pushed to exceeding boundaries, and her being caught red-handed at Rasheed's house was probably the last straw. She was sure of it.

When Sierra got into Lamont's car that night, he tried to slap her. Sierra went off, digging her nails into his right cheek. Lamont's hand went to his face, and when he saw the blood, he tried to go ballistic on Sierra, only she wasn't having it. She fought Lamont like she was Tina and he was Ike Turner. In retrospect, she was. She was tired of being a doormat and a magnet for drama. She was sick of revolving her life around what other people thought of her. She was done with being a do girl for the New York City Department of Correction, and she had it with being controlled by the men in her life.

Lamont pulled his truck over near an abandoned lot on Broadway, and they were really going at it. He got a few hits off, but Sierra was fighting dirty.

"You wanna put hands on me? I told you about puttin' your fuckin' hands on me!" Sierra yelled at Lamont.

She realized that domestic violence had also played a big part in most of her relationships. But she was just as guilty. She was quick to put her hands on a man.

Lamont tried to grab her by the throat, but she punched him in his mouth. His lip was already busted, and she was just finishing Rasheed's work. He finally stopped after that and his hand went to his bloody mouth.

"Get the fuck outta my truck!" he yelled. "Get out!"

Sierra's nose began flaring. "Yeah, the bitch is back!" Sierra responded. "I'm so tired of your cheatin', jealous ass and when I see your bitch, India, I'm whippin' her ass too!"

Lamont tried to reach across her and open the pas-

senger door. Sierra began beating him upside his head
with her fists. "Leave the damn door alone! I'm not
gettin' out! If I get out of this truck, I'm callin' the cops
on you!"

Lamont was pissed. "You're threatenin' me? You
would put my job on the line after I saved yours so
many times?"

"I'm promisin' you, Lamont! If you kick me out this
truck, you are goin' down! You wanna beat on me when
things aren't goin' your fuckin' way? I knew that you
were nothin' but a dirty dick-slingin' bastard!"

Lamont shook his head. "Since I'm such a bastard,
you can pack your shit and get the fuck out my house.
Take your inmate-lovin' ghetto ass back to the projects
then!"

"Gladly, you punk motherfucker! I'm packin' me and
my son's shit and gettin' as far away from your dumb
ass as I can!"

Lamont sighed, and from the look on his face, she
could tell that he regretted his words. But it was too late
for him to take them back. He grabbed a napkin from
the glove compartment and placed it on his bloody lip.
Sierra fixed her tousled hair in the visor mirror, daring
him to say one more word to her about getting out of
his truck. Lamont pulled off and they sat in silence for
the rest of the ride to Queens.

When they pulled up in their driveway, Lamont tried
to grab her, but she pushed him away. Sierra had a
feeling that he was going to try to make it right once
they arrived home.

Sierra marched into the house and pulled out her
luggage. She began packing most of her things. After
doing that, she went into the boys' room and began
packing some of Messiah's things into smaller suitcases.

Lamont was sitting in the living room when she
appeared with the suitcases and the look on his face

was priceless. He immediately got up from the couch and walked over to her.

"Si, I am so sorry, I didn't mean to—" he pleaded.

"Get away from me, Lamont," she angrily replied.

"But I wanted to explain my behavior."

"You don't have to explain nothin' to me. It's over. The jealousy, the insecurity, I just can't deal with it anymore. You just got on me about these same things a few weeks ago and I switched it up. I told myself that I was goin' to learn to trust you and prepare for our life together with our children, but, once again, you sabotaged us with your lies and your deceit. Pussy came between us—again."

Lamont sucked his teeth. "But what about you and Rasheed? Are you gonna stand here and tell me that you and him didn't have sex with each other?"

"Wouldn't you like to know?" Lamont had a blank look on his face when Sierra said that. "So how long were you fuckin' India, huh, Lamont? It's funny because I wasn't involved with Rasheed since he moved back, and, until today, we had never been intimate with each other. I'm sayin' that to say this: I don't want this anymore. You can have India Charles, you can have Deja, you can have whoever you want. But me? Sierra is so done with this. I'm gonna miss my baby, Trey, but if he asks you why me and Messiah left, he has no one to thank but his fucked-up father."

"So who you're gonna fuck with now, huh? Rasheed, the crook? Maybe I should go ahead and report your ass!"

Sierra chuckled. "Sorry, but you may just have to stand in line to do that, baby!"

Sierra gathered up whatever she could carry and went out to her car. Being that Lamont took her car keys, she had to use her spare set of keys. She piled the suitcases into the truck and went back inside once more for the rest of her things. This time, Lamont wasn't in the living room. Sierra figured he must have been in the bedroom, sulking and feeling sorry for himself. She shrugged, and left her house keys on the coffee table. Then she got into her truck, pulled off, and did not look back. After driving a few miles, she finally broke down. She had to pull over to get herself together. After crying her eyes out for at least five minutes, she retrieved her cell phone from her bag and dialed a phone number.

"Hello? Mommy?" she said. "I'm not okay. I will tell you about it when I get there. I am leavin' Lamont and I need somewhere to stay for a little while. I'll be there in about twenty minutes."

Sierra hung up the phone and saw that Lamont was calling her. She pressed the ignore button and steered her vehicle toward the Belt Parkway. All she could think about was how Lamont had pulled his gun out on Rasheed and put her in danger as well. His narcissism and overinflated ego had taken a complete toll on their relationship. When she had ended up back in the arms of Rasheed, she knew that it was over.

For the last two and a half years, she thought that Lamont had finally evolved as a man and wanted to make their relationship work. Then Rasheed told her that he'd been fooling around with India Charles, a woman who had tried to befriend her just to make her life miserable. How could he say that he loved her, but sleep with someone right under her nose?

Sierra shook her head thinking about everything that had transpired in the past weeks. She thought about Lamont's overtime hours at work. He thought about him disappearing for hours with no explanation of where he had been during those times. All of these actions became apparent around the time that Rasheed moved back to Brooklyn from Atlanta.

Fuckin' insecure jackass, Sierra thought.

She also thought about how India had played her. The assistant deputy warden India had talked about was Lamont. And what she had said about the guy having a girlfriend who was possibly having an affair with her baby's father? India was talking about her all that time! Monique had warned her about the woman but she didn't listen and now Sierra felt like a complete fool.

It was almost two o'clock in the morning when she arrived at her mother's house and she was exhausted. Sierra knew that her mother wasn't going to allow her to go to sleep until she filled her in on why she was leaving Lamont.

After Sierra piled all of her luggage into her mother's small two-bedroom apartment, she plopped down on the couch. Marjorie Howell sat in the chair across from Sierra, sipping on a cup of coffee.

"First of all, are you okay?" her mother asked with a look of suspicion on her face. "You look a little swollen around the facial area. Is that man hittin' on you?"

Sierra sighed. "No, Mommy. My face is just swollen from all the cryin' and whatnot."

Marjorie took another loud sip of her coffee. "Mm-hmm." They both paused. "Anyway, where's my grandbaby?" Marjorie asked.

"Messiah is at Pops's house."

"Okay, so if you left Lamont then why is your son at Charles Simmon's house while you're over here?" Sierra couldn't answer that question. "I don't get it, Sierra. Does this mean that Messiah is stayin' with his father while you get yourself together?" Marjorie asked, not knowing that her grandson's father wasn't Lamont.

"Mommy, I don't wanna—" Sierra began to protest.

"I've been standin' by and watchin' what's goin' on

with you, Sierra. You have been hidin' shit from me for too long! I know that you're a grown-ass woman, but you are not gonna keep runnin' to me with your problems and then come with a half-ass story. I wanna hear what is really goin' on with you. I don't give a shit if we gotta be up all damn mornin'!" Marjorie put her coffee mug on the side table. "Um, do I need to make you a cup of this here coffee?"

Sierra shook her head. "No, Mommy, I'm okay," she replied, holding her head down in humiliation.

Marjorie snapped her fingers. "So let's get to it then. Let's go!" Marjorie continued to sip on her coffee, and watched as Sierra collected her thoughts.

Sierra began telling her mother everything. She star-ted from Tyquan Williams, then she went into Lamont Simmons, then she finally got to Rasheed Gordon, whom her mother had never met since he'd been in her life. At the end of her hour-long story, Sierra prepared to tell Marjorie the naked truth about Messiah's paternity.

"And, Mommy, I have one more thing to tell you," Sierra said.

Marjorie held her chest. "I think I heard enough, Sierra. I mean, here I was thinkin' that my only child was a complete angel and you're tellin' me about how you've been datin' Tyke, the murderer; Lamont, the man whore; and a freakin' inmate named Rasheed who you met in Five East!"

"It's Five North, Mommy, I met Rasheed in Five North."

Marjorie waved her hand at Sierra. "Whatever. Now, what else do you have to tell me? You damn near about to give me a heart attack, child!"

Sierra swallowed. "It's about Messiah. Um, Mommy, Messiah is not Lamont's son."

Marjorie's mouth fell open. "But we had y'all a baby

shower! And Lamont looked so happy!" She shook her head. "Well, whose child is he? The dead murderer's son?"

Sierra looked up at the ceiling then looked at her mother. "No, Messiah is Rasheed Gordon's son, Mommy."

"Rasheed, the inmate?"

Sierra nodded.

"So why the hell did you have everybody else thinkin' that Lamont was the father of your child? Does Lamont even know?"

"Yes, he knows Messiah is Rasheed's son. He knew when I first got pregnant. Rasheed and I had a blood test done and everything."

"Why did you hide this from me, Sierra? Does Charles know about this?"

"Yes, he knows."

"So you mean to tell me that I'm the only grandparent walkin' around here lookin' like a damn fool? I thought we were so much closer than that, Sierra!"

"Mommy, we are close! I felt humiliated and embarrassed. Do you think that I want people to know that I had an affair with an inmate when I'm a correction officer? I could deny the rumors before, because there was no evidence. Now Messiah is livin' proof. Lamont was goin' for a promotion, and with me bein' his woman, I didn't want to take the chance of him bein' passed over because of my situation."

"Forget Lamont and his promotion, Sierra! What about your son? What about you? You laid up with Rasheed and you didn't have a problem with that, but you wanna deny your son the right to know his biological father because of the Department of Correction? You should have thought about that back then. Now my grandbaby is bein' pulled in different directions because you, Lamont, and Rasheed can't get y'all shit together. Out there fightin' and carryin' on like a bunch of high school chaps. I'm done with this conversation, Sierra. You need to go in that room and think about how you're goin' to give Messiah the life that he deserves, and then think about gettin' yours together! Good night."

Marjorie looked at Sierra and stood up. She shook her head, and a look of disappointment came over her face. Marjorie then walked toward the back of her apartment to her bedroom, and slammed the door.

Sierra sat on the couch for a few more moments, taking in everything that had just happened. There was just no end to her disgrace. She finally pried herself from the couch, gone into the spare bedroom, and fallen into a deep slumber.

So here she was at work, twenty-four hours later. She was dealing with the mess in her life, and now Anwar had violated her in the worst way. Sierra didn't want to say that it never happened, but it probably wasn't reported, and for good reason. Being that it was unheard of, she wasn't going to be the one to come forward. She would just have to deal with it.

She wiped her tears and prayed under her breath as she continued to write on yet another tear stained page in her logbook. Anwar was going to pay for what he did to her. She promised herself that.

Chapter 33

Lamont

Meanwhile, on the other side of the facility, Lamont had managed to avoid Sierra. He'd seen her walk toward her post after the five o'clock a.m. roll call, and practically hid in his office until she disappeared down the corridor. He knew that he couldn't face her right now after everything that happened between them.

While Lamont sat in his office, trying to figure out what was going on in his life, his phone rang.

"Hello, ADW Simmons here," he answered in a melancholy tone.

"Hello, Lamont, why haven't I heard from you?" asked the female on the other end of the phone.

"Who is this?" he asked. He knew who it was, but, of course, he had to play it off.

"It's India, Lamont," she replied.

"Oh, yeah, what's up," he said dryly.

"So you weren't gonna call me anymore, huh?"

"Look, India, I'm dealin' with a lot right now. I don't think I'm in a mood to be discussin' this."

"Why? Is it because of your girlfriend, Sierra?"

Lamont sighed. When did India become such a pain in the ass? "She's not my girlfriend anymore, India. She moved out. I'm sure that you'll be happy to know that she left."

India laughed. "She did?"

"Yeah, she did."

"So what's up?"

"What do you mean, 'what's up'?"

"What's up with me and you?"

"India, I just can't do this with you anymore."

"You can't do this with me anymore? So you're not fuckin' with me now?"

"You heard me. I have a lot on my mind and I don't have the time for this."

"So tell me, Lamont, is it Sierra you're thinkin' about?"

"India, why do we have to discuss this? I mean, you knew that I was in a relationship with her, right?"

"Yeah, so?"

"So what's up with you, girl? Why are you goin' so hard to be with me then? What is it about me that makes you wanna be with me?"

"Huh? What do you mean?" asked India, sounding like she was confused.

"You heard me. What is it about me that makes you want to be with me?"

"Um, you're cool, Lamont. I think that you are a, um, nice man, and I, um, like you."

"Why do you like me?" Lamont asked. He knew when someone was full of it.

"Why do you keep askin' me all these stupid questions, Lamont?"

"Because I want to know why you chose me. You could have had any man you wanted, but you chose me. I don't know if I should be flattered or fuckin' pissed. "

India sighed. "Look, I just called to find out if you were okay."

"No, you called to find out if I went to Rasheed's house the other night. You wanna find out what happened. If you would have never called me and told me that Sierra was over there, to be honest, I probably would have been in the dark about everything."

"So that must mean that you're thankin' me, right?"

"No, that means that I'm not fuckin' with you anym-ore. You wanted to break up my relationship thinking that I was goin' to rock with you, but that ain't happenin'. Why did you lie about knowin' Rasheed?"

"What are you talkin' about?"

"Remember when I asked you how well do you know Rasheed? You told me that you had never talked to him like that, that he was just some guy from around the way. Tell me the truth. I'm gonna find out eventually."

"Well, um, we're from the same neighborhood. He used to date a friend of mine."

"Who was the friend?"

"Why is that important, Lamont?" India protested.

"Are you gonna tell me the fuckin' friend's name or not?" he asked in a stern voice.

"Her name was Tamir. Tamir Armstrong. Does that answer your question?"

Lamont was silent. Everything was coming together. India had used him as a pawn in her dirty game. All the sexcapades they'd had with each other and all the phone conversations they'd had with each other were just part of some ploy to get back at Sierra. Lamont knew that story all to well. After all, Sierra had shared most of the details about Tamir with him.

"You know you're real fucked-up, right?" Lamont said. "You just used me to get back at my girl."

"Lamont, you don't understand. It may have started out like that, but I really do like you. I want you—"

Lamont hung up the phone on India while she was still talking.

He buried his head in hands. What had he done? He had lost one of the best things that had happened to him, not once, but twice. He was definitely one of the biggest fools ever. There was no way that Sierra would be coming back now, and if she ran into the arms of

Rasheed, he would not be surprised. Lamont was so adamant about Rasheed not winning Sierra back that he had practically dropped Sierra into his lap. Pops had told him so.

There was no looking back now, but he had to do something. First of all, he had to get rid of India. He couldn't bear to look her in the face without wanting to kill her. Someone in the department owed him a big favor, and he was going to definitely utilize it to get India transferred out of the facility.

Lamont grabbed the radio from his desk and prepared to make his routine tour throughout the jail. As he walked through the corridors, new jack officers saluted him, and Lamont attempted to smile. It was hard to do because he kept thinking about Sierra. He made his rounds talking to various officers and captains, making sure that everything was running smoothly on his watch.

Lamont walked toward the end of the hallway. His heart began to palpitate as he approached Five North. He looked at his watch and sucked his teeth. Sierra was still on post. Not wanting her to see him sweat, Lamont intended to just keep it as professional as possible.

The officer opened the gate to Five North. Before Lamont could even step through the door, Sierra ran out and practically fell into his arms, sobbing uncontrollably. Lamont walked her into the staircase in an attempt to console her.

Chapter 34

Rasheed

After speaking to Anwar the other day, Rasheed realized that the years of abuse that Anwar had endured during his childhood had finally caught up with him.

For some reason, Rasheed's instinct kept telling him that he needed to go to Rikers because he couldn't rest until he got to the bottom of what was really going on. Rasheed knew that Anwar was bad news and extremely dangerous. He also knew that his Sierra was mouthy and sarcastic, and Anwar was unaccustomed to a woman talking to him in an authoritative manner. Rasheed could only imagine the hell that Anwar was giving her.

Rasheed found the strength to get up, take a quick shower, and get dressed. After gathering his belongings, he rushed to get in his truck. Rasheed sighed as he headed for the Jackie Robinson Parkway. He was on his way to Rikers Island to see Anwar face-to-face. They had some things to discuss.

Rasheed arrived on Rikers within the hour. He parked his car in the visitors' parking lot and took the Q101 bus over the bridge to the registration building. As he got on the facility visit bus, he felt his chest tighten up. As they proceeded down Hazen Street, he glanced at the various jails on the island: C-74, where he started his jail career as a sixteen-year-old knucklehead; then C-95, where he had graduated to professional jailbird at the tender age of twenty. He sighed as he thought about being in every jail on Rikers, except Rosie's, which was the women's facility. Rasheed was not proud of how many years he spent running the streets doing whatever he wanted. Too bad; Nana had died never seeing him become the man he was supposed to be.

Forty-five minutes later, Rasheed sat in the visit area and waited for Anwar to come out. Depending on his friend's reaction, he was unsure of what he was going to do. Anwar walked from behind the metal doors with a smug look on his face. Rasheed knew that this visit wasn't going to be a good one.

"What's up, A?" Rasheed greeted Anwar without cracking a smile. "What's good with you?"

"I'm a'ight, nigga. What's good with you?" Anwar replied, plopping down in the seat with a slight attitude. "To what do I owe this visit?"

"You hung up the damn phone on me, remember?" Rasheed said.

"Yeah, I remember. You was talkin' some other shit. That's why I hung up on you."

Rasheed sighed. "Yo, A, I don't know what's goin' on in that bugged-ass head of yours, but I'm tryin' to figure out where all this animosity is comin' from—the animosity toward my son's mother and now toward me. "

Anwar leaned back in his chair and then abruptly sat upright. "Look, Rah, I'm at the point in my life where I don't give a fuck about nothin' and about nobody. I don't care anymore. Yeah, you murked that nigga, Russell, for me, but that shit didn't ease my pain, man."

Rasheed's nose began to flare. "Listen, A, I never said that me doin' that for you would ease your emotional scars, but your physical pain was no more!" Rasheed got in Anwar's face. "Now the healing part is up to you. I can't help you get over what happened to you as a youngster. At the time, in my twelve-year-old mind, I'm thinkin' that I was helpin' my best friend. I'm thinkin' that I'm helpin' a nigga who was more like my brother if anything. But damn, A, you gotta find a way to work through this shit. You can't get fuckin' revenge on everybody because of that nigga, Russell. Sierra wasn't there; she didn't even know you existed when all that shit was goin' on. Why the fuck are you—" Rasheed said.

Anwar cut him off. He had tears in his eyes. "Rah, you don't understand, man. That nigga raped me, Rah," he whispered through tears. "He raped me! He took my manhood, yo. I don't like men, Rah, I ain't no fuckin' faggot! Why did he fuckin' do that to me?"

Rasheed put his hand on Anwar's shoulder to comfort him. He looked around and noticed other people watching them. He felt bad about coming on the visit with the intention of giving his friend a piece of his mind. He saw that Anwar was at his breaking point, and Rasheed felt sorry for him.

Anwar wiped the tears from his eyes. "I can't go home, Rah. I don't wanna go back out there and deal with all the shit out there. I ain't got no mother, my sister hates me, I can't be no real man to Deja, I can't function, son. I'm never gettin' a job, never havin' kids, I can't deal with that shit out there in the real world, Rah."

Rasheed held his head down, and then looked Anwar in the eyes. All he saw was mania. He had known Anwar too long, long enough to know when he was up to no good.

"Is there somethin' else that you need to tell me, Anwar?" Rasheed asked.

Anwar sniffled. "What you mean?"

"You got somethin' else to tell me because I know you like a book!"

Anwar sat upright with his chest sticking out. His eyes were darting all across the room and he looked very uncomfortable.

"I don't know what you're talkin' about."

Rasheed squinted. "I don't know. Somethin' just ain't right about the look in your eyes. You got the guilty look. Did you do somethin' to Sierra?"

All of a sudden, Anwar jumped up and tried to cut Rasheed with the same shank he had used to terrorize Sierra. The female correction officers pressed their personal alarms and ran for cover. Visitors scattered all over the place and cowered in the corners of the visit area. Inmates protected their loved ones by keeping them away from the melee.

Rasheed was caught off guard, but he was able hit Anwar so hard that he fell over the desk. The shank fell out of Anwar's hand and he scrambled on the floor to retrieve it. Rasheed stepped on Anwar's hand, feeling the bones crush under the impact of his foot. He kicked Anwar in his face, watching as his blood spewed all over the tiled floor. The stronger Rasheed picked Anwar's limp body up and threw him against the brick wall.

The response team rushed into visits, and in minutes, they managed to break up the fighting match between the two cons. They shoved their batons into Rasheed's stomach, knocking him to the floor, and they hemmed up the bleeding Anwar.

After taking control of the disruptive situation, correction officers made sure that everything was back to normal in the visit area. Rasheed and Anwar were led out of the area into the vestibule of the visit area in plastic flex cuffs. At this point, Lamont walked in.

"Ah, shit!" Rasheed said aloud. He knew that he was in for it now. "Fuckin' Lamont!"

The officers on the response team looked at Lamont with suspicious looks on their faces. They were probably wondering how Lamont and Rasheed knew each other.

A few minutes after Anwar was removed from the area, Rasheed saw that Lamont had retrieved the weapon. Visits were almost back to normal and three muscular correction officers were waiting around with Rasheed, who was still in restraints. Lamont whispered in one of the officers' ears, and he immediately let Rasheed go. They had to cut the tight plastic cuffs off his wrists with wirecutters. Then Lamont told Rasheed to go into the bathroom and wash his face. Rasheed did just that, and followed Lamont into the visit captain's office so that they could talk. Rasheed wondered what Lamont was up to, because he didn't need any more problems.

"Sit down, Gordon," Lamont instructed him. Rasheed did as he was told. He wasn't too happy about taking orders from the man but at this point, he was just trying to avoid being arrested.

"Look, man, that nigga, Anwar—" Rasheed began. Lamont held his hand up to stop him from explaining. The expression on Lamont's face told him that there was something that he needed to get off his chest. He looked as if he was on the verge of tears.

"Look, Rasheed, even though I try to deny it, you and I have somethin' in common and that's our love for Sierra," Lamont said. He put his hand to his chest, as if he was in pain. "I'm gonna be a man about mine and sincerely apologize for the way I acted the other day. But it's just that I love Sierra, you probably won't understand how much. She means the world to me and always has meant the world to me. I know I fucked up plenty of times but . . . but . . ." Lamont plopped down in the chair behind the desk, and covered his eyes with his hands.

Rasheed didn't know what to say or do. It was obvious that Lamont had more to tell him.

Rasheed frowned. "Okay, so you're in love with Sierra, but what that got to do with me? We've been battlin' over this shit for the last few years, and I'm tired of it, man. You didn't even want me to see my son, so I don't know what you expect me to say about what you're tellin' me right now."

Lamont looked at Rasheed and changed the subject. "Look, I'm not gettin' you arrested, Gordon. I'm just gonna keep this incident in-house. That motherfucker, Jones, deserved that shit. I wish I would have gotten to his ass!"

Rasheed grinned. "Is that right?" Then he turned serious. "Is Sierra all right though?"

Lamont held his head down and began punching his hand. "No, she's not all right. That motherfucker, Jones, forced himself on Sierra today."

Rasheed stood up. "He did what?"

"He forced himself on Sierra—he raped her, man, in the Five North dayroom with a weapon to her throat. He did this during breakfast."

Rasheed paced around the office. He was crushed, thinking about what Sierra was going through. He also thought about how Anwar had violated her, after all he had done for him.

"How the hell did he manage to do that?" Rasheed covered his eyes. "And somethin' told me that this nigga had done somethin' to her! He killed Scooter, now he done went and violated Sierra!" Rasheed looked at Lamont. "Yo, man, me and Anwar grew up together. It's like this dude don't have no sense of right and wrong. He's a walkin' time bomb!"

"But what does he have against Sierra? I could see him tryin' to get back at me before her but even that is a little strange. I never had a run-in with him until now."

Rasheed shook his head. "Nah, Lamont this isn't about you, me, or even Sierra. I did somethin' for Anwar when we were younger. I'm not gonna get into it, but ever since I did it, he's spent half of our lives tellin' me that he owes me, that he wants to repay me. If I got love for somebody and I help them, then that's what it is—you don't 'owe' me shit. His stepfather abused him in every way known to man. His mother stood by and didn't do anything to stop it."

Rasheed continued. "You see, Anwar's problem with Sierra is that she's not with me so that we can raise Messiah together. He had a problem with her raisin' Messiah with another man. He has convinced himself that you are abusin' Messiah, just like his stepfather abused him when he was younger, and he thinks that Sierra is allowin' this to go down, like his mother did. I tried to tell him that it's not like that. Just because me and you have our disagreements, that doesn't mean that I think that you aren't good to Messiah."

Lamont shook his head. "Damn. I would never hurt Messiah. He's like a son to me and I love him. I'm just glad that I was able to get Trey away from his mother and this fool, Anwar. But, Gordon, man, I feel bad about everything, about the way I acted with Sierra, and the way I barged into your house the other night. I feel bad about not wantin' you to be in Messiah's life. With all this shit that's goin' on between me and Sierra, I can't blame you or her for anything that happened between y'all. This is all on me, man. I see that you're workin' on you and now it's time for me to work on me. Can we shake on it?"

Lamont extended his hand and Rasheed hesitated for a moment. He still was upset at the fact that Lamont came into his home and acted a fool, not to mention almost killed him and Sierra.

Rasheed wasn't sure if he wanted to shake on anything, but he knew that he had to start somewhere. He finally shook Lamont's hand.

"So, you're not gettin' me arrested, right?" Rasheed asked.

Lamont waved it off. "Nah, Gordon. I ain't gonna press no charges. If anything, you were protectin' yourself. Now, the officer who let him enter this visit area without searchin' him? They're in trouble! I don't know how they let this individual get by with that weapon on him."

Rasheed wiped the sweat from his brow and put his hands on his hips. "Damn, yo, I feel so bad about Sierra." He covered his face in frustration.

"Yeah, me too, but workin' here, me and her gotta put on a façade. Don't want none of these grimy motherfuckers in here to know what's goin' on. I'm gonna make sure I get her all the help that she needs, and I'm gonna get her out of Five North. She's been on that post long enough. Now, Jones? He violated my sweetheart in the worst way!"

"And this is why that nigga has to die," said Rasheed.

Lamont and Rasheed looked at each other. There was nothing more to be said when they knew what the other one was thinking.

Chapter 35

India

When the response team headed back to the intake area with the belligerent Anwar in shackles and his mouth all busted up, India breathed a sigh of relief. She hated to get suited up for alarms. Along with several other officers, she was relieved to remove the heavy vest and place her baton and helmet back into the wooden cubby that they were stored in. While her coworkers huddled together, asking questions about the incident, India made her way back to her post. She had her own problems to think about.

As India got closer to her post, she decided to ask an officer if he had seen Lamont.

"Um, excuse me," she said, stopping the male officer. "You didn't happen to see Deputy Simmons anywhere, did you?"

"Oh, yeah, I did. He's in visits talkin' to the visitor who was involved in an altercation with that inmate. You had to suit up for the alarm, right?" he asked.

"Yeah, I did. That inmate had a fight with a visitor, huh? Male or female?"

"Male. I heard the inmate pulled out a weapon on the visitor!"

India was seriously taken aback. "What? Oh, my God! Did anyone get hurt?"

"Yeah, the inmate did!" the officer replied with a laugh. "The visitor beat his ass. I saw it with my own two eyes!"

India smiled. "Wow! Good for his dumb ass. So Deputy Simmons is in visits. . . . Okay, thank you."

The officer nodded and proceeded to walk off. India looked at the open door leading to visits and headed straight for it. Her meal relief could wait. She had some unfinished business to handle.

India walked through the visits area, following the droplets of blood down the hallway. She entered the visit floor and saw that it was almost cleared out; half of the visitors must have left after the fight. She waved at the female correction officers at the desk and headed straight for the captain's office. She was sure that if Lamont was anywhere, it would be there. India just hoped that Captain Phillips wasn't in there with him. They couldn't stand each other.

India knocked on the door and as she obeyed Lamont's order to come in, she stopped short when she saw Rasheed Gordon sitting there. She wanted to run back out of the office.

"Uh-uh, come on in, India, you're just who I needed to see," Lamont said with a smile on his face. "I'm pretty sure that you know Rasheed Gordon, don't you?"

India stood in the corner by the closed door. There was nowhere to hide, so she had no other choice but to put on her bad girl armor.

"Yeah, I told you that I knew Rasheed . . . and what about it?" India replied with a blank expression on her face.

Rasheed chimed in. "Yo, you told Lamont where I live? You told him that Sierra was with me that night, didn't you?" Rasheed asked.

A smirk came over India's face. "And so what if I did? I don't give a fuck about no Sierra! Did she give a fuck about Tamir?"

Rasheed jumped up and tried to grab her. India co-wered behind a file cabinet. Lamont stepped in between the two. She managed to slide over to the door and put her hand on the doorknob.

Lamont turned to India. "I was on the phone with some of my peoples and we agreed that you should be transferred to Rosie's," he said, referring to the Rose M. Singer Center, the women's facility that was located on Rikers. "So you can start packin' your shit. You're outta here today!"

"But, Lamont, I love you!" she said with tears in her eyes. "Are you gonna let this bitch come between us?" She rolled her eyes at Rasheed, who was standing there, shaking his head. "How are you gonna do this to me?"

"Get out of this office, India, and just go to the locker room and pack your shit, please," Lamont said without a hint of compassion. "And if I hear you utter one word about any of my business, you and your sister are goin' to be out in the street on y'all ass! Is that understood?"

"Yes," she replied in a meek voice.

"Yeah, go pack your shit, India! Bye, bye!" Rasheed added, waving at her.

India wiped the tears from her face and slowly walked out of the office. If her sister's job wasn't on the line as well, she would have gone off on Lamont. But she owed Asia that much. After all, she had already sabotaged the connection with her and Rasheed.

Back in the locker room, India shoved all of her belongings into a large duffle bag. When she was finished, she closed the door and took the combination lock off her locker door. As India turned around to leave, she was surprised to see Sierra standing there, watching her.

Chapter 36

Sierra

An hour before India was ordered to pack her things; Sierra was sitting on a wooden bench in front of her own locker, crying her eyes out.

When Lamont came to her post after the incident with Anwar, it was like he sensed something was wrong. He walked through the gates of Five North; she collapsed into his arms and cried silent tears. She was so happy to see him. He immediately pulled her into the staircase for some privacy.

"Si, what's wrong? What's wrong?" he asked with a look of concern on his face. When she didn't answer, he began apologizing. "I am so sorry, baby, I am so sorry I hurt you!" It sounded as if Lamont thought she was crying over him at the time.

Sierra could barely catch her breath. Lamont wiped the tears away with a tissue from his pocket. Her uniform was in disarray.

Sierra tried to say something but nothing would come out of her mouth. After a few seconds, she was finally able to talk.

"It's not about you, Lamont! It's not about us!"

Lamont looked confused. "I don't understand. What is it? Or who is it?"

She collapsed into Lamont's muscular arms once again. "It's Jones."

Lamont frowned. "Jones? What about that clown now?"

"He forced himself on me," she whispered as her lips trembled.

Lamont's body instantly froze. He stared into space, and, looking at him, Sierra knew that he had blacked out. He had to regroup, for fear that if he reacted, the whole incident would be damaging to Sierra's already shady reputation and his position. The rumors had subsided a little, but everyone in the jail would be back on the premise that Sierra slept with inmates. The Anwar story would only prove that to be true, regardless of whether she was forced to have sex with him or not. It was a sticky situation that no female officer wanted to be in.

Lamont held her face and kissed her tenderly all over her eyes, mouth, nose, and forehead.

"Oh, my God, baby! What did this animal do to you?" he said, tears falling from his eyes as well.

Sierra wiped her face. "He violated me in the worst way, Lamont. He violated me, but I can't do this to myself, I can't do this to us. My life is on the line, our life together, our careers—I can't risk everything that we built by sayin' anything. Please, just get me out of this place! I can't be here anymore, baby, I just can't!"

Sierra began crying again and Lamont hugged her. His body was shaking with anger. She knew that it must have taken everything in Lamont's power to keep him from walking into Five North and killing Anwar with his bare hands.

As Sierra sat on the bench in front of her locker, staring into space, she heard a ruckus in the front of the locker room. She crept up to the front to see what all the commotion was about, and saw India packing her things. After thinking about the part that India had played in some of her misery, Sierra felt that a much-needed confrontation was overdue.

"Hello, Miss Charles," Sierra said. Her tearstained face gave her a deranged look.

"What do you want?" India asked with an attitude.

"I want your fuckin' head," Sierra snarled. "That's what I want!"

India laughed. "Yeah? And I want your man! Now what the fuck are you goin' to do about that?"

Out of nowhere, Sierra grabbed India by her hair and began banging her head into a combination lock on one of the metal lockers. India tried to hold on to Sierra's uniform shirt, but was slowly dwindling into unconsciousness. Sierra saw blood oozing from the gash on top of India's head, but instead of stopping, she began choking her.

Sierra was so angry; all she could see was red. She wanted to hurt someone and India was her target. India represented all the people who had hurt her over the years: Tyke, Rasheed, Lamont, Deja, Tamir, and, last but not least, Anwar Jones.

To Sierra, India was the correction officers who shunned her and talked about her behind her back. India was the inmates who cut their eyes at her because she didn't choose to sleep with them. She wasn't listening as India begged for her life, pleading with Sierra to loosen the vice grip on her neck. Sierra wanted India to die. At that moment, she had no conscience. Anwar had taken her soul with him when he forced himself on her.

"I'm gonna kill you, bitch," Sierra whispered. "You done fucked with the wrong one."

Luckily, two female correction officers walked into the locker room and managed to pull Sierra off India. India fell to the floor and scurried into a corner like the little rat she was. Their coworkers stood there in shock as they looked at the crazed Sierra and the battered and bloodied India. Stressed out from the chain of events,

Sierra began hyperventilating, and fainted in their
arms.

A half hour later, Sierra was awakened by two inspector general officers in the clinic. Lamont was
pacing around the room with a worried look on his
face. Sierra closed her eyes, hoping that when she
opened them again everything that had happened to
her would only be a bad dream.

"Officer Howell?" said one of the officers. "Officer
Howell? Are you okay?"

Sierra was in no mood for the questions. She was
about to take her spanking like a champ. Sierra was
sick of the Department of Correction running her life.

She was getting impatient. "Yeah, that's me, damn!"
she yelled. "Who wants to know?"

"I'm Officer Tavares and this is Officer Patterson,
and we're from the—" he said when Sierra cut him
short.

"I know, I know!" yelled Sierra. "You're from the
inspector general's office! Blah, blah, blah!" Sierra
tried to sit up, but her body was sore. Lamont walked
over to her to help her sit upright. "Listen, if you wanna
talk about me whippin' Officer India Charles's ass in
the locker room, yes, I tried to do some damage to that
bitch! She wanted to ruin my life so she got what was
comin' to her ass! So if you're gonna suspend me or
modify me, just do it then! I don't feel like answerin' a
hundred questions!"

The officers looked at each other, then looked at
Lamont. "Um, are you the tour commander, sir?" CO
Tavares asked.

"Yes, I am," Lamont said calmly.

"So isn't she one of your officers? I don't understand
what's goin' on with her," he added. He obviously
wanted an explanation for Sierra's behavior.

"Look, what are you gonna do? Are you gonna suspend her or what?" Lamont asked.

"It's not up to us to do that, sir. She would have to have a hearing and—" CO Tavares started to explain.

Sierra jumped down from the gurney that she had been lying on. "Fuck you, I'm outta here!" she screamed at CO Tavares. "I'm bangin' in, yep, I'm goin' out on sick leave. If y'all IG motherfuckers want me, come to my house and get me! I'm outta here. Peace!" Sierra walked to the clinic door. "Lamont, I will see you at home, babe," she said, giving him a kiss on the lips.

Sierra left Lamont standing there in the clinic to deal with the two shocked IG officers. They looked at him as if they were surprised that someone in his rank would be with a woman of Sierra's caliber.

"That's my fiancée, so all questions should be directed to me," Lamont said, showing his loyalty and devotion to Sierra. Little did Sierra know, her man had a trick for the Department of Correction.

Chapter 37

Anwar

Meanwhile, Anwar screamed to the top of his lungs from the "Why Me?" pen in the intake area.

"Fuck all of y'all motherfuckers!" he shouted at the officers.

Anwar had become so problematic while being detained at the facility, that the intake officers had grown accustomed to seeing him in there all the time.

"Yo, Jones, shut the fuck up, man!" yelled out one slim CO. "Ain't nobody even botherin' your ass! What is wrong with you?"

Anwar spat through the open bars. It barely missed the slim officer's boot.

"Fuck you, nigga! Suit up and come make me shut up!" Anwar yelled. This time, the entire intake staff laughed at Anwar. He was making a fool of himself.

The slim officer was not impressed. "Duke, you don't really want it. Y'all motherfuckin' crooks think that we all scared of y'all asses. I don't care nothin' about your rap sheet. I will whoop your ass in this intake. And trust me, I will make sure that you're a stat run to Elmhurst Hospital emergency room!" The other officers laughed hysterically.

"Fuck you, CO, fuckin' punk-ass po-lice nigga!" Anwar replied. He was smart enough to know who not to mess with.

A smirk formed on the officer's face. He walked up to

Anwar's pen, daring him to spit at him again. "Bitch-ass motherfucker! Can't stand some of y'all bitch-ass motherfuckers, thinkin' y'all are the only cats who come from the streets! Shit, I was just smart enough to not get caught out there, and got a job instead of gettin' locked up all the time. Now I'm gettin' paid almost a hundred thousand a year to do twenty years in jail and go home every day! Dummy!"

The intake officers began laughing at Anwar again, and he retreated to the hard bench in the pen. It was useless to take his frustration out on other people when he was really pissed off about the incident with Rasheed. He thought he knew the man he considered his brother, but obviously he didn't. He didn't appreciate Rasheed accusing him of being a nutcase, even though he secretly was and taking up for Sierra, that slut of a baby mother of his. Now, because of his erratic behavior, he and Rasheed were at the point of no return.

Anwar banged his head on the brick wall in the pen. Before he passed out, he came to the conclusion that he didn't have anyone to blame but himself.

Chapter 38

Lamont

"Roll call! Roll call!" shouted the captain, standing at the podium. About forty officers slowly walked into position and prepared for an inspection. Another captain walked through the three rows of officers, making sure that everyone was in full uniform. Lamont stood beside the podium, waiting for the roll call captain to debrief the midnight staff and give them their assigned posts.

Shortly after, Lamont looked at the watch on his wrist and saw that it was only 11:25 p.m. He figured that he would sit in his office until around 2:00 a.m. on the midnight tour. Even though it was against the rules, almost everyone should have been fast asleep by then.

Lamont attempted to do some paperwork, and chatted on the phone for a little while. He tried to keep busy so that he wouldn't over think the deed that he was about to carry out. The clock on the wall was moving so slowly. Lamont took a deep breath. His heart was beating so fast, he could almost hear it. He managed to doze off for a brief moment, and by the time he looked up at the clock again, it was 2:30 a.m.

Lamont walked out of his office and into the control room area. He saw that everyone had wound down and had returned to normal duties. He quietly walked out of the control room, instructing the officers who

worked there that he had to make a run to the kitchen
for a snack. Lamont didn't want them to start calling
housing area officers on their posts. This would only
have officers wide awake and eagerly awaiting his
arrival. He didn't want anyone awake while he took
care of his business.

Lamont walked into the kitchen and chatted with a
few staff members until 2:45 a.m. When he walked out
of the kitchen, Lamont looked down the long corridor
to make sure the coast was clear. He sighed as he
headed toward Five North. Normally, the walk to Five
North was short, but at that moment, Lamont felt as
if he were walking for miles. By the time he got to the
door of the housing area, he was almost out of breath.

Lamont stood by the staircase, forced himself to
relax, and put on some latex gloves. He saw that the
steady midnight officers, Crawford and Madison, were
out cold, which was what he expected. They could have
been on the verge of losing their jobs for sleeping on
post when they were supposed to be watching inmates.
But Lamont wasn't stressing that tonight.

Lamont shook his head as he thought about what he
was about to put them through. He didn't care about
any of that. He just cared about getting to Anwar.
He tiptoed into the control room and stood near the
control panel. He needed to crack open a cell. He
remembered that Anwar was moved to cell fifteen in
Five North earlier that day, and Lamont looked on the
panel for the number.

What made it even better was that cell fifteen was the
last cell in the back of Five North. He smiled, thinking
about how easy he had it tonight. The door to Anwar's
cell was slightly ajar due to an inoperable control
switch. Lamont couldn't believe his luck.

He eased his way into the housing area. It was
almost pitch black, with the exception of the moonlight

coming from the back window. Not wanting to be noticed, Lamont creeped down the steps to the bottom tier.

Some inmates were listening to Walkmans or talking to themselves inside of their cells. Most of the windows were covered with towels, sheets, or newspaper, which was not allowed. Correction officers had to be able to have a visual of the inmates inside of the cells at all times, but tonight, Lamont didn't give a damn. He was on another mis When he arrived at Anwar's cell, he peeked inside the sion.

uncovered cell window. All that he could see was the outline of Anwar's frame laying on the foam mattress and snoring very loudly. As the reality of what he was about to do hit him, he silently prayed, asking for God's forgiveness. He just hoped that Anwar wouldn't wake up before he could do it. Now that would be ugly, and everything that he had worked for would go down the drain.

Lamont removed the scalpel from his pocket. Now it was time to spring into action.

The lights illuminating the outside of the cell window provided the perfect lighting for what Lamont was about to do. He knew that all he had to do was slit his throat straight across, push his head forward, and watch him die.

It took Lamont a few minutes to push the cell door open. He didn't want to startle his would-be victim or alert anybody to his presence. He practically tiptoed inside the cell, and stood over the sleeping Anwar. Suddenly, Anwar opened his eyes. Lamont was startled as he prepared to either run out of the cell or fight the man to his death.

"Who's there? Who's in my room?" Anwar whispered. The crook wasn't even looking at him, and Lamont was confused. It seemed as if Anwar was hallucinating.

"Russell, is that you?" Anwar asked no one in particular. "Why are you in my room?"

Lamont held the scalpel up in the air, preparing to attack. *Who is Russell?* he thought.

He was going to play the game just so that he could carry out his mission. Anwar swung his legs over the side of the bed. He was only inches from where Lamont was standing. He still was staring into darkness. It was then that Lamont was convinced that Anwar's episode was a lot more than a bad dream. It sounded as if he was having a schizophrenic episode.

"You came to kill me, didn't you, Russell? Is that why you keep hauntin' me?"

Lamont waited to see what was going to happen next. He felt his hands getting sweaty from wearing the latex gloves, so he tightened his grip on the scalpel.

"Why don't you just go ahead and kill me, Russell? I lost everything because of you. There's no one left to love me so you got what you wanted. Truth is, I wanna die, Russell. I should have died that day, not you. You should have killed me. Is that what you wanna do to me, Russell? Do you wanna kill me?"

All of a sudden, Anwar got up and faced him. He grabbed Lamont's hand with the scalpel in it. Lamont pushed Anwar, who was surprisingly weak, back onto the bed. They struggled for the weapon for a brief second, but Lamont was getting the best of him. He had not anticipated coming into Anwar's cell and getting into a scuffle with the con.

"I wanna die, Russell! I wanna die! Kill me, Russell!" Anwar yelled. He could hear the inmate in the next cell banging on the wall. Lamont began panicking.

"Yo, A," screamed the inmate. "Shut the fuck up, nigga! I'm tryin' to get some sleep over here!"

Other inmates chimed in. They were not happy with their quiet night being disturbed by someone who had obviously lost his mind.

"I wanna die!" Anwar yelled again, looking at Lamont with a distant gaze in his eyes.

"Yeah, Jones, tell that nigga, Russell, to kill you so we can have our peace and quiet back! Nobody like your ass anyway!" said an inmate from the top tier. The others began laughing.

Two minutes had passed, and it was now or never. After slightly resisting, Anwar finally succumbed to Lamont's strength. Lamont held his head up with his right hand under Anwar's chin. He then took the scalpel and made a clean slit right across Anwar's throat. Anwar's eyes almost popped out of his head, as Lamont pushed his chin forward with one hand and held his mouth with the other.

He watched as Anwar moved around for a few seconds, then his body went limp. He actually got instant gratification, looking at Anwar's lifeless body lying before him. Lamont smirked.

"Bitch motherfucker," he whispered to himself. He eased the gloves off his hands, and turned them inside out with the scalpel wrapped up in them. He unzipped the black Windbreaker that he had worn over his white uniform shirt. Lamont slowly walked out of the cell and used his upper arm to slowly slide the door closed. He didn't want any of his fingerprints in the cell.

Lucky for him, the other inmates went back to what they were doing. He glanced at a few cells as he eased out of the housing area. Most of them still had their cell windows covered. As far as he knew, no one saw him exiting Anwar's cell. His knees felt as they were about to buckle as he crept out of Five North, with the bloody gloves and the scalpel wrapped up in the jacket. Now it was time to get rid of the evidence.

Lamont walked past the snoozing Crawford and Madison. He looked at his watch and saw that the time was 3:18 a.m. As he walked down the corridor, Lamont waved at the sanitation officer, hiding the evidence behind his back. The officer gave Lamont a quick salute and continued to supervise the inmates as they picked up trash throughout the facility. Lamont noticed a large, open garbage bag that was waiting to be disposed of, and quickly walked near it.

While the sanitation crew and the officer weren't looking, he was able to drop the gloves, the jacket, and the scalpel inside of the bag without detection. He breathed a sigh of relief as he watched one of the sanitation inmates tie up the bag so that he could dispose of it along with the rest of the trash.

Lamont wiped the beads of sweat from his forehead and walked briskly toward the control room. He stood outside the door and waited until an officer buzzed him inside. He nodded at her, went into his office, and closed the door. He was drained. Before he closed his eyes, he looked at the date on the calendar. It was July 17, 2009. It was that time.

A few hours later, at 6:00 a.m., Lamont emerged from his office with a large duffel bag in his hand. He was supposed to have worked a few hours of overtime that morning, but, instead, Lamont said good night to the bewildered officers. They watched him walk out of the control room with all of his personal items in tow.

It wasn't until the next afternoon that they found out that Assistant Deputy Warden Lamont Simmons had officially retired from the NYC Department of Correction.

Chapter 39

India

That same morning, India woke up in her bed. It was 6:30 a.m. She felt an excruciating pain shooting through her head.

India reached for her cell phone and attempted to call Lamont's cell phone over and over again. He didn't answer her call. She even called the jail, but the only thing they told her was that he was not in the area.

She sighed and attempted to sit up in the bed. India winced as more pain shot through her head like a bullet. Once again, Sierra had come out as the winner. India didn't know what to think at this point. She wondered if Lamont had gone back to Sierra or if she was with Rasheed.

It was about an hour later when India found the strength to get out of bed to take some Aleve for the pain. While doing this, she just happened to peep inside of Asia's bedroom and saw that she wasn't in there.

"She must have had to work the mornin' shift," India said to herself. Suddenly the bell rang. India frowned and tiptoed to the door. She looked through the peephole and smiled when she saw who it was.

She opened the door and Lamont walked in. His eyes were bloodshot. He looked around when he stepped into the living room.

"Don't worry, Lamont. I'm home alone."

"Why do you keep callin' my phone? What do you want?" he asked with an attitude.

She threw her arms around his neck. "I wanted to see you! I missed you so much." She kissed Lamont on the lips. "I'm so happy that you finally made the right choice. Now that Sierra's out the way, we can be together!"

Lamont smiled again and put his arms around her small waist. "You sure you wanna be with a nigga like me?"

India kissed him on the lips again. "Yeah, for sure. I mean, Sierra is out of the picture and why can't we be together? When I press charges on her, she will probably be losin' her job, too. You don't need to be with a broke, unemployed bitch anyway!"

"So she ain't gonna have a job after you report her to the police?" replied Lamont.

"Yeah, baby! After what she did to me, I'm reportin' her ass, that's right, I'm gonna tell the cops and IG everything that I know about her."

Lamont nodded. "Wow. You must really love me, don't you?"

India kissed him all over his face and she began running her hands all over his tight body. "Yes, I do, baby, yes, I do! Make love to me, Lamont, please!"

Lamont smirked. "I got somethin' even better than that for your ass."

India let him go and stood back with an enticing smile on her face. "And what is that?"

Lamont reached around his waist and pulled out his gun. He pointed it at India's neck. "I should blow your brains out, you bitch," he said calmly.

India held up her hands. "Lamont, why—" she whispered.

He didn't let her finish her sentence. "Be quiet, India! And if you scream, I swear to God, I will blow your brains out!"

India felt warm pee roll down her legs. "I didn't do anything to you, Lamont!" she said, looking down at the urine that had formed a puddle on the floor.

He grabbed her by her hair and pushed the muzzle of the gun into her neck. "So you wanna report my girl, huh? You're tryin' to make this shit that we had into a fuckin' relationship when you was just a piece of pussy to me! I knew that you wasn't shit when I found out you tried to befriend my woman, tried to make a fool of her and me. Did you think that I was gonna let you get away with that shit? Then you had me come over here just so I could run into Rasheed. Do you think I couldn't see what you were tryin' to do to me, bitch?"

India mumbled something, and Lamont gripped her hair even harder. "Bitch, I should kill you right now!" he continued. "You tried to make my life a livin' hell, tried to get one of the best things that ever happened to me to leave! I can't afford for that shit to happen to me again, India, that's why I'm gonna tell you this. You stay the hell away from me. Stay the hell away from Sierra, and, fuck it, stay away from Rasheed too, while you're at it! And if I so much as see or hear my name or Sierra's name come across anybody's desk in the fuckin' inspector general's office or any complaint report in any precinct in this city, I will fuckin' murder you. Do you hear me?"

India nodded. Lamont pushed her onto the couch. She was frozen with fear. He looked like he meant business, and, for the first time in India's life, she was going to comply with someone's demands.

Lamont walked out the door without looking back. India slid off the couch onto the floor, and began crying hysterically.

Chapter 40

Rasheed

At 7:40 that morning, Rasheed was smiling as he swept his son into his arms.

"Dah-dee! Dah-dee!" Messiah said, reaching for his father. Ironically, Lamont had dropped off Messiah to Rasheed's house the night before he went to work. He had to work the midnight shift, and Sierra was in no mood to be bothered with children after all the things that had occurred that day. Rasheed completely understood how she felt, and he was more than happy to be with his son.

The day before, for everyone's sake, Lamont and Rasheed had buried the hatchet. They realized that their contempt for each other wasn't doing anything but hurting two of the people they claimed to love so much: Sierra and Messiah.

Rasheed agreed that it was time to move on from the notion that he and Sierra were going to get back together. Lamont agreed to work on his jealousy issues and allow Rasheed to be a father to his only son.

"What are you doin' up so early, man?" Rasheed asked the toddler, kissing Messiah on his chubby cheeks. "You wake up this early all the time?"

"I want juice!" Messiah replied. Rasheed laughed and they walked down the stairs to the kitchen. While opening the refrigerator door, his house phone rang.

"Hello?" he answered with a yawn.

"What's up, Rah? It's me, Si," Sierra said.

"I know who it is. How do you feel this mornin'? Are you all right?" he asked. Sierra sighed. "I'm as well as can be expected. I'm workin' through everything, but I don't wanna talk about it." Sierra changed the subject. "I can hear Messiah in the background. Got you up early, huh?"

"Hell yeah!" replied Rasheed. "Does he always wake up this early?"

"We're usually up this early so that we can take him to school. He's on a strict schedule."

"Well, damn, you know my no-job-havin' ass ain't never up this early, but that's okay. This is my boy. I'm lovin' every minute of it." He paused. "I don't wanna keep askin', but I'm worried about you. You okay?"

"My body is sore. My spirit is broken. I feel like I'm about to lose my mind, but I'm prayin' on it."

"Prayer is good. I do that myself sometimes, believe it or not. But I think you need to say somethin', Sierra. You could probably help somebody else who went through the same thing."

"Rah, I can't bring myself to say anything. I don't wanna be the fall guy. Me, you, and Lamont are in a good place right now. Hopefully we all can just get on with our lives after everything that happened."

Rasheed gave Messiah some juice in his sippy cup. "No doubt. A lot of shit has happened these last few weeks. I know that I'm partly to blame."

"There's no need to go there, Rah. I put you through some shit, too. I guess we're two of a kind when it comes to drama." Sierra's other line beeped. "Hold on, my other line is beepin'." After a few minutes, Sierra came back on the line with Rasheed.

"Oh, my God!" she said in a hurried tone. "Rah, Anwar is dead."

Rasheed was silent. "What? What are you talkin' about?"

"Anwar is dead," she repeated. "Lamont just told me that he just got a phone call about it. He was on his way home from work when somebody called and told him what went down. He was found dead in his cell during the morning shift."

Messiah was tugging on Rasheed's basketball shorts. Sierra was talking to him on the other end of the phone, but he wasn't listening, and he wasn't paying attention to his son. He was shocked that Lamont actually went through with it.

"Did he kill himself? I mean, how did he die?"

"Lamont said somethin' about him bein' found in his cell with his throat cut."

"When did it happen?"

"He didn't say, but who knows? I just can't believe it. Karma is a motherfucker," she said. There was silence on Rasheed's end of the phone. He had to agree with her. "Hello, are you there?"

"Damn, Si, I'm sorry but I didn't expect to hear that that fool was dead. Not in no cell on Rikers Island anyway. Damn."

"I know that Anwar was your friend and everything—" she began.

Rasheed cut her off. "He was my boy, but he had some psychological and mental issues. It's like he finally snapped after all these years. I'm surprised he held out this long."

"You said that you saved his life. How did you . . ."

Messiah began tugging at his shorts again. Rasheed picked up Messiah and immediately put the toddler on the phone with Sierra. He knew that she wanted to ask him how he had saved Anwar's life. He was pretty sure she'd figured it out but wanted him to confirm her thoughts. He was putting behind him all of those negative memories of the crimes he had committed.

After a few seconds passed, Messiah climbed out of his lap and Rasheed got back on the phone with Sierra.

"Are you upset about Anwar's death?"

"Man, fuck Anwar!" Rasheed's eyes went to Messiah. He didn't like cussing in front of him. "I mean, forget Anwar! He violated so he deserved everything he got, abuse victim or not. I can't feel sorry for him when he disrespected our friendship, and, most of all, violated you."

"I feel you, Rah. It's okay to be upset, though. I wouldn't be mad if you were. Y'all were childhood friends."

"I'm good, Si, trust me, I'm good. He's better off where he is."

"So let me ask you another question."

"Go ahead."

"Are you responsible for this?" Sierra asked, referring to Anwar's murder. Rasheed knew that she would think that he had something to do with it. But this time she was way off.

"Nah, baby girl, don't thank me. Thank your man for that when he walks through the front door of your house."

Rasheed listened as Sierra dropped the phone. Then it went dead. He shrugged, and put his cordless phone back on the base. Not bothering to call her back, he wanted to give her a moment to digest the alarming news. Right after he hung up the phone, Rasheed scooped up his son and went back upstairs to his bedroom to get some much-needed rest.

Chapter 41

Lamont

Lamont had committed the ultimate sin, but had done something that, as a real man, he felt that he'd had to do. In order to protect his family, he had killed a man.

When Lamont arose from his nap the night of his last shift at work, he glanced at Sierra while she was asleep and decided that she was the woman he wanted to be with for the rest of his life. They had created a family, and regardless of the mistakes that they had made in their pasts, they were still going strong. This was another reason why he felt Anwar had to go.

Lamont glanced at the clock on his nightstand. It was 9:00 p.m. This meant he had about an hour to get dressed and arrive at work for the eleven o'clock roll call. He shook Sierra lightly.

"Babe," he whispered. "Babe, wake up for a second."

Sierra rolled over and yawned. He knew that she was exhausted from her ordeal with Anwar and India earlier that day. She held her arms out to hug him.

"Yes, baby, what's up? What you need?" she asked, her voice groggy from sleep.

Lamont planted a kiss on Sierra's forehead. "I don't need anything, baby girl. I just wanted to tell you that I'm about to go to work. Trey is at Mo's house for the night and Messiah is in the bedroom. He was asleep when Monique came to pick up Trey and I didn't want to disturb him."

Sierra sighed. "Babe, could you take Messiah to my mother's? I love my booga bear but I just can't deal right now. I need a moment to myself, you know what I'm sayin'?" she said with an apologetic look on her face.

Lamont smiled. "I know, baby, I know. You've been through a lot this past week. I done put you through my shit and then this fuckery with Anwar and India . . . It was a lot. I can't let this shit hold us back." They both paused. "I got an idea. What if I take him to his father's house?"

Sierra sat upright. "If you take him where?"

"I said what if I was to take Messiah to his father's house?"

She shook her head in disbelief. "You would really do that, Lamont?"

He held his head down. "Yeah, I would. At this point, I would do anything to make you and Messiah and Trey happy. I really want us to work. I don't wanna lose you to Rasheed or any other man for that matter. I want us to work out our problems, and I promise you that I will never, ever put my hands on you again. I guess I got so much anger in me that I lash out at the people I love the most. That's not cool."

Sierra's eyes began to get watery. She kissed him on the lips. "You are one of the best things that has ever happened to me."

Lamont sighed. "I love you, Sierra, and I promise you that I'm gonna make sure that no one or nothin' stops us from bein' happy."

"I love you too, baby." They shared an intimate kiss, and Lamont prepared for work. While he got ready, Sierra packed an overnight bag for Messiah. By the time Lamont was dressed Sierra had already called Rasheed to let him know that Messiah was on his way there.

Before Lamont walked out the door with the drowsy Messiah in his arms, Sierra kissed them tenderly. She waved to them from the doorway as Lamont strapped the baby into his car seat. Meanwhile, his mind was going a mile a minute. From the outside looking in, they looked like an average family with not a dilemma in the world.

Twenty minutes later, Lamont dropped Messiah off with Rasheed, and they slapped each other five. From a working Joe to a reformed gangster, they knew what had to be done. For once, Lamont was able to relate to Rasheed and understood why he had chosen to do some of the things he had done in life. There was always someone who could take you there, and for Lamont, that someone was Anwar.

"Thanks, Lamont," Rasheed said, taking his sleeping son into his arms. "Good lookin' out, man."

"Nah, thank you, man," Lamont replied. "Sierra will probably call you later on in the mornin'.

"So you ain't had a chance to tell her about the plans, huh?"

"Nah, man, don't know how to tell her. Maybe you can give her the heads-up when you speak to her."

Rasheed smirked. "Yeah, I will. And remember how we planned it. You ain't nervous, are you?"

"A little bit, but, fuck it, I gotta do what I gotta do. He don't need to walk out of that jail, he needs to come out in a body bag."

Rasheed gave Lamont five again and went inside with Messiah. Lamont walked to his truck, anticipating what was gonna go down that night.

Now, after leaving India's apartment that morning,

he knew that there would no longer going to be any derogatory talk about crooks and gangsters; for, now, he was no better than they were.

Epilogue

It was the middle of April. The sun was shining brightly and it was an unusually warm day. The First Baptist Church of Jamaica, Queens was packed with at least 150 guests. They were anxiously waiting for the groom and the bride to arrive for the ceremony. It was a joyous occasion, and a feeling of serenity was definitely in the air.

The first vehicle arrived at the church. The groomsmen and the groom emerged from the stretch Hummer, looking dapper as ever. Everything about the men were meticulous, and they were estatic. The six men, including the groom, were all dressed in black tuxedoes with light gold cummerbunds. The photographers took pictures of the men before they walked into the church.

Once the groom and his party arrived and the guests were inside, a late-model stretch Mercedes-Benz limo pulled up. Inside of this vehicle was the bridal party. The last of the guests were quickly hustled inside, for no one was to see the bride before she walked down the aisle.

After everyone was inside the church and seated, the bride finally stepped out of the vehicle. Sierra was absolutely stunning in her beautiful wedding dress. It was the color of French vanilla, with a lace bodice and pearl beading. The dress fit every curve of her body, and the train was approximately four feet long. Her bridesmaids looked amazing in their magenta dresses. They wore ankle-length strapless gowns and metallic gold peep-toe shoes. Every last one of the women was just as gorgeous as the bride herself. Sierra wouldn't have wanted it any other way.

As Sierra walked up the stairs to the church's door, two of her bridesmaids held the train for her. She wanted to be careful not to get it dirty before making her entrance.

Lamont's groomsmen were lined up by the door waiting to escort their bridesmaid partners down the aisle. The reverend was waiting at the podium to preside over the ceremony, along with Lamont. After twenty minutes passed, the music began to play, and the guests turned around in their seats. Finally, the ceremony was about to begin.

The bridesmaids filed out through the large doors, with beautiful smiles on their faces. They took the arms of the groomsmen they were partnered with, and walked in to the tune of "Don't Change" by Musiq. Many guests began to tear up as they walked down the aisle.

Finally, Monique, Lamont's half sister, who was the maid of honor, walked down the aisle with the best man, Lamont's friend, Kaseem. The ringbearer, Trey, and the flower girl, Sierra's little cousin, spread white rose petals on the carpeted floor.

Once everyone was in their rightful places, Sierra came through the door with the lacy veil covering her stunning face. She felt all kinds of emotions, and it felt as if she were about to explode with joy. She inhaled, and locked her eyes with her husband-to-be.

Sierra began walking as soon as the music began. As they played "You're My Latest, My Greatest Inspiration" by Teddy Pendergrass, she strolled toward the front of the church.

If only Daddy could be here to give me away, she thought. The tears began flowing as she thought about her deceased father. He would have been so proud of her.

Sierra felt as if she was going to faint, unable to believe that she was about to marry her man. She was unsure of how she was even containing herself at that euphoric moment.

Sierra arrived at the podium and nervously took Lamont's hand. They stood together before the reverend, who blessed their union and addressed the guests about the institution of marriage. By this time, Lamont wasn't able to take his eyes off Sierra. She just smiled as she glanced at Pops and Miss Ann, Monique's mother, sitting in the front pew. Her mother, Marjorie, sat next to her boyfriend and held Messiah in her lap.

The reverend instructed them on their vows. Lamont turned to Sierra and lifted her chin. He looked her directly in the eyes.

"Sierra, I love you so much. You have made me the man I am today, and I love you with every breath that I take. I don't ever want to lose you, and I promise that I will be the best husband and father to our children you can ever wish for."

Sierra had to compose herself before she said her vows. As she got herself together, the guests could be heard cheering her on in the background.

"Take your time, girl, it's okay."

"Go on, Sierra, you can do it, baby girl."

Sierra's lip trembled and she took a deep breath. "I want to thank you, Lamont, for being there for me at my lowest point and my roughest times. You helped me appreciate the love that we have for one another, and I promise you that I am going to be the best wife and mother to our children, as well. I love you so much."

Trey walked up and gave Lamont and Sierra their platinum wedding bands. Their initials were engraved on the inside. Lamont slid the band onto Sierra's left index finger along with her platinum, four-carat engagement ring. Sierra slid the wedding band on Lamont's index finger as well.

"Now that this couple has recited their vows and the church bears witness to their love for one another, I now pronounce you husband and wife. Lamont, you may now kiss the bride," ordered the reverend. Lamont pulled the veil from over Sierra's face and they kissed each other passionately. Everyone applauded. After a few seconds, they turned to the guests.

"Introducing Mr. and Mrs. Lamont Terrell Simmons!" shouted the reverend. Lamont took Sierra's hand and they jumped over the broom. Everyone applauded again. They walked down the aisle, waving to their family and loved ones. The bridal party followed them outside to the Bentley Phantom that was waiting to whisk them to the reception. The guests slowly filed out of the church behind them.

Later on that evening, at the wedding reception at Antun's in Queens, everyone partied hard. The newlyweds received many toasts, and roasts, as well. They walked around to greet all of the guests, collecting cards filled with money, and thanking everyone for participating in their nuptials.

At some point, Lamont went his separate way to talk to a few of his coworkers who had been invited. Sierra and Monique sat side by side to do a recap of the day. While the ladies sat there, drinking champagne and chatting up a storm with a few guests, Rasheed walked up to Sierra. Needless to say, she was surprised to see him there.

"Congratulations, Sierra," he said. He handed her an envelope with money in it. "I wish you the best. I really do." Rasheed looked at Monique and smiled. She smiled back. "Hey, Miss Phillips."

Monique chuckled. "Hey, Gordon, I mean, Rasheed. You know you don't have to call me Phillips no more. It's Monique to you."

Rasheed grinned. "Okay, Monique, it is." Monique excused herself. He looked at Sierra. "You look gorgeous."

She held her head down. "Thank you, Rah. I sent you the invite but I am really surprised to see you. Didn't think that you were comin'."

He sighed. "Nah, I had to come. I had to come to see what I could have had. I'm not gonna lie, a part of me is a little jealous. I wanted you to be my wife one day. But the circumstances . . . the fuckin' circumstances." He went into a zone. "Sierra, I'm gonna keep it real. A part of me still loves you. I don't think that I will ever find another woman who will touch my heart like you."

Sierra looked around. Everyone was engrossed in conversation and wasn't paying attention to her and Rasheed.

"A part of me still loves you too, Rah. We have a son together, so we will always have a special place with each other."

"I know that this may not be the time, but I do have someone in my life I'm kind of diggin' for the moment."

Sierra frowned. She felt the butterflies in her stomach, selfishly annoyed at the fact that Rasheed shared that with her, but what could she say on her wedding day?

"Um, so, who's this special person? Is she, um, here with you?" Sierra asked, looking around.

"Yeah, she is. You sent me the invitation and it said two people. So bein' that I was kinda hollerin' at her at the time, I thought it would be all right if I brought her with me. She wanted to talk to you anyway."

Sierra knew that she was going to have to go through this one day, but she didn't expect for it to be that soon.

"Hello, Sierra," the woman said.

"Wow. Asia," Sierra replied, shaking her head in the process.

"I know you're buggin' out at the fact that I'm here, at your weddin', considerin' all the things that happened between us."

"Not only you and me, but me and your sister, too," Sierra responded. She looked at Rasheed. "So are y'all seein' each other now?"

"Yes, we are." They all paused. Lamont made his way back over to Sierra, and he froze when he saw Asia.

"Hello, Lamont," Asia said, greeting Lamont with a smile. He nodded at her and shook Rasheed's hand.

"Can I talk to you alone, Sierra?" Asia asked.

Sierra looked at Lamont then Rasheed. "Okay."

Asia and Sierra walked outside of the reception area. There were a few stragglers walking in and out to go the bathroom, but, otherwise, the hallway was empty.

"Sierra, my intentions were never to hurt you. The motive for all of the drama was my sister wantin' to get back at you because of Tamir. I felt the same way at first, but to be honest, I really was feelin' Rasheed. I always had feelings for him, but, of course, you know that Tamir was a good friend to my sister and me, so I just left it alone."

Asia continued. "I wanted to tell you that I have no ill will toward you. India took all of this too far by wantin' to break up your happy home. She had me doin' things that I didn't want to do. I just wanted to apologize to you, and I am happy that Rasheed and I are finally gettin' together. I don't want you to think that there is an ulterior motive. Now, as far as me and my sister are concerned, I feed her with a long-handled spoon. I'm on my own now and startin' a new life for myself—without my twin." Asia took Sierra's hand. "Anyway, I wish you and Lamont the best. I'm really happy for both of you."

Sierra managed to smile. "Thank you, Asia. Your apology is accepted. I don't know if I can ever deal with your sister like that, but I do wish you and Rasheed the best."

Asia sighed. "I understand how you feel about India, and I can't say that I blame you. She has to live with the choices that she makes in her life, but I wanna be on the up-and-up. I'm tired, you know? As for Rah and me, we have some plans for the future. I'm goin' to make sure he stays out of trouble and be a good father to his son."

"I appreciate that, Asia. Thank you for takin' the time to come and talk to me."

"You're welcome." They gave each other a quick hug and walked back inside the reception area, where the guests were eating.

Sierra walked over to the table where her mother was sitting. She waved for Rasheed and Asia to come over. She needed to make that formal introduction to her mother and Pops. No longer was she going to be ashamed of her son's father. She had made a choice to have a baby with Rasheed Gordon, and she was gonna stand by that decision.

Messiah was sitting in Marjorie's lap, and when he saw his father, his eyes instantly lit up.

"Dah-dee, Dah-dee!" chirped Messiah excitedly. Marjorie had a confused look on her face. She laughed.

"Boy, your father just got married! He don't have no time for you right now!" she said.

Sierra interrupted her joke. "Um, Mommy, this is Rasheed Gordon, Messiah's father, and his friend, Asia."

Marjorie looked up with a shocked expression on her face. Messiah reached for Rasheed and he picked him up.

"Hello, Ms. Howell. I heard a lot about you," Rasheed said.

Marjorie looked Rasheed up and down. "And I heard absolutely nothin' about you—until a few months ago! So this is Messiah's father?"

"Yes, Mommy," said Sierra.

"Well, he's very handsome. I can see the resemblance. Nice to finally meet you, Rasheed." Everyone greeted Asia, too.

Rasheed smiled. "You, too, Ms. Howell."

"Call me Miss Marjorie, sweetie. That is fine."

Pops stood up and shook Rasheed's hand. "Well, hello, young man, I'm Charles Simmons, Lamont's father, but everybody calls me Pops. You got a fine young lad right there," Pops said, pointing at Messiah, who was in Rasheed's arms. "That's my buddy."

Rasheed smiled. "Yeah, he is somethin' else. Nice to meet you . . . Pops."

Monique's mother, Miss Ann, shook Rasheed's hand too. "I'm Monique Phillips's mother, Miss Ann. How are you, baby?"

"I'm well, and you?" Rasheed asked.

"He's so mannerable, Sierra," Miss Marjorie said. "Why you had to hide him under that rock for so long?" Everyone at the table laughed, and Sierra felt her face flush with embarrassment.

"Mommy, please!" Sierra took Messiah out of Rasheed's arms. She kissed her son and gave him back to her mother. Rasheed excused himself and looked at Sierra.

"I love you, Si. I guess I'll be seein' you around when I come get Messiah or you bring him over. You know the drill."

"Yeah, I know." Sierra saw Lamont waving her over to him. "Rasheed, I wanna thank you."

"Thank me for what?" he asked, looking confused.

"For teachin' me how to appreciate myself and the people in my life. When I said my vows, I know I mentioned that Lamont made me into the woman I am today, but you are equally responsible for the change in me. I will always love you for that."

Rasheed hugged Sierra tightly. After a few seconds, she gingerly kissed him on the cheek and pulled away from him. He stood there for a moment and watched as she walked over to her husband. Rasheed looked for Asia through the crowd of guests. She was waiting for him back at their table. She waved and smiled at him, not noticing that he wiped a few tears from his eyes as he made his way back to her.

As Sierra held Lamont's hand, she took a quick glance at Rasheed and wiped a tear from her eye too. It was at that moment that they both realized that their taboo love affair had finally come to an end.

ORDER FORM
URBAN BOOKS, LLC
78 E. Industry Ct
Deer Park, NY 11729

Name: (please print):_____

Address: _____

City/State: _____

Zip: _____

QTY	TITLES	PRICE
	The Cartel	$14.95
	The Cartel#2	$14.95
	The Dopeman's Wife	$14.95
	The Prada Plan	$14.95
	Gunz And Roses	$14.95
	Snow White	$14.95
	A Pimp's Life	$14.95
	Hush	$14.95
	Little Black Girl Lost 1	$14.95
	Little Black Girl Lost 2	$14.95
	Little Black Girl Lost 3	$14.95
	Little Black Girl Lost 4	$14.95

Shipping and handling - add $3.50 for 1st book, then $1.75 for each additional book.
Please send a check payable to:
   Urban Books, LLC
Please allow 4 - 6 weeks for delivery